Lisa Heidke studied journalism at Queensland University, fled Brisbane and settled in Sydney where she landed a job as an Acquisitions Editor in book publishing (HBJ). After a while there, she headed to ACP where she worked as a feature writer on several national magazines, including *Practical Parenting* and *Bride to Be*. After many years living in Sydney's inner west, Lisa woke up one morning to find herself married with three children and living on the North Shore (much to her surprise and sometimes horror).

Website: www.lisaheidke.com
Twitter: @lisaheidke
Facebook: Lisa Heidke – author

Stella Makes Good

Also by Lisa Heidke

Lucy Springer Gets Even
What Kate Did Next
Claudia's Big Break

Stella Makes Good

LISA HEIDKE

ARENA
ALLEN&UNWIN

This edition published in 2013
First published in 2012

Arena Books, an imprint of Allen & Unwin
Sydney, Melbourne, Auckland, London

83 Alexander Street
Crows Nest NSW 2065
Australia
Phone: (61 2) 8425 0100
Email: info@allenandunwin.com
Web: www.allenandunwin.com

Cataloguing-in-Publication details are available
from the National Library of Australia
www.trove.nla.gov.au

ISBN 978 1 74331 183 7

Typeset in Granjon by Bookhouse, Sydney
Printed and bound in Australia by the SOS Print & Media Group

10 9 8 7 6 5 4 3 2

To Louise Thurtell

1

When I said 'I do' forever, I never thought I'd end up saying 'I don't any more'. Divorce? Not me. Ever.

And I'm not divorced . . . yet. But my husband and I are separated. Terry has a girlfriend. Actually, he's living with her. I'm not feeling sorry for myself, though. I'm in a good place. Happy with my life, friends.

Terry and I met in the early nineties at an inner-city bar. He came out with a ridiculous pick-up line, something like, 'Do you believe in love at first sight or should I walk past you again?' Yes, it was dumb and cheesy, but obviously I was in the mood for dumb and cheesy because I laughed. I thought he was cute. It helped that he was unsure of himself and nervous as hell. And at least he didn't say, 'What time do you have to be back in heaven?' I have standards.

Within a week, we decided we were in love. Three months later, we moved in together. The following year, Ben was born. I often wonder if we'd have stayed together if Ben hadn't been conceived. We met, fell in love, shacked up, got pregnant. In short, we were running on a treadmill of relentless forward motion. Then I fell pregnant with Hannah. Two kids! Marriage would complete the circle. So, Terry and I did what was expected. Three months before Hannah was born, we united as Mr and Mrs. I was ready to forgo my maiden name—Templeton. I know that's not politically correct, but I liked Terry's surname, Sparks.

Stella Sparks. It had a glamorous ring to it. Besides, the name Stella Templeton had never done me any favours. I hoped Stella Sparks would.

Our marriage was good, really good . . . until it ran out of steam.

The bartender coughed and handed over my change.

It was my shout. Place? Local pub. Three girlfriends hanging out at nine o'clock on a Thursday night, catching up for New Year's drinks. Date? January thirtieth, two days after the start of the school year. It felt more like two weeks. Teenagers!

I picked up the bottle of wine and headed back to the girls.

'So,' Carly was saying as I sat down, 'what's everyone's mantra for the year?'

She'd asked the same question for the last three years and I couldn't for the life of me remember what I'd said twelve months ago. I poured the wine instead of answering.

Jesse groaned. 'I'm not playing this game.'

'Why not?' Carly snapped. 'What else are you doing?'

We clinked glasses and she took a large gulp of wine before continuing. 'Anyway, I've got mine—fuck buddy.'

'Carly!' Jesse cried.

I shook my head. Carly could be a loose cannon, especially after a few drinks. She liked to shock people and Jesse always fell for it. I wasn't sure if Carly was serious or not. Her marriage had been through its ups and downs over the years, but I hadn't heard her complain about Brett recently.

'That's not a mantra,' I told her.

She smiled and flicked her long blonde hair behind her shoulders. 'My game, my rules.'

With a slow, deliberate movement, Jesse picked up her glass. 'I know what I want.'

'What does that mean?' I asked.

'It means I know what I want from life and this is my year to go for it. That and maintenance. I'm finding wrinkles on my ears. I can't wing it any more. I have to look after myself, otherwise . . .' She trailed off.

Jesse thought her husband, Steve, was having a mid-life crisis because he was arrogant, rude and hated her friends. He wasn't having a crisis, he was just a prick, full stop. But Jesse seemed devoted to him and did everything she could to keep him happy, including Botox, beauty care and endless sexual favours. I knew she hoped that if she kept herself looking gorgeous and him feeling manly, one day he might tell her he loves her—like he used to years ago. And she does look great—flawless, unlined olive complexion, intense green eyes, wavy, sandy-coloured hair. Jesse's a real catch, unlike Steve, who's rather ordinary.

'What about you?' Carly asked me, snapping her fingers to bring me back from my mental drifting. 'We need your mantra.'

'I can only commit to a month,' I said. 'Anything beyond that is a bonus.'

She sighed. 'Get on with it.'

I took a sip of wine. 'Fun.'

'Too short,' Carly said.

'How about "I take control of my life".'

Jesse and Carly looked at each other. Carly swigged her wine before answering. 'You can do better.'

'What? It's not like maintenance and fuck buddy are so great.'

Carly shrugged and cast her eyes around the room.

'What about "I choose to be happy"?' said Jesse, looking anything but.

Jesse sometimes had great highs, where she was on top of the world, all smiles, hugs and good times, tempered by times when she felt low, sad and uninteresting. She'd been in a depressed phase since before Christmas and was finding it hard to pull herself together. I'd noticed that her little quirks had returned too—the foot tapping, repetitive counting.

'Finding a suitable fuck buddy would definitely make me happy!' Carly cut in.

'What's gotten into you tonight?' I asked.

'Nothing. Just being honest.' She nodded towards a group of men at a nearby table. 'Maybe one of them would be up for the job.'

I rolled my eyes, then turned a deep shade of pink when I followed her gaze and realised who she was talking about.

I'd met Mike seven weeks ago at my son's end-of-year speech night. We were both seated towards the back of the hall and I'd immediately noticed him. He was tall and tanned, with collar-length salt and pepper hair with a bit of a fringe thing happening and an easy smile. Even more interesting was the absence of a wedding ring . . .

After the speeches were over, I made a point of bumping into him.

'Come here often?' I'd asked. It was a pathetic opening but it was all I had.

'Only when I'm certain there'll be attractive women here,' he said, smiling broadly.

I extended my hand and smiled self-consciously. 'Stella Sparks.'

'Mike Thompson,' he replied, taking it. 'Divorced?'

'Presumptuous,' I said, then grinned. 'Separated.'

'Me, too.' His tone was light. 'Sorry. People talk. You're in good company, though.'

'I dread to think what else you've heard.'

'All good, I promise.'

Instant rapport? I wouldn't go that far, but he was easy to talk to and handsome. Bonus points: he didn't appear up himself or sleazy. Another thought had struck me then: if he knew about my marital status, he must have noticed me before.

We got to talking, and the following week we met for coffee ... And that was as far as it had gone. The coffee date was a disaster. It was almost Christmas, the kids were on school holidays, and I was nervous—worried people would see us and talk. I hardly remembered our conversation ... I guessed I came across as some moronic twit. But I'd put it behind me, determined to focus on my children and newly found freedom.

Then, horror of horrors, I'd run into him in Woolies two days ago in the fruit and vegie section. I'd stammered something about how nice it was to see him again and that I was meeting friends tonight and it would be great if he could come along. Lo and behold, there he was, barely three metres away and smiling at me.

I smiled back. Jesus! I felt sixteen again. And I had absolutely no intention of revisiting that annus horribilis.

'See,' said Carly. 'You're eyeing them off, too.'

'You're all talk,' I said, dismissing several erotic thoughts from my head. I wasn't looking for a romantic interlude. I liked Mike, but I was terrified of falling in lust only to have it all fall apart. Yes, I was getting ahead of myself, but that's me.

'I'm not and I'll prove it to you.' Carly stood up and walked towards their table.

As she did, several men turned to look at her. Despite her often excessive consumption of alcohol, Carly's a stunner—athletic, tall, a bit like a greyhound. A good-looking greyhound with long blonde hair. Lately, though, when we're out together, I feel as though I'm minding an eighteen-year-old. It gets tiring, especially when I then have to go home and deal with my own teenagers.

'Everything okay with you?' Jesse asked, refilling my glass.

'Sure,' I said.

'Kids doing okay?'

'They're teenagers. Their lives revolve around themselves and their friends. They're not happy with the disruption of the separation and Terry's new girlfriend, but they're handling it.'

'It can't be easy.'

'No, but there's no alternative.'

Truthfully, my and Terry's romantic life had been kaput for several years. Occasionally, we'd tried to reignite the flame by having weekends away from the domesticity that had engulfed our lives, but the passion never lasted. Then, seven months ago, we'd gone to Fiji, just the two of us. Without Hannah and Ben, we'd quickly realised what we'd known, deep down, for years. The kids were the glue holding us together, and when they weren't with us? Well, we wished they were.

Terry and I had never been the sort to hold hands while walking along the beach, cuddle at the movies or kiss spontaneously. There were rarely any public displays of affection. That just wasn't us. At least, it wasn't me. But it seemed these were the exact intimacies Terry had been missing. Soon after Fiji, his idle lunchroom chat with a colleague turned into coffee at a nearby cafe . . . which turned into lunch, and the lunches quickly progressed to dinners. Thankfully, the affair wasn't drawn out. Terry had the decency to tell me he had feelings for Amanda.

I didn't blame him. In fact, I felt relieved. I wouldn't say I was happy that our marriage was over, but I understood where he was coming from.

So far, relations between us had been cordial. I was staying in the family home with the kids, so life hadn't changed too dramatically. I just had one less person to wash for, prepare dinner for and generally clean up after. I was under no illusions it would always be so, especially once we started negotiating the financial and property settlement, but for now Terry and I were fine.

Last week, he'd moved into Amanda's apartment. I couldn't think of anything worse than shacking up with someone new minutes after leaving a long-term relationship, but there you go. It was what Terry wanted, so good luck to him. The kids weren't as accepting of his new life. It was incredibly stressful for me having to coax them into ringing their dad or having a meal with him. As for staying the weekend with him and Amanda, forget it. That meant that when the kids weren't at school or with their friends, they were my responsibility. It was wearing me down.

Then there was Terry's mum, June. A few months ago when Terry and I told her we were separating, she wasn't impressed. She actually clipped Terry around the ears. That was a sight—a seventy-year-old woman hitting her forty-year-old son about the head. Looked like it hurt too. Poor June. When I'd taken her shopping last week, she hadn't mentioned the separation. When I brought up the subject, she threw me a blank look, like she didn't understand what I was talking about. She'd been a bit forgetful of late so I hadn't pursued the conversation, but thought, wait until she finds out about Amanda!

Anyway, the upshot was I wasn't looking for anyone new, and definitely not a fuck buddy as Carly claimed she wanted. That's why it took me by surprise when I noticed my toes tingling when I thought about Mike.

'Should we do something about her?' Jesse said, drawing me back to the present.

Carly was flirting up a storm with her new friends.

'She's a big girl. Give her ten minutes.'

Jesse nodded. 'Sometimes I envy you,' she said. 'You're free. You have no one to answer to.'

'Except my kids,' I cut in.

'That's different. They won't always be living with you. You can have your own headspace. You can please yourself, not always be worrying about what your husband thinks.'

'How's it going with Steve?'

'Same old, same old. He can't get enough sex, but he doesn't care about me enough to introduce me to his colleagues. I had to beg him to take me to the company Christmas party. A couple of times when I joined in the conversation, he frowned, as if I was going to say something wildly inappropriate.' She sighed and looked up from her glass. 'And you know what, Stella? I never do. I keep it all hidden.'

I wanted to tell her to wake up to herself and dump her dickhead husband. But I'd told her that a couple of times already. I wasn't going to add anything to this conversation by suggesting it a third time.

She sighed. 'I'm just being dramatic.'

I wasn't so sure. And I wondered what she'd meant about keeping things hidden.

From what Jesse had told me, Steve spent a lot of time working late and hardly ever gave her the time of day when he was around, except for when he was after a blow job. I knew he hadn't always been so dismissive of her. When I'd met him several years ago, he'd been open, accommodating and much kinder to Jesse. These days, I hardly ever saw him. Before Terry and I split, we'd occasionally had them over for a barbeque, but Steve had usually ended up drifting away from the conversation towards whatever the kids were watching on television, or else he'd sit there looking superior and raising an eyebrow if he didn't agree with what was being said. It gave us the impression he thought he was better than us, and that we should be honoured that he'd deigned to be in our company.

'And,' Jesse said, drawing me back into the conversation, 'I really want another baby.'

I took her hand. 'You any closer?'

She took the last sip from her wine glass and shook her head. 'I don't blame Steve. I know he's busy, tired and fed up. He doesn't want to add to the pressure by having another mouth to feed.'

'You can afford it,' I said.

'Emotionally, Stella. Steve says he doesn't have the energy or time to devote to raising another child. But yes, he says it wouldn't be financially viable either.'

'You're talking about a baby here, not a new car.'

She shrugged and we both looked at the empty bottle on the table.

'Should I buy another one?' she asked, just as Carly bounced back.

'I've met the most amazing guys,' she told us. 'Mike's a dad from school, and the others work with him. We're all heading out to this other place later. Want to come?'

I glanced over at Mike who was looking sheepish.

'Which place?' asked Jesse.

'Party! I meant party,' Carly said, slurring slightly.

'I don't think it's a good idea,' I said, feeling nervous.

'But they're doctors,' she added huskily, leaning over the table. 'Who's for more wine?'

'I'm in,' I said distractedly. 'They don't look like axe murderers, but you never know.'

Jesse nodded. 'Looks can be deceptive.'

'Please!' Carly snorted, and headed towards the bar.

Jesse's mobile rang. She took it from her bag and walked outside.

Carly returned with a new bottle of wine and poured a couple of glasses. 'Want to join them?' she said, looking over at Mike and his friends.

I shook my head, suddenly feeling shy as I remembered the disastrous coffee date. 'You go. I'll wait for Jesse.'

'Whatever.' And she was off.

I watched as she flirted with Mike's friend. He had dark curly hair that sat just below his collar, sort of messy and unkempt, a three-day growth, and he was tanned and tall, just like her. Mike was probably a bit older than we were, but the other two looked young, well under thirty. I felt a bit rude not going over to say hello. I had asked Mike here, after all. But I was nervous. It was better to say nothing than to start a conversation and say something stupid.

I glanced at my watch, conscious of the time. I was working tomorrow. I was a librarian; so was Jesse. That was how we met, ten years ago, working together at the library, cataloguing non-fiction.

When I told people my profession, they immediately gave me a sly—or in many cases, not-so-sly—once-over, then they'd say, 'But you don't look like a librarian.' As if it was a compliment.

'Really,' I'd say. 'And what are librarians supposed to look like?'

Then they'd throw me a few stereotypes from the fifties, which was when my eyes glazed over. No, I didn't wear thick, horn-rimmed glasses. No, I'd never worn my hair in a bun, nor was I mean or a spinster. I did wear cardigans, though.

'Hey,' said Jesse, walking back to our table, 'Steve's just rung. He's been held up at work. I told the babysitter someone would be home by ten, so it looks like I'm done for the night.'

'But this is our night. We've been planning this for ages. Can't you ring the babysitter?'

'Truthfully, Stella, it's not worth it. Besides, I'm tired.'

There was a squealing sound and we both looked over to where Carly was standing with Mike and his friends.

'Sorry to dump her on you,' Jesse said.

'Yeah, don't worry. I'll see she gets home in one piece.'

I watched Jesse push her way through the crowd towards the exit sign, then turned my attention back to Carly. She was sitting on the doctor guy's lap now.

Mike smiled at me, stood up, beer in hand, and came over. 'This seat taken?'

I stammered something unintelligible and smiled. Where was my brain?

'It was clear you weren't going to join me,' he said, and sat down. 'So, do you want to talk about the coffee date?'

I blushed. 'It wasn't a date, and no, not really.'

'Pity. I thought it had gone well, that was until you stopped responding to my text messages.'

'I sent you messages.'

'*Thanks* and *Nice to see you again* weren't the kind of messages I had in mind.'

'Look, I'm no good at this. I'm . . .' I trailed off, embarrassed.

'You're what? Gorgeous? Interesting? Have a great smile?'

'Stop. I'm too old for games, and besides, you're only saying those things to get me into bed.'

Shit. I couldn't believe I'd just said that.

Mike smiled. 'I am not.'

Great! Not only had I said something wildly inappropriate, but he didn't even fancy me.

'Not that the thought of kissing you hasn't crossed my mind, but I'm not trying to race you off.' He drained the last of his beer. 'Not right now, anyway.'

I grinned, pretty sure I'd turned a bright shade of beetroot.

'Stella, Stella, the night is young. Toby's taking me to a party.'

I swung around. Carly was swaying about ten centimetres from my head. Quickly standing and steadying her so she wouldn't fall, I said, 'You don't even know the guy. Let's go home.'

'Yes, I do. He's Toby and he's a doctor, and he feeds monkeys at the zoo in his spare time.'

I glanced at Mike, who was conveniently preoccupied with reading a crumpled docket from inside his wallet.

'Right,' I said, turning back to Carly. 'Toby sounds like fun and if you feel the same way about him tomorrow, you two can meet up. But,' I whispered, 'you have a husband and child waiting for you at home.'

She slumped into a chair. 'Piffle. You're such a party pooper.'

At that moment, Toby appeared. 'No pressure, but we're taking off,' he said.

'Hold your horses,' squealed Carly, standing up again. She looked at Mike and me. 'You coming?'

I couldn't let her go to the party by herself, so I followed her outside. Mike followed me.

'There's really no need,' I said to him.

'It's cool. Besides, I'm sure you could use an extra hand.'

He was right. I needed to stay with Carly, but I hadn't driven tonight and I couldn't fit into the car she was about to climb into, a black Lexus hybrid.

Mike leaned over to Toby. 'We'll follow you.'

Toby nodded and told him an address. Carly got in beside him, which completely foiled my plan because I'd been hoping to get her into Mike's car and then ask him to drive us straight home. And then I'd planned on ditching Mike, too—I needed some distance from him.

'Carly,' I hissed. 'You don't know these people.'

'Sure I do,' she slurred. 'They're from some hospital.'

She closed the door and Toby pulled away from the kerb. Bloody hell! This wasn't the scenario I'd imagined.

Within minutes, I was in the passenger seat of Mike's car and we were following Toby up the Pacific Highway towards Turramurra. At least we were heading in the right direction for home.

2

ike and I made small talk as he concentrated on keeping up with the zippy Lexus. I glanced at his dashboard clock: 10.39. Where I really wanted to be right now was tucked up in bed, not chasing Carly to God knows where.

As I listened to Mike, my thoughts kept drifting back to what he'd said earlier about wanting to kiss me. Did he actually *say* he wanted to kiss me or just that the thought had crossed his mind? Maybe my fantasies were getting in the way of reality. Either way, surely kissing couldn't be a bad thing? Or maybe it could. I was confused.

'Tell me,' Mike said, 'what do you do when not trying to keep up with your party-loving friend?'

'Besides trying to keep up with my kids and my job at the library?'

He glanced across. 'I still can't picture you as a librarian. You're too . . .'

'What?'

'I was going to say sexy but thought you might slap me.'

'Good call.'

'Okay, alluring . . . feisty? Can I get away with feisty?' he asked as we pulled up behind Carly and her new mates.

We were parked in an ordinary-looking suburban street barely a kilometre from my mother-in-law's retirement village and possibly three kilometres from my home. No loud music filtered from any of the houses, which all looked the same—low-set, blond-brick homes with well-kept, green front gardens. There was nothing unusual in sight; nothing to suggest a party was going off inside one of them.

I looked over at Carly, who was leaning against Toby's car. She wasn't making a hell of a lot of sense, but at least she was standing.

'Now what?' I asked her.

She looked at me, then at Toby, then at Toby's friend, Pete, who had been in the car with them. Pete winked and started off along the pavement towards a white gate attached to a white picket fence. 'This is it,' he said.

'Doesn't look like much of a party,' Mike said next to me.

I nodded. 'Feels like we're popping in to visit grandma.'

Pete led us down a side pathway. Halfway along, he stopped at an ordinary red wooden door. This is it, I thought. This is where we find out there's been a severe case of mistaken identity; we've arrived at the wrong address in the wrong suburb and we're actually crashing an elderly couple's home. They've probably been asleep for hours.

I expected Pete to knock, only to be confronted by angry pensioners. What I didn't expect was for him to extract a key from his jeans pocket.

'Voila,' he said, unlocking the door and pushing it open. He stepped inside, urging us to follow.

Common sense told me to step away and head back up to the road, but before I could grab Carly, she'd stumbled inside. I followed. It was dark and I strained to make out anything. There were lights but they were dim, giving off a soft red glow. As my eyes adjusted, I could see we were in a big room—a living room? There were several oversized lounges, and lamps of various shapes and sizes draped in fine chiffon scarves; there even seemed to be a smoke machine . . .

'Pete!' The voice belonged to a woman. At first it was too dark to see her properly, but then . . . what the fuck? She was practically naked apart from a sheer black baby-doll top and fluffy black high heels. She had huge breasts and was wearing a thong. Playboy Bunny was the first thought that came to mind.

I looked around the room, noticing couples and threesomes on the lounges. What the hell had we walked into?

'You've brought new playmates,' the Bunny said, hugging Pete.

Mike nudged me.

'This is a bit different,' I said, leaning against a wall for support. We'd stumbled into Hugh Hefner's suburban counterpart.

Pete wasted no time. In an instant, he was naked and had joined several others on a nearby couch.

To be fair, Toby seemed as shocked as we were. 'Don't look at me,' he said. 'I had no idea Pete was into this . . . whatever this is.'

Carly put her head on my shoulder. 'This isn't quite what I had in mind when I said I wanted a fuck buddy.'

'Be careful what you wish for,' I told her.

'I've been to an orgy once or twice,' she went on, 'but I was nineteen. It was pretty overwhelming so I had a few lines of coke. But this . . . wow!'

'Coke?' I said. 'You're kidding me!'

'Look around you, Stella. These people aren't just drinking Red Bull and vodka.'

I looked more closely at the trays of drinks that were being passed around. They did seem to hold small dishes that probably contained other substances. I glanced at Mike and Toby. I couldn't hear what they were saying to each other but they looked uncomfortable.

'I could go for it,' Carly continued. 'Anonymous sex.'

'Carly!'

'What? I could be persuaded. Look at Pete—he's just dropped his dacks and gotten into it.'

I glanced at Pete, who was receiving a massage and a bit more.

'Yeah, I'd need the coke, though, or maybe an eckie,' Carly mused. 'And it'd have to be with someone attractive. I couldn't do it with anyone who had bad breath or belly fluff.'

'This is turning you on, isn't it,' Toby said, leaning into her.

She grinned. 'Of course not. I'm shocked. Don't know where to look.'

Pete and a woman holding a pulsating strobe-lit phallic-shaped vibrator started doing some things to another woman that were possibly illegal. She seemed to be enjoying herself, though, given her shrieks.

When a naked man with a gold fringed tassel attached to his flaccid penis bounced up to us with a tray of drinks, I was too shocked to refuse.

'We like to make the newbies feel welcome,' he said, looking each of us up and down.

'I'm Trevor, by the way. After your drink, you'll feel more comfortable. When you're ready, I'll introduce you around.' He smiled and bounded off down the corridor.

Drink spiking? I caught Mike's eye and he shrugged. Suddenly I wasn't thirsty any more. I definitely didn't want to lose control, not here. I put my untasted drink down on a nearby table. Mike did the same. Carly and Toby looked at us, peered at their drinks and downed them in one go.

'I needed that,' said Carly with a giggle. 'Wait till the school mums hear about this. It'll really rock their world.'

Understatement.

What was a party like this doing in Warrawee, I wondered. Wasn't it better suited to Newtown or Paddington? As I looked around at the entwined bodies, it occurred to me that maybe these people lived in the area. I thought about some of the people I knew. I couldn't see Mrs Farns (Year Eight support) or Mr Daniels (Computer Studies) getting into this kind of thing. The school's headmaster, on the other hand, was a dark horse—actually, a dark, quiet and all-too-ready-to-dress-up horse. And maybe there were a few divorcees in the neighbourhood who'd get a kick out of this? Then again, maybe swingers, or whatever these people called themselves, did this kind of thing as far away from their own neighbourhoods as possible.

As for divorcees, what was I thinking? I was soon to be a divorcee. Was this what I expected people to think of me: that I'd turn to orgies to get my kicks as soon as Terry was out the door?

I nudged Mike. 'Ever been to one of these before?'

He shook his head. 'Not sure it's my scene.'

I eyed a dominatrix who was teetering on twelve-centimetre stilettos. She gave a man dressed as a slave a few lashes of her whip, then picked up some kind of paddle and started spanking him with it.

'Electric paddle—won't leave marks,' said Trevor, the tasselledpenis man, back beside us. 'Most people like to be hurt, but no one wants to have to explain the welt marks when they get home.'

'Hmm,' I said, noticing a sign hanging on the wall nearby: *Welcome to Master Mitch's and Mistress Sheri's Haven. Go hard or go home.*

I was thinking about the hundreds of homes I drove past every day, the mums at tuckshop, the fathers at cricket. What did they get up to after hours? How would you know? Everyone was so busy with their own lives, tending to their gardens and weekly agendas. How did anyone have time to go these parties, let alone source costumes and accessories? Maybe it was all done online or by mail order.

I glanced at one couple who seemed heavily into the domination and submission routine. He looked absurd, crawling around like a baby, sucking a dummy, wearing a nappy, a thick spiked dog collar around his neck. A few more people joined them—grown men in nappies on their hands and knees, sucking on dummies, being dragged along by their red-lipsticked, black-corseted mistresses.

I nudged Carly. 'You don't see that every day on the North Shore, do you?'

What kind of people subjected themselves to this treatment, I wondered. How could they enjoy it? Was the butcher from my local supermarket crawling around in a nappy? Or perhaps the guy who owned the pizzeria? The local bank manager?

'Anything goes,' I overheard Trevor say to Mike. 'As long as it's consensual. We're all adults. But remember your safe words.'

Safe words?

I listened as Trevor explained. 'Red means stop, yellow means this is getting intense and green means keep it up, buddy.' He slapped Mike on the back and disappeared into the throng.

'You wanna get out of here?' Mike asked.

I was about to say 'yes' when Carly whacked me on the arm.

'What is it?' I said when she hit me a second time.

'Look,' she said, pointing.

I was staring at a dominatrix who looked slightly familiar—Tami from the newsagency?—when I noticed one of the nappy men look up. At first I thought I was mistaken. Shit! I wasn't. It was Steve. Jesse's husband.

Everything around me seemed to stop suddenly. Steve? Was I hallucinating? How long had this been going on? Was it legal? Did Jesse know?

I had to make a split-second decision. Stay still and hopefully remain invisible? Or make a run for the door? If we moved too quickly, we'd be spotted for sure, but if we stayed where we were, the group, including Steve, would walk—crawl—straight into us.

'The door,' I whispered to Carly.

She turned to follow me, but tripped on a rug and fell into my back. She cried out. I turned and pulled at her arm to keep her moving, but it was too late. Steve had seen us.

I could tell he was trying to place us, to figure out where he knew us from. Seconds later, it clicked. It probably didn't help that Carly was staring at him open-mouthed.

Steve was one cool customer. Only for the briefest of seconds did he looked horrified. Then he winked. Did he really think we were players?

'Let's keep this to ourselves, ladies,' he said, standing up. 'We wouldn't want anyone else finding out about your nocturnal activities, would we?'

'Our nocturnal activities?' Carly hit back. 'What about yours?'

It was hard to take Steve seriously considering he was wearing a studded dog collar and a nappy. Thank God for the nappy, I thought. I had no desire to see my friend's husband's penis.

His mistress tugged on his collar and he dropped to his hands and knees and she dragged him away. Poor Jesse. Imagine being married to that.

Toby, Mike, Carly and I made a hasty exit out onto the street.

'What do we tell Jesse?' Carly asked, sounding exhausted.

I had no idea. How could we bring it up? Invite her for coffee and say, 'By the way, do you know your husband frequents sadomasochistic sex parties?' Or maybe, 'When your kids were babies, did you notice Steve getting unusually excited by the sight of their dummies and nappies?' I thought not. And would Jesse believe us anyway? I could hardly believe it and I'd seen it for myself.

'We let it be,' I told Carly.

'I can't believe you're saying that.'

I couldn't believe I was saying it either, but would Jesse thank us for telling her?

'Let's sit on it a few days before we do anything,' I added.

3

Jesse drove like a maniac the two kilometres to her house and then felt guilty. She'd had two glasses of wine. Imagine if she got pulled up for drink driving and lost her licence. She'd never live it down.

She drove into the garage, then took three deep breaths before getting out of the car and walking inside the house. As she neared the family room, she could hear Anna, the babysitter, talking on her mobile. She stopped outside, exhaled deeply, clenched her hands tightly and entered the room.

Anna looked up and smiled. 'Gotta go,' she said into her mobile, before putting it in her handbag and standing up. 'Good night?'

Jesse nodded. 'Sorry about the mix-up. I thought Steve would be home by now.'

Anna shrugged. 'No drama.'

Jesse walked her to the front door, paid her sixty dollars and said goodnight. Then she started her nightly routine. First, she checked on her nine-year-old twins, Ollie and Emily. She kissed them both lightly on their foreheads and whispered, 'I love you.' In the darkness, she picked up discarded clothes and toys scattered on the floor, then went about checking that all the doors and windows were securely locked.

Satisfied her home was in order, Jesse texted Steve and got ready for bed. But she couldn't settle, annoyed that once again Steve had ruined her night out. She flipped the light switch on and off three times before climbing into bed.

Light on again, she reached across to her bedside cabinet, pulled a leaflet from the top drawer and scanned its headline. *Take charge of your life TODAY! Join the Secret Women's Business society. Let US help YOU make a difference!* Jesse's head was nodding. Yes! She desperately wanted to take charge of her life. *Don't put your life on hold. Start living TODAY, in the NOW!* The words spoke directly to her, compelling her to take action.

She slumped back against the headboard. Who was she kidding? Jesse couldn't imagine going to a meeting, or getting along with the types of women who would frequent such gatherings. Deflated, she shoved the leaflet back in the drawer.

She checked to see if Steve had returned her text. Nothing. No doubt he was angry with her. She shook her head. That was the wrong way round: it should be Jesse who was angry at him. It wasn't as if her going out should have posed a problem. Anna was more than willing to babysit, and Jesse was the one who had organised her, as well as cooked dinner for the twins. The house was tidy—as it always was. No, the real problem was that Steve was a control freak. He didn't like her going out, and he hated her friends. The last time Jesse had been out with the girls was close to three months ago.

Her last social outing with Steve had been his work Christmas party, but that had been a fizzer. Jesse would have liked to have had more fun; she was certainly open to it. It was a Hawaiian theme so she'd worn a hula skirt, a coconut bra, the whole bit.

Everyone had made an effort to dress up. But Steve was on edge the whole night. Every time she opened her mouth, he'd stared at her, silently urging her to keep quiet. So she'd sipped her soda and limes (of course, it was expected she would be the designated driver, as always), made superficial chat with a few people and spent the rest of the time on the outskirts of conversations.

At one point, she'd overheard some of Steve's work colleagues complaining about the hours he kept. 'His lack of commitment rivals Max's in accounts,' said one sales guy, who Jesse recognised but didn't know by name. She'd put it down to jealousy. Steve knew how to network—he'd spent most of the night doing just that, talking 'global economies' with various people.

After ignoring her most of the evening, a pissed Steve had demanded a head job in the kitchen when they'd arrived home, fluorescent lights and all. Yes, they still had regular sex, but sometimes it felt to Jesse that they were just two bodies going at it. Steve didn't like to kiss, so they hadn't for the last couple of years. It was all about getting on with the job and getting his rocks off. She thought it would be nice if he occasionally returned the favour, but he wasn't interested. That's what her marriage seemed like to Jesse most of the time—a job. And not a very fulfilling one at that.

Still, she reasoned, she lived in a lovely home and they had two adorable children. At least she wasn't Stella who was about to go through a divorce. Okay, Stella actually seemed quite fine with it, but who wanted to live with a divorce under their belt?

Jesse shook her head. Despite her reluctance to acknowledge it, sometimes she thought that was where her marriage might be heading, too. She and Steve hadn't been entirely happy for months. His moods had been getting worse and she was losing patience trying to figure out why. He seemed to have lost interest in her—they never talked properly any more—but at the same time he'd become completely paranoid about what she was doing, where she was going, who she was seeing. The combination of his neglect, his increasing absences and his obsessive need to know what she was doing twenty-four hours a day had brought on Jesse's quirks again. Then again, Jesse believed marriage was for life. Her own parents had stuck it out, so why couldn't she? She had children, after all.

She'd been truly shocked when Stella and Terry split. They were like one another's best friend. She laughed at his jokes; he listened attentively when she told stories. Their kids were well-adjusted, normal. If it had been Carly and Brett who were divorcing, Jesse wouldn't have blinked. But Stella and Terry? They'd seemed solid.

The way Stella had explained it, they were friends more than lovers these days. 'Terry's like a pair of old slippers,' she'd said. 'And they're not comfortable any more. They're tired, thin and worn. I still love him, but I'm not in love with him.'

But wasn't that what marriage was supposed to be, Jesse thought. Best friends who have sex?

She checked the bedside clock: 1 am! She considered phoning Louisa in San Francisco, but thought better of it. Her sister would be rushing out the door for work. Instead, she ran through the next day's to-do list in her mind. There was an open morning for Ollie's class; she had to shop for dinner; and Valentine's Day was fast approaching. What to buy Steve?

She must have dozed off because she woke with a start when Steve climbed into bed.

'Hey,' she said, reaching over to cuddle him.

'Tired,' he grunted and turned his back on her, falling almost instantly to sleep.

Jesse sighed, relieved that he didn't want sex. She was tired and still annoyed with him for ruining her night out. She rolled over, thinking back to the leaflet and the phrase *Start living TODAY, in the NOW!* How impossible that seemed.

Carly woke up with a killer hangover. Brett wasn't beside her, but there was a full glass of water on the bedside table. She gulped it down before looking at the clock. Eight o'clock. Shit! Brett would have left for work over an hour ago.

She struggled out of bed and wrapped a light dressing-gown around herself. A quick survey of the house revealed that Will had also departed for school. She walked back into the bedroom, and was about to flop down on the bed when she saw her phone flashing—a text message from Toby. Instantly, she was transported back to her drunken flirting of the night before when she'd been not so secretly rebelling against her mundane suburban life. It had seemed like a good idea at the time . . .

'We're heading to party,' cute Toby had told her. 'You keen?'

Was she keen? He could have told her he was off to wrestle crocodiles and she'd have joined him.

But now? In the harsh light of day, it was a different story.

Hands shaking, she read his message. *What a night, hey? Not what I expected. Dinner next week?*

God! She shook her head, deleted the text, and dialled Stella's number.

'Please tell me we didn't end up at a suburban sex party last night where we sprang Steve dressed as a baby,' she said.

'Okay.'

'Good. I was hoping it was all a bad dream.' Carly paused. 'I've driven along that street so many times.'

'Same,' Stella said.

Carly took a breath. 'Toby was cute.'

'Yeah. Not so sure about his friend Pete.'

'He sent me a text.'

'Who? Pete?'

'No. Toby.'

'I'm not surprised. You were all over him.'

Carly shook her head at the memory. 'Don't remind me. I'm an idiot. What are we going to do about Jesse?'

'Like I said last night, let's leave it for the moment. It's too bizarre. How are you feeling?'

'Disgusting. Ashamed. Embarrassed. Hungover.'

'Okay,' said Stella, 'you've painted a pretty clear picture. Take two Nurofen Plus and go back to bed.'

After hanging up, Carly curled up on the bed and slowly pieced the events of the night together. After their awkward run-in with Steve, the four of them had hightailed it out of the house, leaving Pete behind. Last Carly had seen, he'd been enjoying the attentions of three women dressed up as headmistresses. Where did people find the energy? All she'd wanted to do last night was cut loose—drink some wine, maybe dance. Then she'd met Toby and now he'd texted her.

What the hell had she been thinking, flirting with him? Things weren't great with Brett, but that was no reason to behave the way she had. Carly wanted to die of shame.

She remembered that, earlier in the night, Stella had been annoying her about behaving inappropriately. Sometimes she really should listen to Stella. But Carly had been having a good time and had wanted to forget for a couple of hours everything that was going on in her life. Forget that her oldest son, Nicholas, had gone overseas for the year; and that her other son, William, had less than two years left of school before he'd be taking off as well. Then what? She'd float around alone in this big empty house while Brett continued to work twenty hours a day, seven days a week.

She missed Nicky intensely. He said he hated her using the pet name, but when she did and he was in a receptive mood, his whole face lit up like he was seven years old again. It made Carly feel like she was dancing on clouds. It broke her heart that she wouldn't get to see that gorgeous face for another ten months.

She got up from the bed and walked into the kitchen, searching for something to make her feel better. She ate a banana and instantly wanted to throw up.

Had she really told Stella and Jesse she wanted a fuck buddy? She'd only been joking . . . sort of. Bloody hell, she wasn't a bad person. It was just that Brett spent more time at work than he did at home. And when he was here, he was preoccupied and tense. He had two Blackberries and it wasn't uncommon for both to be glued to his ears at all hours—when he wasn't chained to his iPad. The closest sexual companion Carly had these days was her vibrator, the Rockin Rooster. Brett was too busy keeping track of the money market, too concerned about 'hostile takeovers' and 'significant mergers', to trifle with her.

It hadn't always been this way. She thought back to the beginning of their relationship when everything was brand new and exciting. The first few times they'd had sex had been awkward: both of them were inexperienced and they'd had to work out how to kiss so their teeth didn't collide, and how to make their bodies fit together. But six weeks into their friendship, it had all clicked. That was one day she'd never forget.

They'd met up during Carly's lunch break. As soon as she saw him, the palpitations had started: nerves, excitement, desire. When they'd kissed hello, she'd felt the frisson between them.

'Hungry?' Brett had asked, staring at the menu.

Carly had been hungry, but not for food. Underneath the table her foot nudged his. Boldly, she'd placed her trembling hand on his thigh under his shorts, desperate to touch him skin to skin.

He'd reached over and kissed her. 'I'm already hard,' he'd whispered. 'Let's get out of here.'

She'd smiled, allowing him to take her by the hand and lead her back to his car. They'd leaned against the bonnet and he'd kissed her deep and slow, his hands cupping her butt, their legs entwined.

'Get in,' he'd said softly.

Irresistible desire . . . she couldn't even think about refusing.

Less than ten minutes later, they'd arrived at Lane Cove National Park and he was parking on a secluded track.

'What about rangers?' Carly had managed half-heartedly as he'd tilted the front passenger seat back as far as it would go and angled himself above her.

'Live dangerously.' He was already pushing up her skirt.

She'd grinned, grabbing at his shorts, pulling them down. It had felt so naughty, fucking in broad daylight where anyone could walk by and catch them. But Carly didn't care. Neither of them did. They were young, possibly falling in love, so what the hell did it matter? Brett was right. *Live dangerously.*

Carly had wriggled down the seat till her bum was practically on the floor.

'What are you . . . oh,' said Brett, as she took his penis in her mouth.

God knows what it must have looked like from the outside: Brett gripping the headrest, rocking back and forwards, Carly thankfully hidden from view.

He'd been almost delirious as he reached down and pulled at her hair. 'Come up, I want to fuck you now. I can't wait any longer.'

They'd manoeuvred themselves into position and he'd thrust inside her, his grip slipping to her waist. Carly had pulled her mouth away from his and tilted her hips into him, allowing maximum penetration. They'd rocked together, Brett sucking her breasts, bringing her to orgasm before letting himself come. That was when Carly had known Brett was her soul mate. They'd be together forever.

She smiled at the memory and looked down at her erect nipples. They hadn't had car sex, or any other kind of sex, in a long time.

In the early days, even though they had two boisterous toddlers and lived in a tiny terrace with a mortgage that made them gag, they were in love, horny and happy. When they went out with other parents from preschool, they'd listen to them complaining about the lack of sleep and sex. Brett and Carly couldn't understand it. They couldn't get enough of each other. She'd felt like the luckiest woman on the planet back then: two adorable boys, and a husband who loved her and loved being a dad as well. She'd hit the jackpot. And when he was away on business—phone sex.

Things had changed around six years ago, when Nicholas had started high school. Brett was increasingly busy with work—lots of travel, late-night conference calls. To alleviate the boredom and loneliness, Carly threw herself into volunteering on several school committees. All of a sudden, they'd stopped talking. Brett hadn't seemed overly concerned by the situation. Whenever Carly mentioned that they had nothing in common except the boys, he'd look at her quizzically and say, 'That's a major common interest, don't you think?' Carly would agree and they'd limp along for another few months.

These days, they were lucky to make love once or twice a month . . . and she'd been dead unlucky since New Year's Eve.

Sometimes Carly wondered if Brett was having an affair. That would certainly answer a lot of questions. She imagined confronting him and asking why he couldn't put his energy into having sex with her rather than nailing some floozy who didn't live with him.

Last week, during one of their discussions, she'd even asked him if he was seeing someone else. He hadn't been shocked because it was a question she asked him every three or four months. He'd said no. When she'd suggested they might like to sleep in separate rooms, he'd just shrugged and mumbled something unintelligible. The next morning she'd apologised and he had too, even suggesting a night out together in the city. Brett had good intentions but they hardly ever came to fruition.

Carly walked into the bathroom, contemplated having a shower and thought better of it. She didn't have the physical energy. Still, her mind wouldn't rest.

She thought again about Toby, the fuck buddy business. She didn't want to fall in love. She just wanted a playmate. A handsome playmate. Then again, she was married. She'd never been unfaithful to Brett in all their nineteen years of marriage and she doubted she'd ever have the courage to. It was all bluff—her fantasy. Yes, she'd fondled Toby's hair last night, but that was as far as it had gone. It wasn't as if she'd tried to take his clothes off and have sex with him in a public toilet. Still, she felt like a tool.

She wandered back into the kitchen. The house felt so empty. God, she missed Nicholas. She kept telling herself the gap year overseas was good for him: he needed to spread his wings;

experience life; find out what it was like not having an automatic dishwasher, cleaner and maid at his beck and call. He'd left on 2 January. He hadn't wanted his parents to drive him to the airport; he'd complained that Carly would cry and cause a scene. 'That's so not cool, Mum,' he'd told her. Carly had had to promise him she wouldn't weep.

On New Year's Day, he'd let her help him pack his suitcase, mainly because he was hungover from the night before. Carly had washed and ironed and packed, and held it together. Nicky's flight the next day was at four thirty in the afternoon, so they'd mooched about in the morning. She'd made him his favourite breakfast—pancakes, bacon, hot chocolate, the whole bit—but all too quickly it had been one o'clock and time to leave.

'Don't touch anything in my room,' Nick had said on the drive to the airport. 'I might come back in a year.'

'What do you mean, "might"?' Carly had asked.

Brett had looked at her. 'What the boy's saying is that after living away from home for a year, he may get a taste for it. There's no guarantee he's ever going to live with us again.'

'If I thought that, Nicholas,' she'd said, her eyes brimming with tears, 'I wouldn't let you leave in the first place.'

'Mum, you promised,' he'd warned.

Inside the terminal, swarms of teenagers from Nicholas's school milled about, far too excited about their upcoming gap-year adventures to consider their heartbroken parents. Carly had recognised most of the parents kissing their sons and daughters goodbye; not all by name but by sight. But she didn't want to socialise. Her entire focus was on her eldest son, who was deserting her, flying the coop . . . You couldn't tell Carly there weren't favourites in families. In Carly's house, it was Nick and her, and Brett and Will. God knows how it worked when couples had more than two children. It didn't mean she loved Will any less; it was just that she and Nicholas were simpatico. They got each other.

For a few years, back when Nicholas and William were at primary school, Carly did think about having another child. Seriously. But Brett was blasé.

'What more could we want?' he'd asked as his boys darted around the soccer field, freezing and covered in mud, but happy.

A baby girl, Carly's mind had responded, but she'd pushed those feelings aside. She had her son, Nicky—the one who had inherited her blue eyes and her habit of rubbing her right shoulder when she felt stressed and the one who wanted to explore life outside his own neighbourhood and take risks. Brett had his son, Will. Will who, with his father's build and temperament, was always ready to defend his dad.

Right from the very start, Nicky had been hers; he'd always gone to her first when he was upset, happy, hungry. She used to have to encourage him to talk to his father, so attached was he to her. But Will . . . well, with Will Carly had found out what it was like being the second wheel. William sought his father out in every situation. William was Brett's and Carly hadn't minded so much . . . until now. Until Nicholas had left her.

Thinking back, another child would surely have caused disequilibrium. She was glad there were just the two boys.

Carly went to the computer, switched it on and logged into Facebook. She checked Nick's status update at least once a day, sometimes more. Apparently, it was bitterly cold and snowing in Wales, but Nicholas was having the time of his life coaching the senior rugby team, or assisting, at least. *Pub night, Friday! Schoolies sneaking out to join us*, he'd reported recently in one of his updates. He certainly sounded busy and happy, as if he'd found his purpose.

There was no update today.

Carly had been banned from writing on his wall—in the early days, she'd written *I love you, Nicky* and he'd heatedly told her never to do that again. How was she to know her post would be read by his 458 friends? Now she sent him an email message: *Missing you, Nicky. Hope the weather isn't getting you down. Love Mum xx*

And Carly did miss him. Norman, the cat, missed him too, and she was sure Brett did as well, although he hadn't said much beyond the fact that it was Nicholas's rite of passage and Carly should stop bombarding him with emails and Facebook messages.

Probably the only one who was happy with the situation was Will, who'd just started Year Eleven. There had always been healthy competition between the boys. They were very different from one another and had always bickered and fought. They couldn't play tennis or eat a meal together without it ending in a brawl. Carly imagined William was quite chuffed about Nick's departure. No more having to share the remote, the computer, or the car once Will got his licence.

Tonight, Will was staying over at a friend's. He'd started going to gatherings nearly every Friday and Saturday night. She wasn't so naive as to think he was all pure and innocent. He'd had a girlfriend for five months last year. That had ended in October and he'd been heartbroken. 'Mum, I was in love,' he'd said.

In love! All of fifteen and he was in love. She'd tried giving him the big sex talk but he hadn't wanted a bar of it, just yelled, 'Mum!' whenever she broached the subject.

Nicholas had had a couple of short-term girlfriends but nothing serious. He'd always had more group friends. And when he'd found out he was going to Wales for twelve months, he'd told her: 'No point finding a girlfriend now and having to break up with her when I leave the country.'

Carly glanced at the clock: 11 am. Long, tedious hours of loneliness stretched ahead. This evening, Brett was attending a business dinner—for a second she wondered if it was anything like the business dinner Steve had supposedly been at last night. Brett had invited Carly along, but she wasn't up to it. She felt too insecure, too lost. In fact, the only time she felt good about herself these days was after a few drinks.

Maybe she needed a hobby. She used to be busy all the time: teaching Nick to drive, volunteering for committees, hosting school functions. This year, she hadn't wanted to do any of that. She'd had enough of committees and morning teas. But she did have to think seriously about what she was going to do for the next forty years. Did she really want to be sitting at home for the rest of her days?

Carly had worked in retail, merchandising, after she'd left college. That was how she'd met Brett. She was setting up a display of the latest Dior fragrances in David Jones and he'd walked up to her seeking advice on what perfume to buy for his mum's birthday. She'd found out later his mother's birthday had been the previous week. Before she knew it, they were married with toddlers. She hadn't given paid work a second thought. When Will started high school four years ago, she'd returned to work, taking a job merchandising for a clothing company. She'd jumped in headfirst: the hours were long but rewarding. It had been exhilarating. But a few months after she started, she'd come home one night when Brett was away to find Nick and a couple of mates drunk. She shuddered at the memory. He was fourteen years old. Carly had made the decision then and there to quit.

She'd become complacent about her parenting and this was the result. Brett had fully supported her. In fact, he'd cut back on his travelling for a few months, too. Since then, Carly hadn't worked. As for Nick, it had appeared to be a one-off incident. She hadn't seen him drunk again for another three years.

Maybe I could do a course at university as a mature-age student, she thought. Wouldn't that be great? Nick was starting a commerce degree next year, not that she wanted to study commerce. But surely she could find an interesting course to keep herself occupied.

Leaving the computer still switched on, Carly walked into Nick's room and opened a cupboard. There were toys shoved at the back from when he was seven. She stared around the crowded room, at the clothes he didn't wear, the paperbacks he had no intention of reading, all his past exam papers, assignments and school texts. She hadn't thrown anything away for years because she'd thought Will might use the past exam papers and the books. But Will didn't read. And for exams, he crammed the night before—when he wasn't on his iPod, computer or mobile.

In the distance, the phone rang. As she reached it, the answering machine kicked in. Just as well. It was Brett and she was way too ashamed to talk to him right now.

4

After the phone call from Carly, I drove to the library. All the way, I couldn't stop thinking about last night. We all knew Steve was odd. Okay, odd's probably not the right word. Smarmy. The Steve I knew was always in control and immaculately dressed: Armani suits, Ralph Lauren polos. He prided himself on his appearance, so clean and neat. For God's sake, he was the Australian marketing director of a huge international pharmaceutical company. But this would totally change everything. How exhausting leading a double life.

Jesse called an hour later, when I was neck deep in cataloguing a swag of new titles.

'Hey,' she said. 'Did you end up going to the party?'

'Jesse, hi. Yeah—'

'Sorry I ditched you. It's just with Steve working late, I didn't think it was fair of me to keep the babysitter waiting.'

I stifled a cough. 'Sure. What time did he get home?'

'Late. Two-ish maybe. He was up at the crack of dawn this morning, bleary-eyed but ready to face another day.'

I was sure he was.

I said I'd fill her in on the details later and tried to end the call. Not only was I uncomfortable talking to her, the cataloguing wasn't progressing as smoothly as I'd hoped.

'About the books I stacked the other day . . .'

'It's okay, Jess. I've fixed them. No need to worry.'

'Maybe I'm becoming a bit preoccupied again.'

'You're fine,' I said. This wasn't a conversation I could have with her over the phone. 'Let's talk about it when you come in next Thursday? Okay?'

The truth was, Jesse was starting to become a problem at work. Although she was thorough and dedicated, once she became fixated on something, like tidying up the magazine racks, it would take her the best part of a morning. Then there were the few times recently when she hadn't been able to stop clenching her hands. I'd taken her into the bathroom and helped calm her down, but it had taken a good half-hour. I knew the situation couldn't continue indefinitely but I was hoping to find a solution to satisfy Liz, the manager, so Jesse's job remained secure.

Then there was Steve. What a fuckwit! Maybe I needed a man's perspective—I could ask Terry. I wondered what he'd have to say about it. Maybe he already knew. I thought about it some more. Nah, Terry couldn't keep a scandal that big to himself.

I had no time to deliberate further. Business at the library was brisk. At eleven, I was running toddler hour and some parents didn't seem to understand that it wasn't a babysitting service. You couldn't dump your kids in front of the reader (twenty-one-year-old Skyla, studying English literature at Macquarie University) and dash off to the shops. Which meant I was on parent patrol.

'Can't you just watch them for a minute?' one particularly hassled mother asked after she was caught trying to bolt out the automatic doors.

'No,' I replied, polite but firm. I really wanted to say, 'Does this look like a day-care centre to you?' The nerve of some people.

She slunk back over to toddler hour and her two-year-old twins, no doubt wishing I was dead.

The rest of the day flew by in a blur. It was two o'clock and I was heading out the door before I'd had time to blink. I had to pick up Terry's mum and take her shopping, which I did most Friday afternoons. Just because Terry and I were divorcing didn't mean I had to divorce June. She'd been good to me over the years, especially when Hannah and Ben were younger, picking them up from day care, babysitting. She'd been a saviour. And after Terry's dad, Jim, died, looking after the children gave her increased purpose and meaning. Running around after little kids doesn't allow much time to wallow in your own grief and misery. So, no: I didn't see why the kids and I had to give up June.

Besides, she wasn't any closer to accepting the separation. It had been a shock for most people. Perhaps it would have been easier for others to understand if we'd had a huge blow-up or showed some warning signs of discontent, and it probably didn't help that I didn't feel the need to tell anyone but family and our closest friends that Terry had hooked up with a colleague.

Aside from telling Hannah and Ben, telling June had definitely been the hardest part.

'What about your father?' she'd said to Terry. 'He's not well; his heart will give out when he hears.'

It had taken us all a few moments to process what June had said. Jim had been dead eight years.

'Silly me,' she'd stammered when she realised. 'You've got me completely worked up. I still think of your father as being with us. It's hard to believe he's been gone all these years.' She'd recovered enough to add, 'You and Stella had such a beautiful wedding! The croquembouche was a culinary masterpiece. I've never tasted anything so delicious.'

That was true but, as we explained, a sublime wedding dessert was no reason to stay together indefinitely. It was a painful dinner, and Terry hadn't even mentioned Amanda.

'You're going to have to tell her,' I said to him afterwards. 'Just introduce them—get it over and done with.'

Terry had been horrified. That conversation had happened in October, over three months ago, and he still hadn't said a word to June. Now he and Amanda were living together.

Aside from the issue with June, things weren't too awkward. Terry had come to both Hannah's and Ben's end-of-year speech nights, though because he'd been running late we didn't sit together. (Hence why I'd first noticed Mike.) We'd chatted amicably after Hannah's dance concert, and watched Ben play his end-of-year cricket match. We'd even ended up having Christmas lunch together—although not with Amanda. I wasn't ready to play happy families with her and neither were the kids.

Terry's new apartment (or, rather, Amanda's apartment) wasn't particularly close, but it was on the train line so if the kids wanted to go there after school or on weekends, they could. I knew Terry would have preferred to see and speak to Hannah and Ben more often, but right now they weren't keen on their dad living with somebody who wasn't their mother. I appreciated that. I keep telling Terry it wouldn't matter who she was: the kids weren't comfortable with their father having a girlfriend, period.

Ben had commented that he already had one mother and 'Two would be torture. A stepmother, ugh!'

I thought that was jumping the gun: Terry hadn't said anything about marrying Amanda. Then again, I was as surprised as they were when Terry had announced he was moving in with her.

'It's just wrong,' Ben had said.

'Totally gross,' Hannah agreed. 'See, Mum! You're not in the loop. You don't know what's going on with Dad anymore.'

She was probably right—not about it being gross, but about me not being in the loop. But I didn't feel bitter or angry. I was sad for the kids that they didn't have two parents living together and raising them, but this was the way it had turned out. It could have been a lot worse. Imagine if Terry and I had hated each other and fought over custody, visitation rights and the house. Ugh, indeed!

The person who seemed to be finding it most difficult was Terry himself. When I'd seen him last weekend, he'd looked as if he was carrying the weight of the world on his shoulders.

'You should be happy. New girlfriend, new life,' I'd told him.

'Yeah, but the kids hate me.'

'They don't hate you. They just don't like seeing their dad slobbering over his younger girlfriend, especially in public.'

'I don't slobber and she's not that young.'

'You know teenagers. They can't stand to think their parents might be having sex, especially with other people. They'll come around. A few of their friends' parents are divorced. A couple have even remarried. It's a sign of the times.'

'How about you, Stella? How are you doing?'

'If that's your subtle way of asking if I'm getting any, the answer is no. And I have no intention of meeting anyone either. I just got rid of you.'

Inside my head, a voice was saying, 'Liar! What about Mike?'

'Don't you get lonely?' Terry asked.

I shook my head. 'Why the sudden interest? I'm doing just fine.'

Maybe Terry had wanted me to ask him about his new life, but I didn't go there. It wasn't my job any more to stroke his ego and tell him what a fabulous catch he was. He was doing okay . . . and if he wasn't? Well, it wasn't my problem.

Rather like Jesse and Steve weren't my problem. Yes, I would prefer not to have seen Steve trussed up like a baby, but that was life. Maybe our chance encounter last night would persuade him to come clean to Jesse. That'd be one hell of a conversation. *Guess what, honey? I love dressing up as a baby, sucking on a dummy and being spanked.*

When I pulled into June's carport, she was all dressed up and waiting for me on her veranda.

'June, hello. What are you doing outside? It's far too hot.'

'Nonsense,' she replied, kissing me briefly on my cheek.

On the road again, I asked about her shopping list.

'The usual,' she said, 'but with Terry's birthday coming up, I want to buy him something special. Golf balls maybe.'

'He hasn't played in a while,' I ventured.

'He played last weekend when David was visiting.'

I took a deep breath. David was Terry's brother and, to the best of my knowledge, the last time he and Terry had played golf together was a good five years ago.

'Are you sure, June? I think it might have been a bit longer.'

'No, we went to the clubhouse afterwards for a barbeque, remember?' She paused a moment, then added, 'You might be right. Golf balls would be wasted on Terry. They all seem to end up in the pond.'

I wasn't sure if she'd remembered how long ago that barbeque had been, or if she had just changed her mind. I didn't want to push it so I simply nodded and drove on.

The rest of the afternoon passed uneventfully. We shopped at Coles, then went to Myer where June bought Terry a navy Country Road shirt. Maybe she was just absent-minded. She had always been eccentric, more so since Jim died. Example: she had plenty of hair but liked wearing headscarves and turbans. Today she was sporting a lime green and orange turban. When Jim was alive she'd only worn them on special occasions because he wasn't overly fond of them, but as soon as he passed, she said, 'Bugger it. I'll be dead a long time. I'm going to wear my drapings every day.'

And that was it. June was famous in the neighbourhood for her fabulous turbans and scarves. I suspected she liked the attention. It was a flamboyant look without being completely over the top.

I dropped June home and helped unpack the groceries, then left her to her books and knitting. I felt guilty: I should spend more time with her. But there were only so many hours in the day and often I found myself running out of time and energy.

As I got back into the car, my mobile rang. The screen flashed 'unknown number' at me.

'Hello,' I said tentatively.

'Stella?' It was Mike. 'I'm ringing to apologise.'

Lightning bolt! My hands were instantly clammy.

'I'm mortified Pete took us to that . . . um . . . place,' he went on. 'Maybe we could meet up again?'

'At another swingers' party?'

'Preferably not.'

'Pity, I kind of enjoyed it.'

What was I saying? I wasn't skilled at impromptu flirting. I felt giddy.

There was silence on the other end of the phone.

'Mike?'

'Yeah?'

'I'm joking. I have to admit though, some of those scenes keep popping into my head.'

'Have you spoken to your friend, the one whose husband—'

'No! How would I go about bringing up the subject?'

'Yeah, not easy. You really don't think she knows anything?'

'Jesse? No way.'

'What about the cocaine?'

'What do you mean?'

'Well, he was probably high. You did see the coke on those trays, didn't you? We're getting a lot more middle-aged men suffering cocaine overdoses in emergency these days. Your friend's husband fits the profile.'

Far out! Steve was using drugs as well as going to these sex parties? It did my head in, just thinking about it. What a mess.

'So should we try meeting up again for coffee?' Mike said, pulling me back into the conversation. 'Or, better still, dinner?'

My heart was pounding and the phone in my hand was shaking. But I had to be sensible. I liked Mike, a lot, but he was a complication I didn't need right now. So, as much as my body hated me, I gave him a vague response, thanked him for dropping me home the previous night and wished him a good weekend.

'You can't avoid me forever,' he said as I went to hang up.

'I can try.'

Mike laughed. 'That's not going to work. You're already hooked.'

'So am not.'

'So are.'

I hung up smiling. I was so hooked, it was ridiculous.

•

Terry phoned later that evening. The kids were happily tapping on their computers—Facebook, MSN, downloading music and no doubt participating in other activities I'd banned them from doing—and I'd just poured myself a glass of cold pinot grigio and was settling in to watch *Pride and Prejudice*, the version with Colin Firth as a buff Mr Darcy.

'We need to talk,' Terry said.

Sounded ominous. Why oh why had I answered the phone? It was Friday night. I'd been enjoying myself.

'What about?' I asked.

'Mum.'

I sat up. 'June? What's the matter? I saw her this afternoon. She's fine.'

'She seems to have a problem with Mandy.'

'Back up. You've introduced them?'

'Tonight. I turned up with Mandy to take Mum to dinner. It was a disaster.'

I looked at my watch. It was only just after eight. 'Jeez, it must have been if you're home already.'

'Mum kept asking for you. Wouldn't let up. I tried explaining but she wouldn't listen. Just kept saying that it wasn't the right way to treat my wife and that Dad would be very disappointed. I think it's going beyond her normal forgetfulness, Stella. I'm worried about her. I knew something was up when I arrived. She wasn't dressed for dinner, and she kept rabbiting on about the garden hedge, saying it needed trimming. I don't know what to do.'

'Trim the hedge for starters.'

Terry sighed.

'How did Amanda react?' I asked.

'She was shocked, obviously, especially as Mum kept calling her a home wrecker and telling her I was old enough to be her father.'

45

'That's harsh. Her much older brother, sure, but father?'

'It's not funny. Mum was rude, Mandy's in tears, and all of a sudden I'm very tired.'

'Okay, well, I'm sorry for you but—'

'Could you check in on her tomorrow?'

I could have said no, but given my feelings for June, I didn't. 'Sure.'

He sighed—again. 'Thanks. I appreciate it. How are the kids?'

'Good. Busy. You know what they're like.'

'I miss them.'

'Want to talk to them?'

'Maybe tomorrow.'

We hung up and I went back to watching Mr Darcy.

Specifically, that scene with Colin Firth carrying on in the lake with the wet shirt. It got me thinking about Mike. Well, fantasising, actually.

What would I do with him if he was in front of me . . . naked?

I'd be terrified . . . almost.

I figure I'd tie him up and have my way with him after I'd teased, kissed and probed my way about his body.

Bondage? Where had those thoughts sprung from? It wasn't like me at all. I was normally so sensible. Obviously the sex party antics had affected me more than I wanted to admit.

I shook my head.

I had children . . . responsibilities. But the thought of Mike's hands and lips caressing . . . Stop it, Stella!

Still, it made me wonder . . . why didn't I just say yes to his invitation to meet up again?

5

*J*esse was in the kitchen on Friday evening, preparing a prawn laksa and waiting for Steve to come home. Wine was chilling in the fridge, and Emmy and Ollie were occupied with the Xbox playing Kinect Adventures. She was looking forward to a nice family evening with the four of them enjoying dinner together and then watching a family movie like *Rango* or *Kung Fu Panda*. But whether that would happen or not largely depended on Steve's mood. These days, any exchange between them had a nasty habit of quickly spiralling into an argument. She'd say something that Steve misinterpreted, or he'd say something that Jesse took the wrong way. There was always something upsetting him—the kids were too loud; the toothpaste wasn't the right brand. She felt as if she was walking on eggshells and didn't understand why.

Her mind jumped to her job at the library. She'd been thinking about asking for more hours. There was a full-time position coming up and she was seriously considering applying for it. But Steve didn't like her working. He was much happier when she was at home all day. She'd done that when the twins were little, but she'd missed the library, missed her tiny slice of independence, being surrounded by books and interesting customers. After the twins had started school, she went back to working part-time.

Stella had got her current position at the library: two days a week, ten until two. Easy. Jesse loved working with Stella and Skyla—not that their rosters always coincided. And they were good to her, helping her out on bad days when she got stressed. And she did get stressed, especially when it was her turn at the customer enquiries desk. Why couldn't people wait in line to be served? Instead, they clustered around the desk and coughed or said 'Ahem' to get her attention. She knew they were there; she wasn't blind. Couldn't they see she was already serving someone? The polite thing to do was to stand back, give the person in front of them space, and wait their turn. It wasn't brain surgery. Then there were the patrons who asked long-winded questions and wouldn't stop talking long enough for her to answer them. They just kept going on and on.

Jesse stirred the laksa. Yes, her job was sometimes stressful, but she was confident her issues could be ironed out, especially if she worked full-time. For starters, she'd have more time to complete all her duties.

She jumped when Steve walked into the kitchen. 'Hello,' she said, giving him a beaming smile. 'I didn't hear you drive in. Good day?'

'Long.' He kissed her on the cheek and peered over her shoulder into the pot on the stove. 'Smells good.'

'Prawn laksa. Drink?' She walked over to the fridge and pulled out a bottle of wine. 'Petaluma, one of your favourites.'

While Steve went into the next room to greet the kids, Jesse poured two glasses. She took a small sip from her own, knowing she'd tip most of it down the sink later.

Steve came back in, picked up his glass and took a mouthful. 'What's new?'

He seemed relaxed and responsive, so Jesse jumped in. Now was as good a time as any to bring up what was on her mind.

'Darling,' she said, 'there's a full-time position coming up at the library.'

She waited for a response . . . Nothing.

'I'm thinking about applying for it.'

He took a longer sip of wine and let her statement hang in the air before replying. 'We've been through this before, Jess. Our family comes first. You can barely manage a part-time job. If anything, you should cut back your hours. The kids are your priority, or at least they should be. I have my doubts after last night.'

'Emily and Ollie *are* my priority, always! You know that.'

'So you say, but what about those afternoons when you've been held up at work?'

'That was one afternoon, Steve. One! And Mum picked them up. The kids were none the wiser.'

'But I was.'

Jesse could feel herself starting to twitch. She needed to turn some switches on and off, but Steve was watching, monitoring her behaviour as always. Her hand reached out sneakily, searching for a button to press.

'It would be nice to have some extra cash coming in,' she said.

She meant it, though she could never hope to match what Steve earned. Her job probably brought in a twentieth of what his did, reducing her to little more than a financial footnote. Money equalled power. Steve earned all the money therefore he had all the power. It played on her mind, especially these days. Whenever she asked him for extra money, say for new cushions, he always questioned it. It wasn't that she didn't have access to his money, she did, but it was assumed she would stick to a monthly budget. But at certain times of the year—like November and December, the Christmas shopping months—it was tough. In January, too, when she had to buy new school shoes, uniforms and so on. Steve had no idea how much everything cost. Jesse put as much as she could on lay-by, but she couldn't lay-by shoes. The kids' feet grew too quickly.

'We have enough money,' said Steve. 'Is this about the new plates you bought last week?'

The kitchen plates—she'd forgotten about those. She'd been shopping at Coles and there'd been a homewares promotion just outside on mid-priced crockery. Jesse had spent sixty dollars on the plates, which were discounted from a hundred and ten, but Steve hadn't been impressed.

'It's not about the plates, Steve, though if I was working more I wouldn't have felt so guilty about buying them.'

'You're not making a sound argument. You did buy them, regardless.'

He stared at her, waiting for her to say something . . . to challenge him. But there was little point in continuing. He was a much better debater than Jesse was. She usually felt like an illiterate imbecile after one of their discussions.

Steve put an arm around her. 'I know you like being at the library, it's your escape. But with my job and the long hours I work, it's not fair on the kids. Is it?'

At that moment, Emily bounded in yelling, 'I beat him. I beat him again at *Stand-Up Rafting*. I can ride the rapids better than anyone in this house!'

'Oh yeah?' shouted Ollie, running in after her. 'Well, I'm better at *Rallyball* than you.'

Just as quickly, they raced out again, Emily screaming 'Are not!'

Jesse sighed. 'You have a point.'

'I know I do,' said Steve triumphantly. 'You barely have enough time for all of us as it is. I run a distant third here.'

'That's not true,' Jesse said. 'It's just that there's always something going on with the kids—homework, excursions, sport, music.' She felt overwhelmed just listing their activities.

'Exactly, so how could you manage a full-time job on top of everything else?'

Jesse gave up and turned back to the laksa. Sometimes she wondered if Steve was jealous of the time she spent with Emily and Oliver. She needed to work harder at getting the balance right so all three of them were happy ninety per cent of the time. But then where did that leave her? How did her personal satisfaction and happiness rate on the scale? Perhaps if she could work up the courage to attend one of those Secret Women's Business meetings, she'd learn the secret to keeping everyone happy and satisfied, including herself.

'At least you're over that silly idea of having another baby,' Steve said, draining his glass.

That took her by surprise. 'Why do you say that?'

He shook his head. 'You're talking about a full-time job at the library?'

'Oh, but I do want another baby. That hasn't changed.'

'Jesus! I'm sorry I brought it up. Make your mind up, Jesse. Do you want a full-time job or do you want another baby? You can't do both! Besides which, you know we can't afford another kid—not even with your minimal financial contribution. When's dinner?'

Jesse stared at the pot, blinking back tears. She hadn't added the green prawns yet. 'Ten minutes.'

Steve put his empty glass down on the bench. 'Right then. I'll have a quick shower.'

Jesse stared as he walked out of the room. She did want another baby. She loved the twins to death and was serious about her library career, but that didn't mean she didn't want another child. But Steve wouldn't hear of it.

'You need to get your nervous habits under control before we can discuss having another child,' he'd said on several occasions. That was when he wasn't telling her they couldn't afford it.

Jesse knew she was only nervous because she didn't know what was up with him. She wouldn't feel so anxious if he treated her better.

She'd had such high hopes for tonight and now they'd already had two disagreements in the space of twenty minutes. The weekend stretched ahead and she couldn't bear the thought of more arguments. The tension and stress was too much; Steve was a footy fanatic but unfortunately the football season hadn't started yet. The Australian Open had finished so there was no tennis to distract him. There would be motor racing and wrestling on Foxtel, but that wouldn't interest him for long. She could always offer the usual massage and blow job to get him into a positive mood, but she was starting to resent performing these favours and getting nothing in return, not even a thank you.

Blinking away more tears, she told herself to get a grip. Steve had a busy schedule. She needed to back off. Be grateful for what she had, who she was, and what they had together as a couple and a family. She was just being greedy. Once Steve was out of the shower, everything would be fine. She just needed to relax.

Giving in to her urge, she opened and closed the fridge door three times and immediately felt the tension ease from her neck and shoulders as she counted down. Ten, nine, eight . . . She knew she shouldn't do it but she always felt more in control afterwards.

'What are you doing?'

She jumped. 'Nothing,' she answered quickly, knowing he'd caught her and wishing she could snatch back the last two minutes.

'Bloody hell! I saw Ollie doing the same thing the other night. Are you taking him back to that psychiatrist?'

'Shush, keep your voice down. Ollie's doing fine. And he was seeing a psychologist!'

Jesse shook her head. Sometimes she almost hated Steve. She stared out the window to her car in the driveway. Sometimes she felt like getting in it and just driving away. People like Carly fantasised about fuck buddies, but when Jesse fantasised, it was about escaping. Grabbing her two kids from school one afternoon, leaving town and never looking back. They'd head north-west into the country, where they'd find a pretty cottage in a friendly town—somewhere with a white picket fence and a few acres. It would be sunny every day and they'd grow fruit trees and be happy. Just the three of them, away from the stress and hassle of city life. Jesse would make jam and bake cakes and biscuits for the local weekend market. Their lives would be idyllic.

'So,' said Steve, bringing her back to the present, 'care to tell me about last night?'

'Last night?' she said, surprised. 'With Carly and Stella?'

He reached for the wine bottle. 'You seem to spend a lot of time with those two.'

'Before last night I hadn't been out with them in months. They're good fun.'

'Isn't Stella getting a divorce? Do you really think she's a good influence, especially given the way things are with you?'

Jesse bit her tongue. Good influence? How old was she? Twelve? 'Are you saying Stella's a bad influence because she's separated? That's ridiculous.'

'Ridiculous? I'm ridiculous because I think you spend too much time with vacuous women who are out on the prowl? God knows what you got up to last night.'

Jesse counted backwards from ten before speaking. 'I was home by ten o'clock. And you know exactly where I was for the two hours before. At the pub.'

'So you say,' and he stalked out of the room.

She took a deep breath, wanting to keep it together for the children's sake. To buy herself a few minutes, she fussed about the kitchen, tidying up, washing dirty dishes, wiping down benches. Finally, she could procrastinate no longer.

As she went to get the bowls for dinner, she noticed her phone flashing to signal a new text message. It was from Carly: *Home alone Friday night, missing my eldest. Either of you keen on the movies tomorrow pm?* The message had obviously been sent to Stella as well.

Had Carly forgotten what it was like having nine-year-olds in the house? As if Jesse could take off to the movies at a moment's notice!

She peeked into the lounge room where Steve was playing with the twins. He was still handsome. Most men his age were losing their hair and gaining a paunch. Carly's husband, Brett, was getting rounder by the day. Terry was a bit like that, too, but Stella had said that since he'd moved out, he'd joined the gym.

'Dinner's ready,' she called out.

She dished up the laksa, determined to stay optimistic and bright. As she sat down to eat, she kept telling herself she could do it. She had to do it. It was her job to ensure harmony. Marriage was a compromise. Sometimes you had to do things you didn't want to, to keep the peace. It was called managing the situation.

Thankfully, Jesse didn't have to work too hard at dinner. The kids had so much news to share and their enthusiasm was contagious. They chattered on about school, swimming classes and sport. Then Ollie mentioned a movie he wanted to see on the weekend because 'all the other guys have seen it'.

'Not me?' said Emily.

Ollie shook his head. 'Of course not you. You're a girl!'

'I'll take you,' said Steve, looking up from his laksa.

Wow, that was a surprise, Jesse thought. Progress.

Ollie beamed and punched his fist into the air. 'Yes! A boys' afternoon.'

Jesse smiled. 'Excellent. Carly's invited me to the movies tomorrow, too. I'm sure we can see something that you'd like, Em, so all three of us can go.'

'Yay,' said Emily, bursting with excitement.

'You see too much of that woman,' Steve cut in. 'She's a bad influence—I don't want her around Emily.'

On and on he went. Jesse couldn't understand it, especially in front of the children. It was only an invitation to the movies, not an invite away on a girls-only weekend to Melbourne. In the end she said, 'Forget I ever mentioned it,' and set about clearing the bowls away.

She put the kids to bed, read them each a story and then took herself off to bed, too. If Steve was in a foul mood and didn't have the decency to explain why, so be it.

But by the time he came to bed, she'd calmed down.

She rubbed his back. 'What's up? Have I done something wrong?'

He shook his head. 'Just tired, that's all.'

'Maybe you need to get away from us for a weekend. Why don't you and your mates go up to the Gold Coast for a golfing weekend?'

Steve loved the Gold Coast, but Jesse found Surfers Paradise seedy and depressing. Too many cracks in the pavements, too. She reasoned that Steve heading up for a weekend with his mates every few months might mean they could avoid a family holiday there later in the year.

'So now you're trying to get rid of me, is that it?'

She couldn't win.

She thought about sneaking out of bed once Steve was asleep and phoning Louisa, but she knew that if she let her guard down and told Louisa her troubles, her sister would say what she always did: 'Get outta there, Jess. Run away. Come over to San Francisco and stay with me.'

It was best just to try to get a good night's sleep. She'd ring Louisa first thing tomorrow.

Louisa shut her laptop at the end of her working day, ready to catch the Nob Hill cable car home to her cat, Ziggy, and boyfriend, Philippe. Ah, Philippe!

She'd only introduced him to a handful of her friends, and those who had met him had instantly started teasing her for being a 'cradle snatcher'.

'So it's just sex, is it?' one of them had asked.

'No . . . and yes,' Louisa had replied.

Philippe made her happy. He massaged her toes, and she liked the feel of his young unwrinkled skin against hers. He didn't have any of the bitterness that came with age and experience. He was free, unburdened. Louisa didn't question why he was with her. He was and that was all that mattered.

She'd wanted him the first time she saw him: when he walked into her Wednesday afternoon tutorial group five months ago, at the start of the semester. He was late. Late and laughing, acting like everyone else in the room had just missed out on hearing the funniest joke. She kept her eye on him. It helped that he had a toned, muscular surfer's physique (those arms!), sun-bleached blond hair and a cheeky broad smile. He was late to other classes too, but was always beaming and full of energy. How did people get to be that sparky? Louisa blamed his youth. Occasionally, he'd disrupted the class with his antics, but she never cautioned him because he was a good student and his assignments were always handed in on time.

In October last year, however, he'd handed in a truly shocking piece of research. There was nothing to it; it was transparent and juvenile. Louisa had failed him. To his credit, he'd come to see her in her office that same afternoon.

'Philippe,' she'd said, 'you can do better than this.'

He'd grinned at her. 'Really? Can you teach me? I don't have any experience but I'm a quick study. If you want me, I'm available.'

Louisa didn't need to be asked twice. She'd locked the door and banged him on her desk right then and there. She'd never done it on a desk before. It was exhilarating. They'd been so frenzied, there was little time for foreplay. He'd whipped out his erect cock, Louisa gasping at the sheer thrill and decadence of it, and that was that!

Eventually, they'd moved from the desk to the carpet, and again the sex had been hurried, hungry.

Despite knowing she was risking her professional reputation, not to mention making a complete fool of herself with a student, Louisa had invited him back to her place.

'I can be there in thirty minutes,' he'd said, tucking himself in and zipping up his jeans.

'Better make it an hour,' she'd replied, doing her best to sound casual.

Fifty-seven minutes later when she buzzed him in, just on dusk, they'd barely made it to her bed, kissing, pulling and tugging at each other's clothes as if they might never see each other again—which was the way Louisa usually played her sex life.

When Philippe ripped off his T-shirt, she'd marvelled at his muscled chest. She'd had her hands all over it barely hours before, but now it was as if she was seeing him properly for the first time. She slid her fingers inside his jeans in search of . . . ah! Her gaze dipped, taking in his tight, tanned body, his obvious arousal.

He pulled her close, slipping her black jersey dress easily off her shoulders. He released her bra and started gently exploring her nipples with his tongue, before moving down to lick her stomach playfully. 'You're perfect,' he murmured, before moving lower and finding her inner thighs . . . He'd kissed her and teased her, his tongue hot and nimble, bringing her right to the edge of orgasm.

Dizzy with a desire she hadn't experienced in a long time, Louisa felt the hot spasms coursing through her body. She groaned as his hands wrapped around her butt, pulling her closer.

He lifted his head. 'I think you're ready for me now.'

Louisa had let out a strangled 'yes' as he snaked his way up her body and kissed her with passionate force. She wrapped her legs around his waist as he thrust into her, loving the feel of him, all of him, deep inside her. She felt desirable, fuckable. Philippe was definitely going to prove to be a distraction at work, no doubt about it.

And he was! He was all she could think about those first couple of months—his skin, his lips, his eyes, his touch. She practically orgasmed looking at him. He was extraordinary. Still, there was no way she was going to fall for him.

Several years before, when Louisa had first started working at the university, she'd fallen in love with an older colleague, an English professor, who had wooed her with all the best lines from the Romantic poets. They had a brilliant two-year affair, right up until his announcement that his tenure was coming to an end and he was moving back to New York City and his wife. Devastated, Louisa had vowed never to fall in love again.

Standing on the cable-car platform, the wind whipping her hair around her face, Louisa smiled to herself as she recalled Jesse asking about Philippe when they'd spoken on the phone last night.

'When am I going to meet him?' Jesse had wanted to know.

Louisa had been her usual non-committal self. 'Maybe during our summer break. It really depends on what courses I'm teaching.'

'Can you at least email me a photo then?'

'I guess I could do that,' Louisa had laughed. 'How are things with you?'

'Busy, the usual.' It wasn't like Jesse to be so brusque.

'And the library?' Louisa had pressed her.

'There's a full-time position coming up that I'd love to get.'

'But?'

'But nothing. Steve doesn't want me to apply for it.'

Louisa had wanted to scream, but it wasn't her place to interfere . . . Though sometimes she just couldn't help herself. 'Jesse, you should go for it if that's what you want.'

'I guess.'

Jesse had changed the subject, clearly not wanting to pursue that conversation. Instead, they'd made small talk while Jesse cleared cereal bowls and fussed over the twins. It was seven in the morning in Sydney and Jesse had sounded tired and fed up.

'How can you stand it, Jesse?' Louisa had asked. 'Day after day? Don't you want to scream?'

'This is my life, I have to get on with it. My home, my kids, my life. No one else is going to live it for me.'

'But some part of you must yearn for freedom and adventure,' Louisa had persisted.

'Maybe. But it's not my time yet. One day it will be, but not today.'

When the call ended, Louisa had put down the phone feeling like she'd missed something important during their conversation.

She couldn't quite believe that her sister had remained married to that prick for so long. If she ever found out the truth . . .

But Louisa quickly put that thought out of her mind. Jesse never would find out the truth—that was why Louisa had stayed out of her life all these years.

6

Usually I was up by seven, even on a weekend, but today I'd slept in until eight thirty. Something of a miracle for me. Must have been all those dreams about Colin Firth, or maybe Mike. It was now mid-morning and I was driving over to see June. Terry had called me half an hour ago to remind me. As if I'd forget.

I'd asked the kids this morning if they'd noticed anything odd when they'd spoken to their nanna recently. They'd looked at me as if I had two heads and gone back to what they'd been doing. Ben and Hannah weren't really in speaking mode these days. They were teenagers, the world revolved around them, and if it didn't? Well, they weren't interested. I got it, but I'd have appreciated more than the occasional grunt from time to time. Ben was the worst. He was attached to his phone, iPod or computer twenty-four seven. Hannah was a bit more communicative: she'd chat about friends, music or the latest movie she'd seen if she was in the mood. But if she wasn't up for a talk, forget it. It was monosyllabic answers all the way. So I hadn't really expected much of a response when I quizzed them about June.

Then I'd moved on to their dad. 'He'd really like it if you both stayed overnight some weekends,' I told them.

'Yeah,' said Hannah.

'Yeah, you will?'

'Yeah, no. Can't this weekend. Lucy's having a party.'

I shook my head. 'Ben?'

He was wolfing down an overflowing bowl of Weet-Bix. 'Nup. Exams.'

'Come on, guys. You need to see your dad and I need a break.'

'Thanks a lot,' said Hannah. 'I'm sorry we're such a burden and ruining your perfect life!'

Perfect life? What the . . . ?

'You're not a burden, darling, but Dad misses both of you. He wants to see you, take you out to dinner, the movies—'

'I'm good,' said Ben. 'Anyway, if he wants to see us why can't he come here?'

'Because he wants to show you his new apartment.'

They'd both rolled their eyes.

'I don't think so,' said Hannah. 'I don't want to stay overnight with Dad's lover.'

Well, when she put it like that.

'Can you at least call him?' I asked. 'Organise to go to the movies or something with him tomorrow?'

They'd both shrugged and scarpered, leaving me to clean up the breakfast mess. As well as that, I had the daunting prospect of baking some scones to take to June's. She loved scones, so as much as baking didn't appeal to me, I'd given it my best shot.

'Hi June,' I said when she opened her front door. 'How are you this morning? Thought you might like some scones. They're still warm.'

Nothing seemed amiss. June was dressed and wearing a purple and cream turban. Clearly, she'd eaten cereal for breakfast—the porridge container was sitting on the bench. She seemed in high spirits as she put the kettle on.

'Go walking this morning?' I asked.

June was one of those people who got up before daybreak every morning without fail and walked every morning without fail, unless there was a cyclone warning or blizzard—both unlikely occurrences in Sydney.

'Of course. Best part of my day,' she said briskly.

I'd never been up before sunrise, except once, to catch a 6 am flight to Darwin. Of course, when Hannah and Ben were babies I was often awake at that time, but I'd worked hard to erase those memories. Sleep deprivation and I did not sit well together.

June pulled out two teacups from the cupboard. 'Beautiful morning, but it's going to be a scorcher.'

I watched as she moved nimbly around the kitchen. 'Terry tells me dinner last night wasn't so good?'

June turned to me and raised her eyebrows.

'What?' I probed.

'I don't know why he had to bring that woman.'

'And which woman would that be?'

'Why? Has he got a few?'

'Good one, June. Not to my knowledge. But seriously, he said you wouldn't talk to Amanda.'

'Did he? Well, what does he expect? Taking up with a woman who wears plunging necklines. They should both be ashamed of themselves. What about you and the children?'

'I'm fine. You know Terry and I are separated, right?'

She looked at me as if I had two heads. I knew which side of the family my kids had inherited that from! 'Of course I know,

63

but that doesn't mean I'm happy about it. In my day, you stayed married until you died. There was no other choice. Marriage or death. End of story.'

'Thankfully, times have changed.'

I covered several scones with strawberry jam and whipped cream while she poured boiling water into the teapot. 'Come and sit down,' I said.

She inspected the spread. 'Lovely. Where did these come from?'

'June! I baked them this morning.'

'Yes, of course. Silly me.'

Over the tea and scones, we talked about June's plans for the following week. I listened carefully to her every word. She certainly seemed to know what was going on with Terry. She dismissed last night's events as him being 'overly sensitive'.

She adjusted her turban. 'Terry's never liked confrontation. One bark and he's off like a dog with his tail between his legs. In some ways, he's still a child.'

I couldn't argue with that—she was spot on.

After an hour and a half, I'd decided that June had her wits about her, but was pissed off with Terry for not staying married and miserable like half the population. Yes, she was unimpressed with Amanda, but I was sure she'd come around.

When I arrived home, the house was empty except for the Cavoodle and the Burmese who were engaged in their familiar Mexican standoff routine, this time over a rogue slice of ham. Don't know why the dog bothered pretending to be brave, the cat always won. Without the kids around, it was almost too quiet. Not that I was complaining. It was nice to have some time to read the papers and play the music I wanted to listen to. However, my peace was shattered a few minutes later when the phone rang.

'Stella? Did you see Mum? Is she okay?'

I'd forgotten about phoning Terry to report back.

'She's fine. She was probably just tired when you saw her, having an off night.'

'I'm so relieved. I mean, it's not good she was rude to Mandy, but I was worried it might be something more.'

'It wouldn't be a bad idea to get her checked out by a doctor . . .' As much as I didn't want to alarm him, I did think June's forgetfulness was more than simple absent-mindedness.

'Really?'

'Yes, really, Terry. As much for your peace of mind as hers. Don't worry, I'll organise it.'

He sighed. 'Thanks. I appreciate it.'

'No worries. Enjoy the rest of your weekend.'

'What are the kids up to?'

'The usual: hanging out with friends, refusing to clean their rooms. Why don't you call them?'

'Because they don't want to talk to me. Are they home?'

'Not right now.'

'See. I'll catch them later.'

Poor Terry. In my kinder moments, I felt sorry for him. The kids didn't really want to spend time with either of us, but at least they were living with me. I could nose my way into their bedrooms occasionally and force them to talk. They weren't about to friend me on Facebook, but they weren't entirely locking me out of their lives either. I needed to get stricter with them about spending time with their dad.

I was settling back down with the papers when I noticed two text messages and a couple of missed calls on my mobile. The first text was from Carly inviting me to the movies this afternoon.

Maybe. The second message was also from her: *OMG! Ring me ASAP.* It had been sent an hour ago.

I checked my voice messages. The first was from Steve. That was a worry. When I heard the message, I couldn't believe what he was saying. I had to play it again.

'Stay the hell away from my wife, hear me? Jesse doesn't need the likes of you putting silly ideas in her head about working full-time at the library. And on that other matter, I'd advise you to keep your mouth shut if you know what's good for you. I repeat, stay away from her.'

The second message was from Carly; she sounded frantic. *'Did Steve call you? I'm still shaking. Ring me!'*

I replayed Steve's message. It was clearly a threat. Under the circumstances, I didn't think he was in any position to be telling us what to do. Besides, regardless of whether we saw Jesse or not, we could still tell her what we'd seen the other night. Steve couldn't stop us ringing her or texting her. She was our friend. I spoke to her practically every day.

I phoned Carly.

'Did he threaten you too?' she gasped.

'Yeah.'

'Stella, I'm still rattled. What are we going to do? Did you actually talk to him?'

'No, he left a message.'

'Same here. The guy's a nutter.'

'Look, I'm shaken, too, but I don't think he's going to do anything silly. He's just scared we're going to tell Jesse.'

'He didn't sound scared. I'm worried,' Carly said. 'Maybe we should steer clear of Jesse for a while? We don't want to make matters worse.'

I was furious, and thankfully that was overriding my fear for the moment. The nerve of him ringing and leaving threatening messages! I forced my voice to remain calm. 'I'm not so sure. We haven't done anything wrong.'

'Shit! I sent her a text message about going to the movies this afternoon.'

'Carly, did you hear me? We've done nothing wrong. If we suddenly stop talking to her, she's going to think it's strange.'

'Yeah, but maybe we should keep a low profile just for the next week.'

'What is this? *Underbelly Four*?'

'Worse.'

'I still can't believe we saw him at that party,' I said.

'Wearing a nappy!'

Despite our unease, we both burst out laughing.

'Did you tell Terry?'

'Nah. You tell Brett?'

'No way. I just keep wondering how long he's been doing this stuff,' said Carly.

I shook my head. 'Who knows? But seriously, I think it's best if we do nothing for the moment. And just try to ignore Steve.'

'And Jesse?'

'Let's take a step back, try to keep things as simple as we can for a while.'

I heard Carly sigh. 'Okay.'

After I'd hung up, I sat for a time thinking about Jesse, worried about what Steve might be capable of. No doubt he would be giving her a hard time right now. Most people would be extra nice if they got caught out like that, but that wasn't Steve's style. He was always right, no matter what. He could be caught with the crown jewels in his pocket and he'd still deny it.

I couldn't begin to imagine Jesse's reaction if she found out. She'd be devastated, her life in tatters.

I deleted Steve's message and then wondered if I'd done the right thing.

On Sunday morning Carly was still feeling shaken by Steve's threatening message. She'd spent yet another sleepless night tossing and turning, thinking about her behaviour with Toby, seeing Steve at the party, and what Jesse would do when she found out.

Over breakfast, Brett looked at her expectantly, as if he knew exactly what was going on in her head. She tried to keep a poker face.

'What are you up to today?' he asked, not unpleasantly.

Carly shook her head, rattled. It was on the tip of her tongue to tell him about Steve, but then she thought better of it. She'd have to explain about the party, why she was there and who she was with. She closed her eyes, imagining the scene.

'You went to a party with three strangers?' he'd say. 'You allowed three men you didn't know to take you to some party in a private house? You actually got into their car? Whatever possessed you to do such a thing? How much had you had to drink? How did you meet them?'

She could always blame Stella, say that she'd dragged Carly along, but Brett would never believe her. He'd quickly realise it was Carly who'd made Stella go. No, she really wasn't up for that discussion. It was better Brett didn't get involved. She and Stella would handle this alone.

'The usual,' she said in the offhanded tone she'd perfected when she didn't feel like talking.

He shrugged. 'Okay, well, I'll see you after Will's basketball game.' He kissed her lightly on the cheek and was gone.

Brett! The distance between them was widening into a chasm. She knew she was as much to blame for it as he was, but really, what did they share these days?

Sometimes, like now, Carly found herself staring into space, into nothingness. Just waiting the day out, for it to end, so she could go to sleep and not have to think anymore. It was like she was wishing her life away.

She sighed and decided to get on with the day. She was planning to tackle Nick's room. She'd asked him to do a big clear-out before he'd flown to the United Kingdom, but after the HSC was over he'd got caught up partying with friends, then it was Christmas, and suddenly he was gone.

It was a big room with built-ins along one complete wall. That would be a major task. The rest of the room was straightforward: bookshelves, bedside drawers, desk. Carly opened the built-in and shook her head. The top shelves were packed with books, toys and God knows what else. She went to get a ladder from the garage and several garbage bags. This was going to take some time, but if she approached it methodically . . .

Most of the things on the top shelves were from Nick's middle school years—school cap, tie, ribbons from sports carnivals, lots of photos stuffed into school diaries. She put them to one side and kept going. What she'd thought were keepers years ago (Year Eight maths books, exercise books crammed with French notes, English and history essays) she decided they could now live without. When on earth was Nick ever going to look at those notes again? She threw book after book down on his bed, pleased with herself to be making space in the cupboard.

Maths! The rows they'd had over that subject. Years Nine and Ten had been a struggle, with the distractions of hormones, first girlfriends and friendship dramas. Study had been well down Nick's list of priorities. But he'd ended up taking the subject right through to Year Twelve and he'd done well. All that torment and heartache had been quickly forgotten. That was why Carly was easier on Will, not that she'd admit it. They'd just gone through the hideousness of Year Ten with him, and she was hoping he'd follow in his brother's footsteps and settle down this year.

Stuffed away at the back of the cupboard, hidden from sight, were Nicholas's two favourite cuddly toys from when he was a toddler: Wags the Dog and Barney, a dinosaur. Carly took them out, smelled them and started getting teary. She looked inside the cupboard again. The top shelf had been cleared, but she was only a third of the way through the total job. She checked her watch. She'd been going for close to two hours.

Climbing down from the ladder, she stared at the mess on Nick's bed and sighed. She'd created far more destruction than she'd thought. Papers and books were strewn everywhere.

'Hey.' It was Will.

She jumped and turned around. 'How'd you go?'

'Smashed 'em. Sixty-four to twelve.'

'Ouch.'

'What are you doing?'

'Cleaning out Nick's room.'

'He'll be pissed.'

'Will.'

'What? He will be. Don't try to do this to my room.'

Carly shook her head. 'Where's Dad?'

'In the kitchen. We bought meat for a barbeque.'

Will wandered off and Carly looked again at the pile of junk on Nicholas's bed. She couldn't do any more right now; she'd lost her enthusiasm.

'Mum,' Will shouted from his room. 'Is it okay if Ben comes over?'

Stella's son, Ben, and Will had been best mates for years.

'Sure,' Carly called back. 'But clean up your room first.' And then let me know when pigs are flying overhead, she added to herself.

An hour later, after some lunch, she was back in Nick's room. She had to practise what she preached. When you start something, see it through till the end.

She gathered up the books and bits of paper off the bed. If she threw it all in the recycling, Nick would never notice, so that was what she was going to do—all those old maths books and notebooks, gone. No point getting sentimental over geography and algebra. But she'd keep his school diaries. She flipped through the one from Year Eight. He'd crammed it with ticket stubs, photos, notes. So cute. Those from Years Nine and Ten were similar, bursting at the seams with paraphernalia.

His Year Eleven diary wasn't as thick: obviously he'd got past the phase of pasting in every photo and note. When she opened it, a couple of pieces of paper fell out of a card. She picked them up and put them back inside, but then curiosity got the better of her and she started reading.

You're a hottie, the card said. *When I see you in class, smiling, wow! Please tell me we'll be friends forever.* It was written in large curly writing and signed '*B*'. Who on earth was B? Brenda, Bridget . . .? She couldn't think of many names starting with B. There was no date, but given that she'd found it in his Year Eleven diary, she assumed it was a couple of years old.

Then she read the notes. Still the same curly, girly writing: *Nicky, I hate it when we argue. Please forgive me. Forever, B xxx*

The next was sad and pleading: *Don't tell me what we have isn't special. This friendship means everything to me. I've seen into your soul. Please talk to me. Forever, B xxx*

Carly sat on the bed. She noticed that on all the notes, just above the B, the girl had drawn a bumble bee. Cute. But who was this poor girl and why hadn't she heard of her before? Nick had dated a Lauren, and an Ella. He'd taken Lucy to the semi-formal in Year Eleven and Maddie to the formal in Year Twelve. But a B? Bernadette? Becky? Carly couldn't come up with a name she remotely recognised. Why hadn't Nicholas told her about B?

She picked up his Year Twelve diary and scanned it. It was much the same as the others, full of scribbled notes, assessment dates, telephone numbers. It was like looking for a needle in a haystack. She shook the diary to see if anything fell out. Success! Several notes—none of them relevant, except the last one. *Nick, you are so cruel. You're the same as all the others. I'm sorry we ever met. No, forget that, I'm not sorry we met. Maybe when you finally grow up you'll realise what you've thrown away. Seeing you is a constant torment. Forever, B xx*

Poor broken-hearted B. Was there anything more devastating than the angst of teenage love? Especially unrequited love. Heartbreak didn't get any easier, but at least when you were older you were more capable of putting things into perspective. B . . . B . . . Brooke? Bree? Bailey?

Carly couldn't stop thinking about B all Sunday afternoon. She kept going over names in her head, trying to remember events, parties, gatherings, meetings of significance. Nicholas was a rugby head and sport took up most of his waking hours. He'd studied only when he had to, and spent most Saturday nights at the movies with his mates. He wasn't into the party scene, going out every other night and getting drunk and cracking onto girls. But maybe that was all a facade, Carly thought. He could have been seeing lots of different girls and just not bringing them home.

The only B Carly could come up with was Bella Anderson, who lived a few streets away. She was around Nicholas's age and they'd gone to the same primary school, but she'd attended a girls' school in the city. It was time to ask a few casual questions . . .

Carly wandered into the kitchen where Will and Ben were scoffing chocolate cake and ice-cream.

'So, I've been clearing out Nicholas's room,' she said.

Will turned to Ben. 'Mum's in a cleaning frenzy.'

'Yes, and I'm starting on yours next.'

Will went to object but Carly got in first. 'Joking. Look, do either of you know a girl whose name begins with B?'

'Totally random, but okay,' said Will.

'We've got a hot chick in our tech class called Bridie,' said Ben, smiling.

'And there's Billie in my English class,' said Will. 'Why do you want to know?'

'Just curious.' She probed further. 'Anyone from Nick's year?'

Will laughed. 'How would we know?'

'I just thought there might have been someone he was close to, whose name started with B.'

'Nup,' said Will, stuffing his face with ice-cream.

Carly busied herself cutting more cake for them and dishing up the rest of the ice-cream. 'Or a girl whose nickname had something to do with a bumble bee?'

The boys started laughing so much that they spat ice-cream and cake over the bench.

'Buzzy bee,' giggled Ben.

'Buzzing around the locker room . . .'

'And the showers . . .'

'Okay, let me in on the joke, boys,' Carly said, pointing her very sharp Global knife at them.

'It's nothing,' Will said, and he and Ben glanced at each other and giggled some more.

'Waiting . . .' she persisted.

Long beat.

'Buzzy Bee was one of the assistant sports coaches at school last year,' Will said.

Carly's mind was racing. Nick had been going out with an older woman? It made sense that she was into sports, but a teacher? That couldn't be good. And she'd been pursuing him? No wonder he hadn't told her about it. Had they done anything illegal? Nick had turned eighteen last June, but if she was . . . Oh. My. God. A teacher!

'Yeah, always hanging around the senior boys' locker room, checking them out,' Ben added.

'That's not very professional,' Carly said, raising her eyebrows, keeping her voice calm.

'No, Mum. Not professional at all.'

Both boys laughed some more.

'We all knew he was gay,' Will said.

'Pardon?'

'Mr Busby—he was always trying to crack onto the senior guys,' explained Will.

Carly put the knife down. 'What?'

'Relax. He only lasted a couple of terms before they shipped him off to Tasmania or Siberia . . . somewhere.'

She took a deep breath. 'Well, you shouldn't say things like that about the teachers. I'm sure he was just being friendly.'

'Yeah,' agreed Will. 'With guys he wanted to pork.'

'Thanks for the cake,' Ben said, licking his fingers. 'It was great.'

'Yeah, Mum, great cake. Ben, you playing COD?'

'Nah, I better get home.'

'Say hi to your mum,' Carly said as Ben scooted out the back door.

'Sure.' He gave her the thumbs up before disappearing into the garden.

In a daze, Carly cleaned up their mess. B was male? B was . . . a man? Nicholas's B was a sports coach called Mr Busby? That made no sense at all. She couldn't believe Nicholas would get involved in something like this. Who was this Mr Busby? Where had he come from? What did he look like? Had he coached Nick? She'd have to take action. Make a formal complaint to the school. Nicholas was obviously being harassed, stalked by a lunatic. There was no way this would have been a mutual attraction.

She raced back up to Nick's room and read the letters again. They made her feel sick. B made his feelings very clear, but clearly Nick didn't feel the same way and had tried to distance himself. The poor child. Why hadn't he told them he was being harassed by a teacher? They could have helped him. Maybe he had tried to talk, but she and Brett had been so caught up with their own problems, they hadn't listened to him. They'd shut him out because they were too busy arguing.

No wonder the kid had been excited about going to Wales—he was escaping B and leaving his parents as well, who'd done nothing whatsoever to protect him from this vile predator. While Carly had been conjuring up imaginary fuck buddies, her son had been pursued by a lunatic and scared out of his mind. It would have been too much for him to handle: a young kid being sexually harassed by a man. Why hadn't he spoken to her about it? Carly had let him down. She had failed him.

Now the question was: what to do with the information? Tell Brett? She didn't want to say anything to him, not yet. She couldn't. Wouldn't know how to start. Maybe she could talk to Stella about it? Although just what evidence did she have? Maybe those letters hadn't been written by this Mr Busby at all. Maybe they'd been written by a girl Will didn't know about. It was possible. Perhaps the best course of action was to send Nicholas an email.

She went into the study and turned on the computer. She stared at the screen a very long time before starting to type.

Hi Nick, how are things in Wales? We miss you. The house is empty and quiet without you. Hope you are doing fine and the weather's not getting you down. Please write soon. Love you, Mum xx (She added one of those ridiculous smiley faces.)

It was impossible to ask the question she desperately wanted to ask. What was she supposed to say?

Hi Nick, I found a bunch of letters from your admirer, Mr Busby. Was this guy harassing you? Or did you have a friendship together? Just wondering if there was anything going on, because at the moment when I put two and two together, I keep coming up with four. Please tell me what's going on.

If she started down that road, she'd never stop. Besides, it really wasn't a conversation they could have via email. The most sensible thing was to let the matter drop, at least until she could talk to Nick.

Sunday had been a disaster. Steve was being a complete misery. Jesse was trying to be supportive—she understood he had a demanding job; he told her often enough—but it was the weekend. Time to let up. But no, nothing Jesse said or did was right. Not only that, he wanted to know what she was doing, where she was going and who she was seeing—even when she'd popped to the local shops to buy a loaf of bread and the morning papers. It was weird. And he was jumpy, as if he was nervous about something. Normally, Jesse was the one who was anxious.

That afternoon, when Emily had been helping Jesse in the garden, planting petunias into clay pots, Steve had come outside just as Emmy had accidentally spilled some potting mix.

'Emily! Would you be more careful?' he'd shouted. 'You're making a huge mess.'

'Settle down,' Jesse had said, seeing that Emmy was about to burst into tears. 'It's just a driveway.'

'She has no respect for other people's property,' he yelled back. 'It's a filthy mess now.'

'It's okay, Steve. We'll wash it down.'

It had been a totally bizarre outburst. He'd calmed down eventually, but his foul mood had lingered.

When Jesse had cooked the kids' favourite, spaghetti bolognaise, for dinner, he'd barked, 'Couldn't you cook a decent meal once in a while?'

Straight after eating, the kids had scurried to their room to play a game of Monopoly by themselves, clearly not wanting to deal with their bickering parents. Jesse was tired and completely fed up. After yet another outburst—this time about his business shirts not being ironed correctly—she lost it.

'Our marriage is hanging by a thread,' she shouted, itching for a scene. Not only had Steve been behaving like a spoilt brat all day, but he'd ruined the kids' day yesterday by reneging on his offer to take Oliver to the movies.

Steve just looked at her like she was insane. 'One minute you want another baby, the next minute you're telling me our marriage is crumbling. You're all over the place, Jesse.'

She shook her head. Maybe she was. She couldn't control herself. She was clenching her fists so she wouldn't start switching lights on and off. Or closing doors, or checking the oven.

Instead, she walked out the front door and got in her car.

'You're not leaving me,' Steve shouted after her as she revved the engine. 'I'll never allow it.'

How could she have let things get out of hand like that, she asked herself as she drove to her mum and dad's. She was the one who needed to keep things running smoothly. Her role was to support Steve and look after the kids, not to storm out of the house. That was definitely not managing the situation.

Arriving at her parents' home, she composed herself to face a barrage of questions.

'Where are Steve and the twins?' her mother asked the minute Jesse walked in. 'Why aren't they with you? What's the matter?'

'Nothing, Mum,' Jesse said wearily. She nodded to her dad, who was watching *MasterChef Unplugged*.

'Have you heard from your sister?' Dot continued, barely stopping for air.

Jesse had needed to go somewhere quiet. Big mistake coming here. She should have gone to the movies.

Thankfully, her grandma, Milly, walked into the room with a pot of tea. 'Jesse, I thought I heard you come in. Cuppa?'

Jesse smiled and took the cup Milly handed her.

'That husband of yours looking after you?'

'Of course,' Jesse replied shakily.

'Hmm. Drink up. We've got apple crumble, too.'

'Thanks.' Apple crumble was the last thing Jesse felt like eating. 'How's church, Grandma?'

'Please don't indulge her, Jesse,' said Dot. 'Her and her happy-clappy new friends!'

'It *is* a church,' replied Milly indignantly.

'Do you even pray there?'

'What are you talking about, Dot? I pray.'

'I'm not talking about your fancy new age church prayers. I'm talking old-fashioned, word in the Lord's ear type praying. The kind of praying that gets answered,' Dot said putting her tea cup down on the coffee table.

'Mum,' Jesse said. 'Don't be mean.'

'Mean? You don't have to live with her.' Dot shook her head. 'Now drink your tea, Mum, and be quiet.'

'See how she bosses me,' Milly said to Jesse. 'I don't know how Tom's put up with her for thirty-six years.'

'Thirty-nine actually,' Tom said, looking up from the television.

Milly walked out of the room whistling an unfamiliar tune. No doubt about it. She was shrinking by the week.

The house was dark when Jesse got home. The kids were asleep and so was Steve, though he rolled over when she lay down beside him. A few moments later, he'd wrapped her in his arms and was pressing his naked body against hers.

'I'm sorry,' he whispered. 'This is the third month in a row that the team haven't made target and I'm taking it out on you and the kids. I can be a moody arsehole.'

Jesse tugged off her T-shirt and underwear and turned to face him. 'It's okay,' she said, stroking his hair.

'Mmm,' he groaned as his hand reached up to take hers and guide it towards his erection.

Moments later, his full weight was upon her and she was grinding into him. She wanted him to kiss her, but he turned his face away and started pumping. She wanted to believe that things would be all right between them, but the hurt and rejection was too much and she cried silently after he'd fallen asleep.

8

Could this weekend get any more bizarre? I'd spent most of Sunday afternoon in the emergency ward. June had taken a fall while doing some gardening and hurt her arm. Her neighbours had driven her to hospital and then rung me. I'd chased around trying to find Terry, without success. I found out later he'd been sailing on the harbour with Amanda. By the time I arrived at the hospital, June was receiving her X-ray results. And one of the attending doctors was Toby, Carly's friend from the other night.

'Small world,' he said.

'Are you looking after her?' I asked in what I hoped was a pleasant manner. Yes, he was old enough to be a doctor, and his name badge said *Dr Toby Mitchell*, but all the same I was nervous.

'Relax, Stella. Yes, your mother-in-law's had a fall, but I've mended many broken arms, mostly belonging to seven-year-old boys and seventy-year-old women. You'll be all right, won't you, June?'

'You scared me,' I said, bending down to kiss her.

'As it turns out,' Toby told June, 'there are no broken bones, but you've got extensive bruising and swelling. I'm going to wrap you up and keep you under observation for the next couple of hours.'

'That won't be necessary, young man,' said June, then winced in pain.

'June,' I said quietly, 'we should let the doctor get on with making you better.'

'I'm not sick.'

Toby gestured to the nurse to wheel June into a nearby examination room, then said to me, 'The other night was weird, hey?'

I nodded and looked around at the other doctors, nurses and orderlies. 'I don't know what I'd say to Pete if I ran into him again.'

'No fear of that. He's not on today. Neither's Mike for that matter.'

'Mike?' It took me a moment to register. 'The three of you work at this hospital? Together?'

Toby nodded.

Small world, indeed.

I left him to get on with wrapping June's arm and sat in the waiting room with a watery cup of tea and a copy of *Woman's Day* circa 2003. I glanced up at the wall mirror. I was a mess: no make-up and my hair was definitely in need of a good wash. I'd left home so quickly, I hadn't changed out of my house clothes. I was wearing cut-off denim shorts and a faded blue T-shirt. I guessed now wasn't the time to be worrying about my appearance, but I was relieved Mike wasn't at work given that I looked so scruffy.

By the time June had been given the all clear—she'd probably badgered Toby into submission—Terry and Amanda had joined me. It didn't surprise me that Amanda looked stunning. Her lipstick had been carefully applied and her short black hair was shiny and neat. She was also wearing a plunging neckline, which, while perhaps inappropriate for the hospital, showed off her generous cleavage.

'Mum,' Terry said, after a nurse had wheeled June into the waiting room, 'what were you doing standing on a ladder in the garden?'

'Trimming hedges. I told you they were growing out of control. Who's this?' she asked, pointing to Amanda.

'June,' I interrupted. 'You know Amanda, Terry's friend.'

Amanda smiled but said nothing.

Toby introduced himself to Terry, and asked him to sign several sheets of paper before handing over a bottle of painkillers.

'Mrs Sparks is free to go,' Toby told Terry and me. 'But she won't be able to do much for herself the next few days.' He turned to June. 'Don't worry, you'll get used to the bandage and sling soon enough.'

Terry nodded and the penny dropped. 'Doctor Mitchell,' he said, 'Mum lives by herself.'

Toby regarded the three of us. 'Mrs Sparks should be fine to go home in four or five days, when the swelling and bruising have subsided, but in the meantime it's best if she stays with family.'

He smiled at me. 'Nice seeing you again, Stella. And, Mrs Sparks, I'll see you in two days' time, okay?'

June nodded and Toby left the room.

Terry did a double-take. 'You know him?'

I didn't answer. 'So, June, what are we going to do with you?'

'I guess you can come back with Mandy and me,' Terry said.

'But I don't have a spare bedroom,' Amanda said, looking anxious.

'That won't be necessary,' June said. 'I don't want to be a burden. Nor do I want to be in the same house as that woman.'

'Mum,' said Terry firmly, 'you should be with me.'

'I'm not a bloody invalid,' June barked. 'My arm's bruised, that's all. I'm sorry I'm such a bother. Anyway, I want to go to my own home. I'll manage quite well on my own, thank you very much.'

Terry sighed. 'You can't do that. The doctor said you need to stay with family for now.'

'That's ridiculous. I don't need a babysitter.'

'Maybe not,' I soothed. 'But we'd all feel a lot happier if you stayed with Terry.'

Amanda shot me a warning look.

'Or perhaps,' I said, thinking aloud. 'You could stay at your mum's, Terry.'

'That wouldn't work,' he replied, genuinely horrified.

'Okay,' said June quietly. 'I'll stay at your house.' She nodded to Terry. 'Yours and Stella's.'

'But, Mum, you know I don't live with Stella any more. It's hardly fair—'

'If your mother wants to go home with Stella,' said Amanda, placing her hand firmly on his arm, 'that's what she should do.'

'I said I want to stay with you, Terry,' said June, her voice rising. 'You and Stella.'

'But—'

'But nothing. You can't expect Stella to look after me while you go off with one of your dalliances.'

Amanda flinched. 'I'd hardly call me a dalliance.'

'Really?' said June, looking her up and down. 'I would.'

'June!' I said, taking her hand. 'It isn't like you to be so rude. Is it the drugs?'

Amanda snorted.

'No, it's not the drugs,' replied June. 'I just don't like her.'

'Mum!' Terry was almost hyperventilating. He took Amanda's hand in his. 'I'm sure it's the medication, sweetie.'

The nurse coughed. 'Shall we go?'

She was waiting to wheel June to the lobby, where she could relieve the hospital of any further duty of care. We followed her and June down the long corridor to the hospital's front doors.

'What are we going to do?' Terry whispered in my ear.

'Well, clearly she's not going to Amanda's, which will be a huge relief to—'

'I'm right here. I can hear you,' Amanda said.

I turned to her. 'And are you relieved?'

'Well, yes, of course, but—'

'Okay so, Terry, if June's not going with you, and you're not prepared to stay at her place for a couple of days, then obviously she'll have to come home with me. It's not as if I don't have the room.'

I patted June's good shoulder. 'The kids will be thrilled to have you stay, darling.'

She rolled her eyes. 'My own son doesn't want me. Is this the way I brought you up, Terry?'

I loved the way she spoke to him as if he was still twelve.

We thanked the nurse and Terry carefully helped June out of the wheelchair. 'Where's your car?' he asked me. Clearly, he'd decided he wasn't up to arguing any more—with his mother or with Amanda. June was coming home with me whether she liked it or not.

'Good question,' I said. 'I was so flustered when I arrived . . .' I looked around. 'I think it might be . . . yes, this way.' I set off down the hill towards the underground car park.

Terry helped June into the car. 'I'll pop in tomorrow to see how you're doing, Mum. Okay?'

'Don't do me any favours,' she said.

He attempted to kiss her cheek, but she turned away and he ended up kissing her very grey hair.

'Right, I'll see you tomorrow,' he called out to me as I got into the driver's seat.

'Sure,' I said. 'Bye, Amanda.'

Terry grimaced again, and the two of them walked back in the direction we'd come, Amanda clinging on to Terry as if he might suddenly float away.

'You okay?' I asked June as I drove out of the car park and turned left onto the Pacific Highway.

'I feel silly.'

'About Amanda? Don't worry—'

'Amanda? Certainly not! I'm talking about falling off my stepladder and into the compost heap. I don't care what she thinks. She's just a woman who looks like a thin Liza Minnelli with a ridiculously large bosom.'

I grinned. She did a bit.

When we arrived home, the kids were waiting for us. Well, waiting was a bit of a stretch. Ben had arrived back from Will's minutes before but was already on the PS3 playing some war game and shouting, and Hannah was doing the Farmville thing on Facebook. Her crop of strawberries had just died and she was distraught—as distraught as you can be over the demise of cyber-fruit.

'So how about you guys stop what you're doing for a moment and say hi to Nanna,' I said when June and I walked into the rumpus room.

'Hey, Nanna, how's your arm?' said Hannah. At least she had the decency to look up momentarily.

Ben grunted, 'Hey', without pausing in his gunning down of enemy soldiers.

I made June a cup of tea and settled her on the deck with the day's newspapers while I went upstairs to make up the spare bedroom. I hadn't stopped to consider how her being here would impact on us. Not that there'd be a problem, but the kids had their routine and I had mine. Everyone was going to have to make some adjustments.

I had to laugh when I thought about Terry. He'd been so hassled at the hospital—his mother, wife and girlfriend in the same room and him trying to keep everyone happy. Amanda looked as if she'd swallowed nails. And Terry's reaction to Toby as it dawned on him that we knew each other . . . I'd almost seen his brain working as he tried to figure out the connection.

Toby! I rang Carly to fill her in. Sure, I could have walked the fifty metres to her house, but I was feeling lazy. Lazy and tired.

'Oh my God! That's so embarrassing,' Carly said. 'What did he say? What did you say? I can't believe the one night I go out and get smashed, I meet toy-boy Toby.'

'The one night?'

'Whatever. What I mean is, I was never supposed to see him again.'

'Even though he's rung you?'

'Twice, actually. I was so out of it, I forgot I'd given him my number.'

'I believe you scribbled it on his arm, several times.'

'I'm married, for Christ's sake.'

'And how's that going?'

'Fine. Good. Not that great. The usual. So June's staying with you?'

'Looks like it.'

'And you'll see Jesse at work on Thursday. What then?'

'Let's see how the next few days pan out.'

I hung up and set about cooking a chicken stir-fry. When Terry was here, he'd done most of the cooking. So far the kids hadn't complained about my average efforts, but they would soon enough.

June was outside resting in the late afternoon sun, the kids were still on their computers, and I had time to think as I chopped broccoli and shelled peas.

I'd felt little emotion when I saw Amanda with Terry today. No jealousy or dislike, envy or sorrow. I'd felt . . . nothing. She was just another person. I was sure she was perfectly nice, but I had no compulsion to get to know her, to find out whether she preferred green tea, Earl Grey or a latte first thing in the morning.

At six o'clock, the phone rang. Speak of the devil.

'How's Mum?' Terry asked.

'Fine. No problem at all.'

'Good, good.'

'And you?'

'Mandy's not happy. We fought the whole way back to her apartment.'

'That's no good.'

I really didn't want to have a conversation about his domestic bickering.

'Anyway, we've decided it would be better if Mum stayed with us,' he went on. 'I am her son, after all.'

'Good luck convincing her to move,' I said as I mixed the vegetables with noodles and chicken.

'I thought you might—'

'Look, I'm happy for her to stay with you, Terry, but I'm

not going to waste my breath trying to convince her to leave, especially when I know she doesn't want to.'

'Please.'

I sighed, and walked out to where June was doing the crossword. 'June,' I said, loudly enough for Terry to hear, 'your son's on the phone. He wants to know whether you'd prefer to stay with him?'

'Only if he's staying here,' she said, then shook her head and went on with her puzzle. 'Now, where was I?'

I walked back into the kitchen. 'As I was saying.'

'Fine. I'll talk to her about it again tomorrow,' he said, sounding tired.

'Listen, I know you're trying to do the right thing, but she's comfortable here. Honestly.'

'It's just that all my family is at my house except me.'

'Terry, this is what you wanted. Besides, you have Amanda.'

'Yes,' he agreed, brightening. 'I do.'

I hung up, and served dinner as everyone straggled to the table. I cut the noodles on June's plate to make it easier for her, but she ate slowly and with difficulty.

'Goodness me, you look like your father did when he was your age,' she said to Ben halfway through the meal.

'Yeah?' Ben mumbled.

'He was handsome, like you. I bet you have to fight off the girls.'

Hannah burst out laughing.

Ben glared at her. 'Shut it.'

'Terry was such a good boy when he was younger, so popular too. Girls were always ringing, badgering him about homework, dances, this, that and the other.'

'I think Ben's handsomer,' I said.

'Mum!' he groaned.

'Maybe,' said June, regarding her grandson thoughtfully. 'Pity he's dead,' she added.

I put down my fork. 'Terry's not dead, June.'

'Metaphorically speaking, darling.'

I couldn't work out whether she was saying it to get a rise out of me, or whether it was the painkillers taking their toll.

'Jimmy and I were forever shooing the girls away,' she went on. 'I miss him.'

'Terry?' I said. Why on earth? We'd only just seen him.

'No, Jimmy! He was such a strong ox of a man. Who would have thought his heart could give up like it did. He wasn't even doing anything extraordinary, just sitting in his chair reading the evening paper. One sip of beer, that's all he'd taken, and plop. He keeled over. The beer went everywhere. My poor carpet. It was never the same after that.'

I glanced at the kids, worried it would upset them hearing about their grandfather dropping dead. I needn't have. Ben and Hannah continued eating. They didn't flinch. Not one bit. Perhaps they'd tuned out or maybe they were just used to their nanna's quirks.

I turned back to June. 'Jim was a great man.'

'Sometimes, I think I see him. When I wake in the middle of the night, he'll be sitting at the end of the bed. He doesn't say anything, just hovers, watching me. I'll look at him and say, "For God's sake, Jimmy, what is it? Is it the turbans? Because I'm not taking them off, you know." And then he disappears.' She snapped her fingers.

'Sounds a bit *Twilight* for me,' said Ben as he stood up.

'Take your plate into the kitchen,' I reminded him.

'Your grandfather's not a vampire, Ben,' June said sharply.

'I think it sounds lovely, Nanna, having Granddad watching over and protecting you,' said Hannah, also standing up from the table.

Bless her. She could be so sweet when she wanted to be. Or wanted something!

'Spying, more like it,' said June.

'You know,' she said to me in a low voice, after the kids were out of earshot, 'Jimmy wasn't such a great man. He played around. He was a philanderer, just like Terry. I ignored it, but those years were hard.'

'Really? I never knew.'

'Why would you? We never talked about things like that back then. It was the era of JFK: your private life was your private life. But Bill Clinton and that Monica woman changed all that. Nothing's sacred any more. There are no secrets. Everyone knows everything about everyone.'

I had to agree. When Terry moved out, it seemed everyone within a ten-kilometre radius knew about it before his car had reversed out the driveway. Add in Facebook and Twitter and even cyber-strangers knew about our personal situation. I kept telling the kids they had to be careful about what they posted online, but apparently it wasn't them who'd spread the news; it was friends, and friends of friends. Almost immediately, my Facebook message page was filled with condolences and notes from people I'd never met. At first I'd started responding to them, saying it was a mutual decision and that I was fine, but I quickly tired of that. After the tenth reply explaining our decision, I thought, what the hell am I doing? Who are these people and why do I care? So I deleted the posts and went about my business.

'Over-sharing,' I said.

Long beat. June looked at me blankly.

'It's called over-sharing,' I repeated.

June nodded. 'Some matters are better kept private. So what are we going to do about it?'

I was about to say, I don't think there's much you can do about Jim's nocturnal visits. If he wants to sit on the end of your bed and watch you, and you believe he's watching you, then so be it, when she went on: 'Terry could do so much better.'

'Pardon?'

'That Amanda woman! How are we going to put a stop to this nonsense?'

I'd just got out the shower around ten thirty on Sunday night when the phone rang. It was an unknown number so I didn't want to answer it. The kids were always getting calls from their friends at odd hours even though I'd told them specifically, no calls after nine o'clock at night. They never listened. But I didn't want the phone to wake everyone in the house, so I eventually answered it in my gruffest mother's voice.

'Enjoy your weekend?' It was Steve.

I wrapped the towel around myself tighter. There was an uncomfortable silence until I said, 'What do you want?'

'You bitches have turned Jesse against me—'

'What? We haven't said a thing about what we saw last Thursday night—'

'And exactly what did you see?'

My hands were shaking. I wanted to hurl the phone to the other side of the room, but I also wanted to confront him, to tell him to back off and leave Carly and me alone.

'You know what I saw. You, playing dress-ups—'

'Your word against mine.'

'Your word against Carly's and mine.'

'That drunken flake? I'm not worried about her. But you say one word—'

'And what? If you don't tell Jesse what's been going on, I will. It's not fair on her.'

'Not fair? I'll tell you what's not fair. Having a wife who taps her foot, clicks her fingers, turns lights on and off—'

'No, this is about you and your perversions. You're the one who's in the wrong here.'

'Think what you like about me, but know this. If you breathe a word to Jesse or anyone else, I'll destroy you.'

The phone went dead.

I sat down on the bed and released my grip on the phone, but the indentation marks on my fingers remained. The smart me said I should call the police, or at least tell Jesse about the calls, but I still had no proof that he'd threatened me.

I'd known Steve for over ten years. We'd never been bosom buddies, but we'd been to school trivia nights together, library Christmas parties. Hell, I'd done the chicken dance with the guy. Okay, so I'd always been a bit wary of him, but only because of what Jesse had told me. If I met him on the street or at a party—a standard party—independently, I'd think he was your run-of-the-mill forty-five-year-old man, even though he carried himself with an arrogance that should only be the privilege of men like Brad Pitt and George Clooney.

But the Steve I'd seen and heard the past couple of days wasn't the Steve I knew. It was no wonder Jesse had been exhibiting physical symptoms of her anxieties: the guy had a split personality. The worrying part was I truly believed he could be capable of anything and I was beginning to fear for Jesse's safety.

I quickly texted her. *Everything okay at your end?*

Her reply was instant. *Of course. And you?*

I thought about telling her about June's arm, and then launching into a tirade about her maniacal husband, but thought better of it. *Yes, just thinking of you.*

I sounded like a deranged stalker, but at least she was okay. Then I considered calling Terry, but stopped myself. I didn't need him adding his two cents' worth.

Instead I wrote down the conversation with Steve, as accurately as I could remember it. I also wrote down what I'd seen last Thursday night. It was midnight before I'd finished. I read over my notes and wondered what to do with them. Send them to my lawyer in case Steve tried to bump me off? I didn't even have a lawyer.

It got me thinking. How long had Steve been involved in these sex parties? It obviously hadn't been his first time, so had it been months? Years? And then there were the people with him. I'd joked with Carly that they might have included the local teacher and butcher—but were we far off? Sixty people didn't just decide to have a night out in Warrawee unless it was for a school fundraiser. They had to be locals. Or were they? Steve was, but did that mean the other fifty-nine were, too?

On Saturday afternoon, I'd driven down party street. In daylight, it had looked even more suburban: immaculately maintained sidewalks, neat kerbing and guttering, and row after row of nondescript brick homes. I'd parked two houses down from the house in question and then walked to its gate. There wasn't a red light by the letterbox, or empty beer bottles on the front lawn . . . In fact, there was a red and purple welcome gnome standing to the side of the gate. The curtains were open. There was nothing to suggest this home was anything but ordinary.

Across the road, a man, maybe my age, was mowing the grass. Had he been at the party on Thursday night? Were all the neighbours involved? I walked back to my car and started the ignition. Maybe I'd come back another day and check out the letterbox to find out if Mitch and Sherri really lived there. Of course, I could have rung Pete—he had a key, after all—but I didn't have his number.

I drifted off to sleep, a new mantra running through my mind: *I will not be bullied*.

I wasn't going to let Steve's harassment get the better of me. Given time, I'd figure out a way of dealing with him.

9

$\mathcal{J}$esse had a restless night. She dreamed she was drowning, reliving a swimming accident from her childhood. She woke lathered in sweat and panicking. She fell back into an uneasy sleep, and when she woke again Steve had already left. That was odd. Normally, he made a big song and dance about getting up so early while she had the luxury of sleeping in till all of 6.30 am.

Before waking Ollie and Emmy, Jesse made herself a strong black coffee. She'd been worrying about the twins lately. They'd started commenting on her habits, especially Emily, and more so since she'd noticed Ollie doing similar things. Ollie was a great kid—sensitive and quiet—but just last week his teacher had told Jesse that he'd started tapping his pencil three times after writing a sentence.

'It's distracting for the other children,' she'd explained.

'I'll talk to him about it,' Jesse had assured her, trying desperately not to tap her foot as she spoke.

At school drop-off, after Emily had dashed off to find her friends, Jesse brought up the subject with Ollie.

'You know how Mummy sometimes taps her feet or checks to see that she's turned the light off?'

'Like a hundred times!'

'That's right. Do you ever do stuff like that?'

'Dunno.'

'Okay,' Jesse said, biting back tears. 'Just remember that if ever something's worrying you, or you want to talk about school or friends, you can tell me. You like school, don't you, Ollie?'

'It's okay.'

'Good.' She drew him close and hugged him.

'Can I get a new game for my DS?' he asked.

That was the extent of their mother/son chat. Jesse didn't want to make a big deal out of it if it didn't need to be a big deal. Everyone had quirks. So what if hers and Ollie's were a little more obvious than other people's?

She watched Ollie run off into the school yard before returning to her car and driving home. It was a gorgeous, sunny day. She should have walked. Maybe yoga was the answer. If she could control her breathing, then maybe she could control other parts of her body. Often, it felt as if her hands and feet had minds of their own, minds she was powerless to control.

She'd only been home a few minutes when Steve rang.

'If you think I'm leaving, you've got another think coming,' he said.

'Pardon?'

What the hell was going on? What had happened to the repentant husband who had apologised for being moody and then made love to her?

'I thought after last night—' Jesse began.

'I'm just reminding you that you have responsibilities: namely, the children and me. Or have you forgotten?'

'How could I forget? I love Ollie and Em more than anything—'

'Glad to hear it. You won't want to lose them then. Given your habits, you need to think very carefully about the consequences of any actions you might take, okay?'

He was making her sound like some mad woman who went around with unkempt hair wearing caftans and mismatched shoes.

'I'm not crazy, you know.'

'Well, if you're not crazy, you'll know what's good for you, won't you?' His tone was threatening.

'I don't know how to respond to that, Steve,' she said, on the verge of tears.

'You don't have to respond. Just think about what I've said.'

After he'd hung up, Jesse sat on the kitchen floor and cried. Steve could be so cold and manipulative. Sometimes she felt like a very small animal trapped in a cage.

She needed to talk about this. She wasn't going to let Steve win. Drying her eyes, she stood up. She needed to call her sister.

'Jesse, what's up?'

She always felt better, just hearing Louisa's voice.

'I've had a fight with Steve. He phoned just now, accusing me of all sorts of things and threatening to take the children away.'

'Why would he say that?'

'We had another fight over the weekend,' Jesse said, fighting back tears. 'I told him our marriage was hanging by a thread.'

'That'd probably do it.'

'But then last night I thought everything was okay again.'

'Don't let him get you down, Jess. You know Steve and his moods. You've lived with him long enough.'

Jesse let the tears flow. 'I feel like I'm teetering on the brink. I don't know what to do—I get so angry and then I get depressed. Sometimes I wish I could disappear forever.'

'You just need some help. Maybe Mum—'

'Mum's the last person I need meddling in my life. Besides, she has her hands full with Grandma.'

'What about your friends?'

'Steve hates all my friends.'

'Jesus, Jesse! How many years has this been going on? He hates me, too. If your marriage is hanging by a thread, then why don't you just leave him?'

'But where would I go? What would I do? It's not like I can take off and fly over to stay with you.'

The silence was almost unbearable.

'The kids have school for starters,' Jesse added.

'If you're going to come up with excuses all the time . . . '

'They're not bloody excuses. This is my life. My kids are in school. There are practicalities to take care of.' Jesse took a deep breath. 'Besides, I'm just ranting. Everything's fine. It's Monday. Mondays are always stressful, everyone's cranky after the end of the weekend. I'm fine. Really. How's everything over there? How's Philippe?'

'He's good. We've had a lazy weekend so far: dinner Friday night, second-hand markets yesterday.'

'Sounds idyllic,' Jesse said. 'Like I've already asked you fifty times, when do I get to meet this guy?'

Louisa didn't answer.

Jesse knew she shouldn't push. Sooner or later the conversation always got around to 'When are you coming home?' or 'The kids miss you. When can I tell them you're visiting?' She knew it made Louisa feel like she was being harassed. Besides, Jesse knew Louisa wasn't coming home anytime soon.

'I really miss you, Lou.'

'I miss you, too. And I will come back, maybe for the summer, like I said.'

'That's months away.'

'I'll do my best, okay? Maybe our spring break.'

'And you'll bring Philippe too?'

'Maybe.'

After the phone call, Jesse still felt empty. Louisa couldn't do a hell of a lot for her on the other side of the world. She thought back to what Steve had said about her responsibilities. There was no way she was going to let her kids down; and she was damned if she was going to let Steve take them away from her. Jesse would suck up her unhappy marriage and live with it. She could do that. Countless other women did. In a few years, when the kids were older and she'd saved enough money, she'd fly away. One day, but not yet. Not while Ollie and Emmy needed her at home.

So, if she was staying, she needed to make the circumstances work for her. She thought back to the Secret Women's Business pamphlet. She was going to a meeting! She had to.

Louisa mulled over Jesse's situation. From where she stood, the solution was clear: take the kids and leave the bastard. She got the guilts every time Jesse rang and sounded so unhappy. It made her want to blurt out everything she knew about Mr Not-So-Perfect. If only Jesse knew the truth, she'd leave him without so much as a backward glance. But Louisa couldn't do it. It was too late. She'd had her opportunity but had kept her mouth shut, believing she was doing the right thing—minding her own business and protecting her sister.

Fifteen years ago, Louisa had come across Steve in her role as Mistress Lola, dominatrix. She'd loved being at university, but it was an age-old story—she had no money. Even though she was working part-time as a waitress, she always spent more than she earned. And she hated being poor. One afternoon, she'd spied an ad in the local paper, and a week later she was hooked up in a black leather corset and brandishing a riding crop. Louisa was on her way. It was the best of both worlds. She could stay at uni and indulge her love of the arts and earn top dollar while doing it. It was fun in the early days, dressing up and being part of someone else's fantasy. Before long, she'd done it all: spanking, caning, whips, chains. She'd pretty much seen it all too: the cages, leather-upholstered beds that doubled as coffins. Nothing fazed her.

Steve was one of her irregular clients. She met with him about three times before he moved on to private parties. She'd never had sex with him—thank God! Louisa shuddered at the thought. He was a crazy bastard, one of those guys who wanted his mummy to spank him when he shat in his nappy or cried liked a baby.

Three years later, he'd turned up on Jesse's arm at a family dinner—Mother's Day. It had taken Louisa a while to recognise him, but she never forgot a face. By the time her mother had wheeled out the crème brûlée, Louisa had known exactly who he was. But she didn't say anything to Jesse. She'd hoped he was a passing phase. Unfortunately, he'd continued hanging around.

One night, after consuming several scotches, he'd asked Louisa if she was still in the business.

'No,' she'd lied. 'You?'

He'd dismissed the question with a shake of his head.

She could tell it had scared the hell out of him when he'd realised for certain that sweet Jesse's older, wilder sister was the woman who had seen him crawling around on the floor in a nappy. He must have been terrified that she might blab about his idiosyncrasies. But why would she? Exposing him would have meant revealing her secret as well. And she wanted to keep that side of her life hidden from her family.

She'd kept out of his way as best she could, which wasn't difficult given that she was working six nights a week. She'd had no social life back then. But, by that stage, she was tiring of the business: it was mentally, as well as physically, exhausting. She was fed up with spanking, whipping and humiliating middle-aged stockbrokers, solicitors and teachers. By the time Steve and Jesse married two years later, Louisa was done, thankfully. She was earning enough money lecturing at uni to give up her night job.

In hindsight, she should have handled things differently; she should have told Jesse what she knew that first time she'd brought Steve home. It killed her to know that her sister was suffering now. And imagine if Jesse found out that Louisa had known all along? If Louisa had something on Steve, then he had something on her, too.

And then, six years ago, everything had blown up in Louisa's face. She had fled Australia and she couldn't go back. It was easier living in San Francisco, even if it meant she was estranged from her family and didn't get to see her niece and nephew. She figured that when they were older, they'd understand. She sipped her wine and glanced at the photo of Emily and Oliver that Jesse had sent her for Christmas. She didn't usually go in for sentimental mementoes, but the photo was sweet. Emily had hand-made the red and green frame and sprinkled glitter on the border.

Louisa went over to her favourite armchair by the window, where Ziggy was curled up on a thick woollen blanket. She stared out into the street. The sky had darkened; the forecast had warned of a wild storm approaching. So far, only a couple of fat drops of rain had hit the windows. In the distance, she could hear the clackety-clack of the cable cars groaning up the hill. This was her home—small, cosy, happy and bright. She loved it. Loved the peace, the quiet, the total joy she felt at being in her own space. She loved her little herb pots on the kitchen and bathroom windowsills, loved the sunlight streaming through the skylight in her bedroom, the quirky Mexican tiles in her tiny bathroom. Why would she want to live anywhere else? She nudged Ziggy and stroked him under his chin.

Last night, over dinner at Fisherman's Wharf, when Philippe had suggested he and Louisa should move in together, she'd almost choked on her clam chowder.

'You know I love living on my own,' she'd told him.

She also liked it that Philippe came over for dinner and sex then went back to his own home afterwards, leaving Louisa in her queen-sized bed to sleep uninterrupted. He'd known the deal when they got together. Yes, she adored Philippe, and there were times when she could almost feel their relationship evolving to the next level, but she always stopped herself. She couldn't go there again. The devastation she had felt after the professor had left her was never far from her mind.

Philippe had told Louisa many times, usually during and after sex, how much he loved her. So far, she'd refrained from offering him the same response. She hadn't told him not to fall in love with her—that would have been presumptuous. But she had said she was with him for a good time, not necessarily a long time. Poor Philippe. Last night he'd looked like a puppy that had been rejected by its mother.

'Don't you even want to talk about it?' he'd asked her.

'Philippe, I'm here with you now, aren't I?'

'But for how long?'

'As long as it's fun.' How more honest could she be?

'But don't you want more?'

'Like what?'

'Like knowing your partner is going to be there for you twenty-four seven. Someone who loves you unconditionally and forever?'

'I have my cat for that.'

Philippe had pushed his plate away and taken a swig of beer. 'I'm being serious.'

'So am I.'

As far as Louisa was concerned, these conversations were becoming tedious. They came up every couple of months. Philippe knew where she stood on all this crap. It annoyed her that he was harping on about it again.

'Louisa, are you telling me that our relationship is going nowhere?' he'd asked.

'I don't know what you mean.'

'I mean, if you're never going to consider a future with me, then maybe we should call it quits before I get in too deep.'

'You can't be serious. We're having fun. Don't spoil it.'

'You might be having fun, but I'm miserable. I want more.' He'd pushed back in his seat. 'Why does commitment frighten you so much?'

'It doesn't.'

'Bullshit it doesn't. You're all about going with the flow until the flow stops suiting you. Don't you want to get married? Have kids?'

Louisa had turned away. This was becoming a spectacle. She liked being in control, doing what suited her, and squabbling like this, especially in public, was definitely not how she wanted to spend her Saturday evening.

'Look at me, Louisa. I want everyone to know we're together.'

Louisa had faced him. 'You're my student.'

'I may be your student but I'm also twenty-five years old.'

'Good for you. I'm pushing thirty-seven.'

'I don't care.'

'I do.'

'I want to be with you, Louisa, but if that's not what you want, so be it.' He'd stood up and thrown twenty dollars on the table.

She'd picked up the notes and handed them back to him. 'I'll pay.'

He'd brushed her hand aside. 'Keep it.' And he'd walked away.

Perhaps he was expecting her to follow, but she hadn't. What would she have said if she'd caught up? *Yes, I love you, darling. I can't live without you. Let's move in together right now!* She simply couldn't tell him what he wanted to hear.

She'd give him a couple of days to calm down. He'd see that she was right. It couldn't be a more ideal situation for him: he had his freedom; Louisa didn't question what he did or where he went when he wasn't with her. Yes, she trusted him, but there was also a part of her that didn't particularly care what he did when he wasn't with her. That was his business. He had his friends and his family and she was happier not getting drawn into that side of his life. Because once families got involved, they could trap you . . . and getting trapped was not on her agenda.

Despite that, she'd met his family once, a few weeks ago at Christmas.

'You can't spend Christmas Day alone,' he'd said.

'I'm perfectly happy on my own.'

'Come on. I left you alone at Thanksgiving, but my parents will never forgive me if I don't take you home on Christmas Day.'

'Philippe, I really don't want to. Look, maybe I'll come for dessert . . .'

'That's not going to work. Are you afraid?'

'Hardly!'

'Then what is it? Why don't you want to meet my family?'

'I do. It's just that Christmas is stressful enough without you introducing your parents to your much older friend.'

'Is that what this is about? Your age?'

'No—'

'Good. Bernie's met you. She adores you.'

Bernie was Philippe's dog, and 'adore' might have been stretching the truth somewhat. But eventually, Louisa had given in. She had to eat, and at least when she spoke to her parents they'd seemed pleased she wasn't spending Christmas alone.

Normally, she didn't tell her parents who she was screwing because since the professor her affairs never seemed to last more than a couple of months. But Philippe was hanging in there. As soon as she'd mentioned his name, her mother had wanted to know all about him—what he did, where he was from.

'He's American, Mum.'

'American? With a name like Philippe? Surely not!'

'Surely is!' Her mother could be so irritating.

'Work, Louisa? What does this gentleman do for a crust?'

'Student.'

'A student? At his age!'

Louisa didn't tell her mother that Philippe was significantly younger than her. She'd never hear the end of it.

'So anyway, I'm having Christmas with him and his family,' she'd said.

'But not your own family?'

'Not this year, no.'

Louisa had wrapped up the conversation pretty quickly after that. Between Jesse's domestic dramas and her mother's agonising concerns about Louisa 'settling down', phone calls home, though few and far between, were exhausting.

On the chair, Ziggy yawned, stretched, and went back to sleep. That was one of the things she loved about him: he was always there, practically on top of her at times, but he still managed to remain aloof, his disinterest in her human affairs bordering on disdain at times. Louisa looked at the hefty box of assignments on the floor next to Ziggy's chair. She was tempted to forget about grading them and watch *Idol* instead. Sighing, she took a seat, reached for the top assignment and started reading.

It crossed her mind to call Philippe and ask if he was okay, but she dismissed the idea. He was a big boy. He could take care of himself. Besides, she had no doubt he would eventually ring her. He always did.

10

*M*onday didn't start well. I'd found it difficult to get to sleep on Sunday night after the threatening call from Steve, and at two this morning I'd woken to hear someone wandering around the house. Initially, I'd been frightened that it might be Steve before common sense kicked in and I got up to find June. She was disorientated and teary about not being at home in her own bed. I'd left it too long before topping up her painkillers, so her arm was aching and she was feeling depressed about her lack of mobility.

'I don't like relying on others to take care of me,' she said.

'June, I'm not an *other*. We're family and we'll always be family.'

Poor old stick. I helped her to her room, and watched while she downed a couple of painkillers.

'My turbans, I need my turbans,' she mumbled. Fifteen minutes later, she was asleep again. She looked mighty uncomfortable but obviously the pain had subsided.

But by the time I walked into the kitchen for breakfast, things were improving. June was well into her second cup of Earl Grey and looking resplendent in a lemon and lime headscarf, a T-shirt that said *Grandmas Are Tops* and her favourite pair of blue jeans.

'You're looking bright,' I said, kissing her cheek.

'Wish I could say the same about you. You look like death.'

'Thanks,' I said, pouring myself some tea.

'Hey,' said Ben as he made a beeline for the fridge. 'Are Will's parents getting a divorce?'

'Not to my knowledge. Why?'

'Nothing. Just something he said yesterday. I told him all parents get divorced eventually.'

'So much cynicism in one so young.'

'Marry an ugly girl,' June told him. 'She'll be so grateful, she'll never leave you.'

I stared at my gorgeous fair-haired boy. He'd changed so much in the last six months. His two years of braces-wearing torture were over, meaning that his teeth were perfectly straight. They were also white and hole-free, despite his love of all things sugary. His complexion was clear, and his body, so gangly and uneven last year, had filled out. He was as tall as Terry and tanned to boot.

'What are you staring at?' he said.

I looked away. 'Nothing.'

He shook his head. 'Women!'

'Now, June,' I said, 'I've been thinking: why don't I drop you home today while I'm at the library? You might as well be in your own house as here.'

'Indeed,' she said, tears pooling in her eyes.

'But you need to rest, okay? No climbing ladders or housework.' She nodded obediently.

I'd barely done up her seatbelt for her before she asked, 'Is your neighbour getting a divorce?'

I shrugged. 'Hope not. They're just going through a tough time.'

'What is it with you young people? Don't you know the rules? You get married and you stay married. The end. You don't run off and have affairs. You don't get divorced. If you want out, you die. End of story.'

'Yes, well, that might have worked in the good old days, June—'

'Did you just hear yourself? Good old days. They were called the good old days for a reason. No one had any bloody time to think about whether they were happy or unhappy, they just were.'

'I understand, but—'

'But nothing. And speaking of no-good husbands, where's yours?'

'Terry's with Amanda, you know that.'

'Why can't he forget about that tramp and come on home?'

'Because, darling,' I said, trying to think of a way to end this absurd conversation, 'we're separated.'

'I don't know why he had to go and break up a perfectly good marriage,' she said, staring out the window. 'It'll end in tears, mark my words. You know what you need, Stella? Fancy lingerie. Edible undies.'

'June!'

'What? I may be old but I know a lot about a man's desires. Take off your Cottontails and slip into some satin. That'll bring him crawling home.'

'We'll talk some more about it later,' I said, thankful to be pulling up outside her home and hoping to hell she'd have forgotten this conversation by the time I picked her up that afternoon.

'Call me if you need anything,' I told her. 'I'm only ten minutes away. And remember what I said. Rest! Don't do any gardening and for heaven's sake don't lift anything or climb stepladders. Oh, and don't overdo the painkillers,' I added as an afterthought.

She nodded meekly.

•

I was at the computer, pounding through overdue notices, when Carly rang about Steve.

'We've got to tell Jesse,' she said.

'Let me think about it some more,' I whispered, mindful that Manager Liz was hovering. I tried to hide my mobile by holding my hand over it, hoping she would assume I enjoyed touching my cheek and ear at the same time. It was an awkward manoeuvre. 'We have to be careful about this. We've got no idea how Jesse's going to respond.'

Honestly, I had no desire to be the messenger. The messenger always got the blame and lost the friendship or her life. But as much as I didn't want to get involved, Carly had a point, especially after Steve's phone call last night.

'Stella, I don't know how you can be so wishy-washy.'

'I'm not wishy-washy. I just want to get my facts straight before we tell her. Look, I have to go.'

Despite Carly's grumbling, I hung up and got on with my job, until Liz tapped me on the shoulder and demanded a word. 'In my office,' she said.

I dutifully followed her, and sat down on the uncomfortable wooden chair in front of her desk.

'How's everything going?' she started.

'Good.'

'How's Jesse doing?'

'Jesse?'

Liz sighed. 'Yes, Jesse. Remember a couple of weeks ago when I took her off the customer relations desk because she was taking too long with the patrons? How is she doing?'

As if I could forget that day. Liz had been keeping an eye on Jesse, monitoring how she was dealing with customers. Unfortunately, it happened to be a morning when Jesse had felt it necessary to tap her foot three times every time a customer handed her a book for scanning. If they were taking out ten or fifteen items, she repeated the process almost every time. Within half an hour, the line stretched back to the periodicals section and Jesse was getting increasingly agitated. I'd felt so sorry for her.

'You understand, I can't put up with her doing that,' Liz said. 'And neither can the customers.'

I nodded. 'But Jesse loves working here.'

'I know she does, but I've been watching you too, Stella. You follow her around cleaning up her messes. I'm not saying she goes around stacking books according to height and colour, but it's touch and go.'

'I'll talk to her.'

'I'm not sure how that's going to help.'

I wanted to mention Jesse's idea for a monthly book club, but now didn't seem the time. 'Maybe she just needs a holiday?'

'Yes, a very long holiday.'

I walked back to my desk feeling helpless. The last thing Jesse needed was more pressure at the library. But I had a feeling Liz was going to step in, which would mean a confrontation, one that Jesse wouldn't win. The minute Liz started talking to her, even if only to ask a simple question like 'How's your day going?', I knew Jesse would get stressed and start tapping her foot. I needed to keep the two of them apart, even if that only meant delaying the inevitable.

Feeling despondent, I sat down at the computer again, then noticed my mobile flashing. It was a text message, from Mike. I felt my pulse leap and was smiling even before I read it. It had been sent an hour ago.

Bored. What are you wearing?

Being a complete doofus, instead of texting back *Naked, apart from Chanel No 5* (which wasn't true, obviously), I told him what I was actually wearing—a navy wrap dress, cream heels. Idiot! I regretted it as soon as I'd hit the send button.

I was shocked when my mobile rang two minutes later.

'Really? You couldn't do better than that, given what we saw the other night?'

'I know,' I said, cringing at my woefulness. 'I thought I'd never hear from you again.'

Mike laughed. 'Takes a bit more than that to put me off. If you must know, I've been having librarian fantasies, so the image of you in a navy wrap isn't altogether unwelcome. But your hair needs to be tied up in one of those bun thingos and—'

'Let me guess, I'm wearing glasses and no underwear?'

'See! Now you're getting the hang of it. Have to go, but let's talk soon, hey?'

He clicked off and I was left staring into space, mortified that I'd just asked him to imagine me sans underwear.

A minute later my mobile beeped and a text message popped up. *Am now imagining you wearing little more than horn-rimmed glasses.*

I was still thinking of an appropriate response when Terry rang.

'What's going on?' he said.

'Hi to you, too. Can you give me a clue? Are we talking about your mum? Hannah? Ben's geography excursion? The lame Christmas present you bought me? What?'

'I've just spoken to Mum. She said you want me to come back home. She also said you were going shopping to buy—I can barely say the words out loud—edible undies.'

'And you believed her?' I was trying hard not to laugh.

'Well, no. That is, I thought . . . Well, you never know. Women of a certain age, they decide they want a divorce and then change their minds again—'

'What are you talking about? It was a mutual decision. Besides, aren't you forgetting Amanda?'

Even after all these years, Terry could exasperate me. You'd think he'd be in heaven living with Amanda, far away from his boring life in the suburbs with a wife and two kids. But more often than not he made it sound like he was doing me a favour—that the only reason he was with Amanda was to make me happy. And I was happy he was occupied with her, but I wouldn't be for much longer if he kept pestering me.

Terry coughed. 'I didn't say I wanted to eat your edible undies.'

'Thank God for that.'

'I only said that Mum said you were going to buy them and that you were getting sentimental about old times.'

'Really? I can see June saying something ludicrous about underwear but the getting sentimental part?'

'Yeah, okay. I made that up. So how is she?'

'Not bad, though evidently she's taking too many painkillers.'

'And?'

Clearly, Terry wasn't in a jovial mood.

'Look, as much as she'd never admit it, I think she's lonely. It gives her a purpose being with the kids and me.'

'Jeez, I could never live with her.'

'No, *you* couldn't.'

'Are you saying you could?'

'Maybe.'

'But you used to hate her. Said she was interfering.'

'A hundred years ago. It's different now. We're friends.'

'United against the common enemy?'

I laughed. 'Something like that.'

He snorted. 'She's been with you half a day. You'll feel differently by the end of the week, trust me. I lived with her for eighteen years, nine months, three days and fifteen hours. I know what I'm talking about. You'll be pleased when the week's up and you can drop her back to her villa, no questions asked.'

It was true that in the early days, long before Jimmy died, June could be a handful. She'd had very definite opinions on everything from toilet paper to chicken seasoning. Most of the time, I'd switched off. I didn't care what brand of toilet paper we used. If it made her happy that we used her preferred brand, so be it. I'd been less accommodating when it came to her suggestions about raising my kids. She was a self-proclaimed expert on breastfeeding, control crying, even banana puree. You name it and June knew all the answers. Dr Spock had nothing on her. It was around that time I'd started making up excuses as to why I couldn't go to dinner with her or meet to see a movie in the city.

All that had changed when Jimmy died. The standard family joke was that Jimmy had died to escape June's nagging, but the truth was, June was lost after that. Gradually, she'd changed from being an overbearing matriarch to a caring, interested and loving grandmother. The more involved she became in our lives, the less she'd tried to interfere in the day-to-day running of the household. In the last couple of years, she'd been great. I really did enjoy her company and I silently hoped we'd still be on speaking terms by the end of her stay.

After work, I picked June up and took her home with me. She'd packed another suitcase overflowing with turbans and scarves.

'You've been doing too much today. What about your arm?' I said as I unpacked them onto two rarely used hat stands.

'Nonsense. My arm's fine. I have painkillers.'

I raised my eyebrows. 'Anyway, when will you get time to wear all of these?'

She smiled. 'The ones I don't wear I like to look at. They're so pretty.'

I couldn't argue. There were exquisitely coloured silk scarves from India and Turkey, and turbans from Egypt. 'Where do you find them?' I asked.

'Mostly on eBay. I'm a very good shopper.'

I left June admiring her scarves and was in the midst of preparing tacos for dinner when Hannah wandered into the kitchen and told me she was thinking about applying for a job at the local video store.

What? My baby?

'Not until you're fifteen,' I said.

'But Ben's got a job, and besides, I need the money.'

Ben had worked at Bunnings over the summer, doing five shifts a week, mad keen on saving for a car. I was happy about it. It kept him focused—and off the streets. I knew where he was pretty much all the time. Now that school had started again, he'd cut back to one four-hour shift on Sundays.

'Hannah, let's talk about it when you turn fifteen.'

That way, I still had a few months' grace.

My first job had been at Hungry Jack's when I was just a little older than Hannah. I'd dressed up for the interview, keen to impress. The manager, who was probably all of twenty-one, had taken me into a tiny grey room that smelled of grease and uncooked meat. I didn't have a resume, of course, but that didn't seem to matter.

'We can start you this weekend,' he'd said. 'Just to let you know, we put the good-looking kids out the back, cooking fries, assembling the burgers.'

I nodded.

'Yeah, customers get too distracted if there's a stunning chick on the registers.'

'Okay,' I said, immediately thinking, Yuck, not only do I have to wear the hideous uniform, I'll be covered in chip fat.

'So anyway,' he said standing up. 'Let's go out the front and I'll give you a quick lesson on the tills.'

I shuddered at the memory. All up, I'd lasted three miserable weeks working on a cash register I never mastered.

I looked at my daughter and thought about the years I'd spent sitting through dance recitals and flute concerts. When Hannah was five, I'd held my breath, tears in my eyes, as she pirouetted fleetingly across the stage, and then I'd sat for a further mind-numbing two hours while all the other little sunbeams did their thing. One minute, I was sitting at her first dance recital, and the next, she was getting a weekend job. Another blink of an eye and she'd be moving out on her own. I wasn't ready for that.

11

*C*arly waited until after Brett and Will had left the house on Tuesday morning before checking her emails. She was hoping Nicholas would have replied. She knew a phone call was out of the question. Nick didn't have a lot of money, and it was unlikely he'd spend what little he did have on an international call to his mother. She turned on the computer and drummed her fingers on the desk as it beeped into life. There were three emails, one from Nick. Thank God! There was also one from Steve. That couldn't be good. And one from an address she didn't recognise. The other two could wait. Carly's boy had written to her.

Hey Mum, What's happening? Freezing here. You'd hate it. Life's really full on but great. Had a mental with the head sports master but he's a freakazoid and getting bent out of shape about nothing. Everything's under control. I'm handling it so don't worry. How are Dad and the bro?

Carly wasn't sure what to read into that. Nick sounded fine, but what was the 'mental' with the sports master about? Was it something that warranted her calling him?

She looked at the other messages. What the hell was Steve doing emailing her? She opened it and quickly found out. One line. Eight words.

I meant what I said the other day.

What had he said? Something about keeping away from Jesse or Stella and Carly would be sorry. The nerve of the guy! Carly was shaking. She wanted to march over to Jesse's house and tell her everything! Steve was threatening her and Stella and it had to stop.

She rang Stella at work and explained about the email.

'We have to tell Jesse what we saw the other night or we'll end up being the bad guys,' she said. She could hear Stella tapping on her keyboard. 'Stella?'

'I got the same email,' she whispered.

'Why are you whispering?'

'Because Liz is on the warpath. She runs this place like a bloody concentration camp.'

'Like you'd know.'

'It's a metaphor!'

'Okay, so what are we going to do about this? Steve's not going to let up.'

'I thought we'd decided not to say anything?'

'That was before,' Carly said. 'It's getting creepy now. Besides, don't you think Jesse has a right to know what her husband's up to?'

No response.

'Stella,' she snapped.

'I think it'll make things worse for her—'

'How much worse can it get? We'll just be giving her more ammunition to use. Besides, think about the diseases he's probably bringing home. Ugh! And you know how available Jesse makes herself. Even if she says she hates him, she certainly doesn't hate him from the waist down.'

Stella groaned. 'Carly! Trust you to say that. Look, gotta go.'

And with that, she hung up.

Carly had wanted to tell her about the notes she'd found in Nick's room, but Stella hadn't given her a chance. Probably a good thing. It wasn't fair to Nicholas. Carly needed to talk to him about the notes first before she spoke to anyone else. And she was still convinced they were from some love-struck girl whom Nicholas had rejected. Of course they were. No doubt it was a crush that he'd crushed and they'd both moved on. Still, he had kept the notes so B must have meant something to him. Nonsense, she argued with herself as she drifted back to the computer. What teenager willingly cleaned up his room and turfed out all the bits of unwanted paper and food scraps? That's what mothers were for.

Carly opened the third email. It was from the sports master Nicholas had mentioned in his email.

Dear Mrs Hindmarsh, I am writing to inform you that your son has been suspended from duty as of Monday, 3 February due to inappropriate locker room behaviour. Pending an investigation, it will be decided whether Nicholas remains on campus for the remainder of the school year or is sent directly home to Australia. Please feel free to contact me on 1090 345 678 to discuss the matter further. Yours, Mr Peter Sinclair, Head Sports Master.

Inappropriate locker room behaviour! What the hell was going on with Nicholas? Carly's heart was pounding and her legs were shaking. What had her boy been caught doing? A thought popped into her mind, which she quickly wiped. She couldn't think like that.

She checked her watch and calculated the time in Wales—10 pm. Both emails had been sent eight hours ago. If she woke up Nick, too bad. She dialled his mobile.

He picked up after a couple of rings. 'Yeah?'

'Nicholas, it's Mum. How's everything?'

'Great. At pub. Can't hear.'

'Is everything all right at school? I had an email from the sports master—'

'Crazy Stinky Sinclair? Everything's cool.'

Carly desperately wanted to believe him, to believe this was all a mistake, whatever 'this' was, and to know her son was safe. 'As long as you're sure . . .' She let the sentence hang.

'Mum . . . dropping out—'

The phone went dead and Carly was no closer to finding out what was going on than she had been before ringing. Nick had sounded in high spirits but was that more to do with the number of beers he'd consumed?

She glanced at Peter Sinclair's number and considered phoning him. But it was too late in the evening. He'd probably be asleep. Besides, if Nicholas was at a pub, he couldn't be in that much trouble. If he'd done something really bad, wouldn't he have been locked up or dispatched on the first plane back to Sydney?

She thought again about the kinds of things he could have been caught doing—fighting and breaking some kid's nose, perhaps? Or stealing? Neither of those sounded like Nick, but she was trying to be open-minded. However, the more open-minded she allowed herself to be, the more outrageous her scenarios became.

She sat down and composed an email to Peter Sinclair.

Dear Mr Sinclair, Thank you for your email regarding Nicholas. It is very concerning. Can I ask what the inappropriate locker room behaviour was? Is there anything I can do? I know Nicholas is a good person by nature and if he has been involved in a brawl I am sure he will have a reasonable explanation. (I have never condoned fighting, but do understand that sometimes rough and tumble can explode into physical warfare.) I will ring you tomorrow morning your time to discuss the matter further. Yours sincerely, Carly Hindmarsh.

She re-read the email, then pushed send, feeling faint and nauseous.

She didn't have time to dwell on those feelings because just then her mobile rang. Toby! Though he was a distraction she didn't need today, she answered it.

'You've been avoiding my calls,' he said.

'Not at all,' she stammered.

'I'm seeing Stella and her mother-in-law in a little while.'

'Small world.'

'So, how's everything with you?'

She didn't answer.

'Your friend?' he prompted. 'Jesse?'

'So-so.'

'You told her?'

'No. Stella thinks we should stay out of it.'

'You don't agree?'

'How did you guess?'

Carly padded over to the fridge, opened the door, pulled out the bottle of wine and poured a glass. It was after midday, so what the hell! She took a quick sip. Heaven.

'Have you thought any more about the other night?' Toby said.

'Toby, you know I'm married, right? And the other night, I was hideously drunk,' she paused. 'And, well . . . I don't think we should see each other again. It's not right.'

'I thought you might say something like that and I'm sorry to hear it. If you change your mind and want to catch up over a drink . . . '

Carly let out an audible sigh. She didn't need another friend.

'Okay,' he said. 'If you're ever at the Royal Hospital, don't be a stranger.'

'Thanks,' she said, making a mental note never to go anywhere near the hospital. 'It was nice meeting you.'

'Likewise,' he said before clicking off.

Carly shook her head. Crisis averted. All going to plan, their paths would never cross again.

She glanced at her glass. What was she thinking? She'd consumed over half of it. She quickly tipped the rest down the sink.

What to do about Nick? Call Brett? He might tell her that the sports master was overreacting. On the other hand, Brett was particularly stressed about work these days. He didn't need the extra burden of knowing that Nick was in trouble overseas. There was little they could do about it anyway, except wait to hear more.

She poured herself another glass of wine and gulped half of it before tipping the rest down the sink. She didn't need alcohol. She needed to talk to Brett, tell him what was going on with Nick.

She dialled his number.

'Brett Hindmarsh.'

'Hey, Big Boy,' she said in a deep, throaty voice that she hoped passed for sexy. 'I'm wearing nothing but black stilettos and I'm all alone in bed just waiting for you to spank me! Hard!' As the words tumbled out of her mouth, she knew it was a huge mistake.

'Carly? Is that you?' Brett sounded confused and a touch concerned.

'Um, yes.'

'What the hell are you on about?'

'Sorry, I thought I'd try some sex chat to liven things up between us.'

'It's twelve thirty in the afternoon. I'm about to go into a strategy meeting. I don't need this now.'

'No, you never need it, do you?'

'We'll talk about this later.'

After she'd hung up, Carly could have screamed. Why had she rung anyway? What had she hoped to achieve? If she'd been wanting to feel better she was out of luck, because all she felt was rejected and weepy. Her sadness turned to anger. Brett was never there for her. Not when she needed him, and she really needed him now.

Jesse double-checked the address on the scrap of paper she'd hastily written it down on that morning. The Scout Hall was at 51 Station Street, several suburbs away from where she lived. She checked her make-up in the rear-vision mirror. Satisfied, she hopped out and started walking.

This is a good thing, she kept telling herself. A positive step in the right direction.

But she was nervous. Several times she went to turn around. She kept thinking, what the hell am I doing here? But she forced herself to put one foot in front of the other and enter the building. Once inside, she exhaled deeply. After weeks of contemplation, she was finally here. She'd made it to a Secret Women's Business meeting. This could change her life, her perspective. She just had to be open to it and go with the flow. Not so easy for a person like her, but she was determined to give it a try.

A woman touched her on the arm and smiled broadly. 'First time?'

Jesse nodded.

The woman, dressed casually in a white shirt and floral skirt, long red beads dangling from her neck, was welcoming but not gushy. She didn't try to invade Jesse's personal space, which Jesse appreciated more than the woman would ever know.

'I'm Rebecca. Come and take a seat. We've all been through a first time,' she said gently.

Jesse did as she was told. Rebecca disappeared, returning minutes later with tea and Scotch Finger biscuits. 'Hope you like English Breakfast?'

Jesse nodded her thanks. It felt nice to be waited on. She drank her tea and surveyed the hall. The women were a mixed bag—some young, some older, some standing or sitting by themselves, others mingling. She felt comfortable, comfortably alone.

When it was time to start, Rebecca got up on the podium to speak. She was obviously the group's leader. She spoke about commitments, prosperity, loving yourself and getting the mix right. She spoke of action plans, to-do lists and about revitalising one's spirit. 'It's time to embrace and celebrate who you are. Let us awaken the spirit within,' she boomed to her captivated audience.

Yes, thought Jesse, that's exactly what I need to do: 'awaken my spirit and recharge myself in an atmosphere that nurtures my feminine energy and being'. She completely understood what Rebecca was talking about; Jesse didn't want to wake up one morning and wonder what it had all been for.

'Isness is the business,' Rebecca shouted. 'Let us embrace the now and live consciously in the moment. Say it with me.'

'Isness is the business,' Jesse yelled, along with one hundred other women. Smiling, she felt herself relax for the first time in a very long time.

The hour flew by so quickly, Jesse could hardly believe it was over. She didn't want to leave, she felt so caught up in the atmosphere of friendship, love and positive energy. But she didn't want to meet the others yet. It was too soon. Later on, when she felt more confident, she might introduce herself to a few women but not now. She was just finding her way.

Baby steps, she told herself as she walked back to her car. And they might have been baby steps but she was feeling lighter and more energised than she had in months. It felt fantastic. As she put her key in the ignition, she realised something else, too. Not once during the entire session had she tapped her foot, clenched her hands or thought about her husband.

Jesse was feeling optimistic and strong, as if she could take on the world and win. She felt confident she could find ways to handle Steve better, to nurture their marriage as well as the kids, and balance those responsibilities with her own ambitions and desires. This was definitely a turning point. Jesse could feel it in her heart.

12

The library was hectic. There were people everywhere, speaking loudly on their mobiles, letting their toddlers scream up and down the shelving aisles. I had a massive to-do list but I'd been stationed at the reference desk for most of the morning, dealing with customer enquiries. At one point it was so busy that the people waiting formed a huddle, inching ever closer to the desk as I tried to deal with them one at a time. One particularly rude man even tapped his keys on the desktop to get my attention. I wanted to ignore him but Liz was standing nearby.

'I'll just be a moment,' I said and turned back to the elderly woman I was helping.

She wanted to know if the book she was holding, a 1969, out-of-print illustrated history of the magnolia flower, was for sale.

'It's not a bookshop,' Key Man barked.

I glared at him, then smiled at her. 'No, I'm sorry, madam, the book isn't for sale.'

She walked away, book clutched firmly against her chest.

Key Man shook his head. 'Bet that book disappears before the end of the day.'

I didn't want to agree with him but he was probably right.

At least Liz was having a good day. Her new-books order had arrived and she was in her element, marvelling over jacket covers, making notes about guest authors she wanted to invite to speak at the library. She hadn't mentioned Jesse and I hoped that meant she'd leave her alone when Jesse came in on Thursday.

After my stint at the reference desk, I got on with my other jobs. By two o'clock I was up-to-date and out the door. June and I had an appointment with Toby.

'I'm perfectly fine,' June said when I picked her up. She was looking resplendent in a Pucci-inspired turban.

'I know, but your arm's still swollen and bruised. The doctor needs to see how it's healing.'

That was true. But I'd also phoned Toby to ask if he could discreetly run some preliminary Alzheimer's memory tests. He'd said it wasn't his area but had agreed to line up another doctor. Just thinking about the possibility of June having Alzheimer's broke my heart, but we needed to get some facts. And then, hopefully, we could just put her memory lapses down to ageing and absent-mindedness.

Toby didn't keep us waiting. 'Mrs Sparks, how are you feeling today?'

'As I told my daughter-in-law, I am feeling perfectly fine. I wish everyone would stop hovering around me like I'm a cripple.'

'Excellent,' he soothed as he took her by her good arm. 'We're just going to have a look at your arm and run a few tests—'

'What sort of tests?'

Toby glanced at me before continuing. 'Nothing to be concerned about. Standard procedure on over seventies. Doctor Gordon is going to assist, but I'll be staying with you.' He nodded to a woman nearby who looked even younger than he did.

'I'm not over seventy, I am seventy.'

'Come on, June,' I said. 'Stop being pedantic.' I felt guilty not telling her the real reason for the tests, but I held my ground. They needed to be done and I knew she'd never agree. 'I'll be here when you're finished.'

I took a seat in the waiting room, cursing myself for not bringing a book. A few minutes later, Toby walked in.

'That was quick!'

'Sorry to disappoint you but we're just getting started.' He crossed his arms. 'I spoke to Carly a little while ago.'

'Ah.'

'Yeah, seems her declarations from last Thursday night aren't about to be followed through. Pity. I thought we hit it off.' He looked over to the closed door of the room he'd taken June into. 'They'll be ready for me now. See you in a little while.'

I turned my attention to an ancient copy of *House & Garden* magazine. I'd almost dozed off when someone tapped me on the shoulder. Mike! With everything that had been going on, I'd almost forgotten about him. Surreptitiously, I checked my appearance.

'Hello, stranger,' he said, smiling broadly. 'I was told you were lurking around the second floor.'

'Nice to see you again,' I said. And it was. I couldn't help smiling as I looked into his incredible blue eyes.

He sat down beside me. 'Not wearing the navy wrap today? Shame.'

I blushed.

'So tell me,' he said, suddenly serious, 'how is your mother-in-law? This isn't my area—trauma and emergency are more my specialty—but Toby called and said you were worried about her.'

'Thanks,' I said, overcoming my shyness. 'Maybe I'm overreacting. June's been a bit forgetful of late, and then with her fall on Sunday and coming in here, I thought it was a good opportunity to have her thoroughly checked out. I hope I'm wrong.'

Mike looked at me closely. 'I hope so, too. What else has been happening?'

I raised my eyebrows and deliberately looked at my watch. 'How long have you got?'

He smiled 'That much?'

Despite the circumstances, I felt happy. Nervous but excited. I had an incredible urge to touch Mike. I wanted to wrap my arms around him and hold him. It certainly wasn't appropriate or in any way rational—and I prided myself on being rational. So I took a deep breath and tried hard to pull back and concentrate on our conversation.

'How's your friend?' he asked.

'We haven't told her,' I said, glancing down at my hands. 'But . . .'

'But?'

'Her husband's been making calls to Carly and me. And he's sent emails.'

'What? Threatening you?'

'Kind of.'

'Stella, that's not good. You need to tell someone—if not the police—'

'No!' I shook my head. 'Jesse has a right to know, but—'

'Yes, she does. And once she knows, she'll be able to deal with it. Something like this is almost impossible to keep secret.'

I nodded, feeling myself drifting from the conversation, imagining Mike and I somewhere, anywhere, ripping each other's clothes off. His naked body and my pure lust driving me . . . hard.

Mike took a moment. 'So, you're not really into texting?'

I blushed again. 'Sorry about that. Don't get me wrong—I like getting your texts,' love getting them, actually, 'it's just that I read your last message and . . . well, I didn't know how to respond.'

He put his hand on my knee and I shivered, hopefully not so much that he noticed.

'We can work on that,' he said. 'Because unless I'm reading this completely wrong—and tell me if I am—there's something between us. I just need to draw your inner wilder Stella out into the open.'

'Hmm.' Again I felt like a mute.

'I'll take that as a "Yes, Mike! I totally agree. Do what you have to do." Am I right?'

I giggled nervously. 'Maybe.'

'Ahem.' It was Toby. 'We're all done, Stella.'

'Oh,' I said, standing up and composing myself. 'How is she?'

'Still in a lot of pain, but she's a tough old bird, that one.'

'Who are you calling old?' said June, coming up beside him.

I'd have expected her to be more affronted by the word 'bird' but she didn't seem to mind.

'June,' I said, 'this is Mike.'

'Another doctor friend, Stella?' June's eyebrows were raised so high her turban wobbled. 'You seem to be gathering a collection.'

Mike held out his hand. 'Nice to meet you, June. Love your headgear.'

June smiled.

'You're in good hands with Toby here,' Mike told her, then turned to me. 'I'll be off. Let me know when we can catch up for that coffee.'

'Sure,' I said nonchalantly and watched him walk away. I suddenly felt deflated. When would I see him again?

June and I thanked Toby and headed towards the elevator.

'Are you going to tell me how you know all these handsome young doctors?' June said as we stepped inside.

'From around,' I replied, a little flustered, sidetracking her with a suggestion about stopping in at Flower Power.

Twenty minutes later, we were wandering amongst the herb seedlings at the nursery. It was a glorious afternoon. All around us, freesias, hydrangeas and lisianthus were in full and abundant colour.

'This was a nice idea,' June said as we breathed in the late summer orange blossoms.

'Should we stop in at your house on the way home?' I asked as we made our way to the car park. I was loaded up with several pots of herbs, three flowering daisy plants and a standard lemon tree.

'No, thank you. I have all I need,' said June, as I helped her into the car.

I thought about Mike as I prepared dinner. Of course I did. He was creeping into my mind more and more. He was handsome but not drop-dead gorgeous. He had charisma, though, buckets of it, and a great smile, piercing blue eyes. Not to mention he was charming and . . . well, the whole Mike package made me swoon.

I'd done a bit of snooping—discreetly, of course—and found out that he'd split acrimoniously from his wife several months ago and she was restricting access to his three kids—two girls, and a son, Jack, the eldest, who was a year above Ben at school. He only saw them every fourth weekend, and sometimes not even then because he was often on call seven days a week. It made me think how lucky I was that the separation was working out so far with Terry. Touch wood. We'd tried hard to keep things amicable for the sake of Hannah and Ben. Not that Terry should be narky, given his situation. Still, he wasn't seeing much of the kids so I needed to gently steer them towards making a greater effort with him. On the other hand, he wasn't the greatest communicator, either.

'Mum,' said Hannah, interrupting my thoughts and passing me the phone. 'It's Dad.'

'Are you seeing him soon?' I whispered.

She nodded. 'This weekend.'

I blew her a kiss. 'Good girl.' I placed the phone to my ear. 'Hi Terry, how's it going?'

'Under the pump.'

Under the pump? What the hell did that mean?

'You're fixing a pool pump? Being pumped by a person or persons? Sounds painful.'

Terry sighed. 'I'm just busy.'

'Oh, okay. Well, what's up? This is becoming a regular habit.'

'Aren't I even allowed to phone my family now?'

I shook my head. Men! 'Of course.' I wasn't up for a confrontation. 'What's news in the last six hours since we spoke?'

'Nothing. Just checking in.'

'You don't need to check in. You do know that, don't you? We're separated.'

I could hear him sighing on the other end of the line. Again.

'I took June back to the hospital for a check-up this afternoon,' I said. 'Her arm's healing but it'll take time.'

'Thanks for looking after her. I . . .'

Silence.

'What's up? You sound terrible.'

'It's Amanda.'

'And?'

More silence.

'Terry? I don't get it. You couldn't wait to leave me and hook up with her.'

'That was before.'

'Before what?'

'Before she wanted to get married.'

'Oh.' That took me by surprise. Terry marrying Amanda? The kids having a stepmother? Wow! Life really did move on quickly. I couldn't begin to imagine how June would take the news. I could just imagine Terry telling Hannah and Ben. They'd have a fit. They'd come around eventually, especially if he lavished them with gifts of iPads and holidays to Fiji, but I didn't relish the idea of sharing my children with another woman permanently.

'But we're not divorced yet,' I said evenly, despite the lump at the back of my throat and the pain at the front of my head.

It wasn't like I wanted Terry back; I didn't. And I wasn't jealous about his relationship with Amanda. I just didn't understand how he could re-partner so quickly. He'd moved from living with his mother to living with me, and now he was living with Amanda. Didn't he want any time alone to enjoy his own company?

'I know, so the longer we stay married, the better,' he said.

'So you don't want to marry Amanda?'

'Of course not! We're only just getting to know each other.'

Okay, so Terry wasn't completely ruled by his penis, at least not yet. He still possessed a modicum of independent thought.

I immediately felt twenty kilos lighter . . . and the headache disappeared.

'Stella?'

'Mmm?'

'I thought I'd lost you.'

I blinked. What was he trying to tell me? 'Pardon?'

'The connection—I thought I'd lost you. Listen, I'd appreciate you not mentioning this to the kids.'

'Sure. Okay.'

Really? I felt like saying. *And just why the hell would I?*

I had just finished clearing the dinner plates and stacking the dishwasher when Jesse rang to ask if she could come over. I was a bit apprehensive. What would Steve say? Would he even let her come once he knew where she was going?

Thankfully, Jesse answered the question before I had a chance to ask. 'Steve's working late—again! And Mum's been pestering me about having Ollie and Em stay overnight, so I thought, why not?'

'Sure. Okay. Sounds excellent.'

'Good! I've had a really great day and I want to talk to you about the library and a bunch of other stuff.'

She certainly sounded in fine spirits, but the library? Ugh. I'd deal with that later.

Half an hour later, she bounded through the door holding a bottle of chardonnay.

'I know it's only Tuesday night but one glass can't hurt us, can it?' she beamed.

'Absolutely! Should I see if Carly's free?'

'Why not? The more the merrier.'

Within minutes, Carly arrived, and soon the three of us were sitting on the outside deck, a glass of wine in hand.

'What's happened to you today?' I asked Jesse. 'Even your hair is bouncing.'

She smiled. 'I told you. I had a good day.'

'Did you win the lottery?' asked Carly.

'Nah, but I have been thinking about a lot of things and I really want to apply for the full-time position at the library.'

'Okay,' I said tentatively.

Liz would never agree, I knew. She was making noises about cutting Jesse's hours.

'I know you're thinking Steve will never agree to it, but I have it all worked out. He'll come around. I'm feeling confident so I may as well put my optimism to good use.'

'That's great,' said Carly, sipping her wine.

'But enough about me,' Jesse continued. 'How's June?'

'Mad as a cut snake,' I said with a grin. 'Feisty, determined and strong. But her fall gave me a huge shock. She is seventy, after all.'

'You're very good to take her in,' said Carly.

I frowned at her. 'Why wouldn't I? She's family.'

Carly shrugged and sipped her wine. 'Not for much longer.'

'June's part of our lives. She'll always be family, regardless.'

'Fair enough.' Carly paused a moment before clearing her throat. 'I'd like to apologise for my behaviour the other night. I don't know what got into me, fuck buddies and all.'

I laughed. 'Yeah, how's that resolution coming along? You could have knocked me over with a feather when I realised Toby was June's doctor.'

'I'm confused,' said Jesse. 'What are you talking about?'

'Toby was one of the guys Carly met at the pub the other night.'

'And he's a doctor. Can you believe it? Small world, hey?' said Carly. 'He's a nice bloke, though. So's Mike.'

'Mike being another guy at the pub?' Jesse chimed in. 'Also a doctor?'

I nodded. 'It's not as complicated as it sounds. Actually, I saw him today at the hospital, but—'

'But what?' Carly demanded. 'He seems like a decent bloke.'

'Yes, but unlike you, I don't want a fuck buddy. I'm happy on my own.'

'You say that now, but when the right man comes along, we'll see.'

'You never told me what happened when you gatecrashed the party,' Jesse said. 'How was it?'

'Interesting,' I said.

'Yes! Interesting,' Carly quickly agreed.

'Come on,' Jesse said. 'Details, please.'

I glanced at Carly who had her hand over her mouth. That's right, I thought. Keep it there. But of course she didn't.

'It wasn't your typical North Shore party,' she started. 'It was a dress-up kind of affair.'

Jesse looked confused. 'Like a Bollywood or Rocky Horror party?'

'Not quite,' said Carly. 'One of the doctors, Pete, is into bondage and fetish stuff, and he took us along with him to see if we'd be interested as well.'

'Carly,' I warned.

'You're kidding?' said Jesse. 'Fascinating. What was everyone doing?'

'There were people in dominatrix gear whipping each other,' I said dismissively. 'Standard stuff.'

'Plenty of naked or near-naked bodies in threesomes and foursomes,' added Carly.

'Oh my God. And what were you guys doing?'

'Pete threw himself into a threesome, but the rest of us just stood and watched in disbelief,' I said.

Carly and I took a gulp of wine. I noticed Jesse's glass was untouched.

Carly nudged me. 'Go on.'

'Not much more to say, really.' I glowered at her.

'Come on, Stella,' Jesse said. 'Don't leave anything out. It's highly unlikely I'll ever get the opportunity—'

Carly burst out laughing. I glared at her but she didn't stop. She was laughing so hard, wine was dribbling from her nose.

'Carly, control yourself,' I said. 'Please.' I wanted to belt her.

'I'm sorry. I just can't get that image out of my head—the nappy, the dummy, the studded collar around his neck—'

'Carly! No,' I yelled.

'She needs to know, Stella.'

Jesse was pale, almost white. 'What do I need to know?'

'Don't do this, Carly,' I begged. 'It's nothing, Jesse.'

Carly snorted and gulped down the rest of her wine. 'Okay, here's the thing.' Her eyes were red-rimmed and wide as saucers, her cheeks flushed and full.

I willed her to stop. 'Now's not the time—'

'We saw your husband,' she blurted.

Jesse looked puzzled. 'Steve? At the party?'

'That's right, Steve. He was there and he was—'

'Stop,' said Jesse. 'This is a joke, right? Ha, ha. Very funny. Just as well I know Steve was working late last Thursday night.'

I glared again at Carly, who was now slouched back in her seat.

'Come on,' said Jesse. 'You're having a laugh, right? Well, you got me. I almost fell for it.'

I put my hand on her arm. 'Jesse—'

'No!' she said, closing her eyes as if to block out my voice. 'I don't want to hear any more. I don't believe you, anyway. Steve was working last Thursday night. He told me.' She hesitated, trying to get her breathing under control. 'There's no way . . .' She pushed her chair back and stood up.

'I'm sorry,' I said quietly. 'But despite Carly's lack of tact, Steve was there. We saw him.'

She shook her head. 'No.'

Silence. Even Carly didn't speak.

'Did he see you?' Jesse asked.

I didn't know what to say. I got up to hug her but she shrank away from me.

'Just tell me,' she demanded.

I nodded.

Jesse scrunched up her face, trying to compose herself. 'I still don't believe you. You've always hated Steve and now you're saying things that aren't true to push me to leave him. Well, guess what? I never will. I'm going to work even harder to get my marriage back on track. I don't need you. Fine friends you are, spreading vicious rumours. How could you?' Tears streamed down her face. 'Steve's a good man, a really good man.'

I tried to stop her from leaving but she pushed past me.

'Just leave me alone,' she said. 'As for you, Carly, you might want to start on my glass next, seeing as you're on a roll. As usual.'

With that, she hurried down the deck stairs and onto the driveway.

'Jesse, please don't go,' I called after her. 'Let me explain.'

But she got into her car and slammed the door shut. The engine revved, she put the gears into reverse and was gone. My heart sank.

'That went well,' Carly said.

I turned to look at her. 'You've got one hell of a big mouth, I'll say that much.'

'She'll forgive us.'

'You reckon?'

'She has to. We're the ones who are going to get her through this nightmare. I don't know why you're being so shitty about it. We're only telling her the truth.'

I shook my head. 'Did you ever stop to consider that she might not have wanted to know the truth? People bury their heads in the sand for all kinds of reasons. Maybe Jesse already had an inkling but chose to ignore it. Now we've forced her to face something she mightn't be ready for. Couldn't you see her foot tapping as soon as we mentioned the party?'

'Yes, but—'

'But it didn't occur to you that we might be making her situation worse?'

'Her tremors, you mean?'

'If that's what you want to call them.'

'Look, I'm sorry. I just thought—'

'Carly, sometimes your insensitivity astounds me.'

Carly left when I told her I didn't want to open another bottle of wine. And she talked about other people being in denial! As soon as she was out the door, I rang Jesse but she had her mobile switched off.

'Jesse, I'm so sorry,' I told her voicemail. 'We shouldn't have said anything, and you're completely right, we were probably mistaken. Maybe it wasn't Steve . . .' I asked her to call me and hung up.

I was so exhausted by the time I slipped into bed, I could hardly move. It had been a long day. I'd just switched off my bedside lamp when the phone rang. I wasn't going to answer it, worried it might be Steve again. But then I recognised the number.

'Stella?' It was Jesse and she was crying.

'Everything okay?' I asked gently.

'Yes. No. Steve's not home. I've left a message on his mobile and called his office phone. No answer. I don't know what else to do.'

'Do you want me to come over?'

'No, I'm okay. Sorry I freaked out. I was shocked. Still am.'

'Of course you are. I could kill Carly.'

'She was just being herself.' Jesse took a moment and her breathing calmed. 'Can you tell me exactly what you saw that night?'

'I'm not sure that's a good idea. The room was dark, there were loads of people—'

'Stop bullshitting and just tell me. I don't need specifics. You can tell me all that on Thursday. I just want you to tell me whether the man you saw at the party was Steve.'

'I'm ninety-nine per cent sure.'

She took another deep breath. 'Was he drunk or . . .' She paused. 'High?'

'He didn't seem drunk but maybe he'd been taking drugs. I really don't know, Jess.'

'Okay.'

'If you want to take Thursday off, it's no problem.'

'No, I'll be in. Ten o'clock as usual.'

'You sure? You sound too calm.'

'Trust me, Stella, I'm okay.'

I wasn't. I hung up feeling decidedly shaky. Jesse was taking the news well, almost too well. She was too calm, her emotions overly controlled. It worried me. I thought about driving over to see her, but it was late. She'd be asleep before long. Besides, Steve was probably pulling into their garage about now. I didn't like to think of Jesse confronting him. He could wither her with a single well-placed gibe. I dreaded to think how he'd react when he found out Jesse knew what he'd been up to.

I couldn't imagine him saying, 'Okay, Jesse, you caught me. I was wrong, I'll do anything you want.' He'd never agree to a divorce if that wasn't part of his own agenda. Jesse had told me once that their home and bank accounts were all in his name. He held all the aces: the money and the power. I found it odd in this day and age, but that summed Steve up. He needed to control every aspect of Jesse's and the kids' lives. She had no money of her own aside from the small amount she earned at the library.

Besides, Steve wasn't the kind of man to give up easily. To him, image was everything. To the outside world, he lived the perfect life: the glamorous wife (even though he kept her apart from his colleagues so they wouldn't notice that she twitched in his presence), the gorgeous twins, one girl, one boy. Steve would rather crawl naked over broken glass than admit he was wrong about anything. He'd probably enjoy it, too.

13

Jesse sat on her bed, hugging her knees to her chest, rocking herself backward and forward, tears streaming down her face. What to do? It had just gone eleven o'clock. She considered ringing Louisa, but she'd only spoken to her a couple of days ago.

Stella was her best friend, but Jesse couldn't continually burden her with her secrets, regrets and desires. She knew too much already. Any more and . . . well, it would be too much for her to keep it to herself. Jesse couldn't ask that of her. She'd get what she wanted in the end. She just had to figure out how to make it happen—how to work it to her advantage.

She stared at the ceiling as she thought back over the evening. The humiliation and shame. She could kill Steve for what he'd done. She could walk out on him tonight. And it had come from Carly, of all people! The least qualified woman Jesse knew to be lecturing her about her marriage.

She remembered a conversation with Louisa years ago. Lou was high on coke and she'd blurted out something to Jesse about how her sex life with Steve 'must be pretty out there, given what he's into'. Jesse had pretended she knew what Louisa was talking about so she'd continue.

'I don't know how you put up with it, all that nappy stuff, having to clean up after him when he shits in it.'

Jesse had thought Louisa was talking about Oliver. The next thing she knew, Louisa was packing her bags and leaving for San Francisco. Jesse had been stunned.

'Tell me what's happened?' she'd begged her sister.

'Nothing, Jesse,' Louisa had assured her, tears streaming down her cheeks. 'I just need a break. I'll be back.'

Famous last words.

Jesse had even resorted to questioning her mum. Dot's response? 'A silly misunderstanding with a friend that got out of control.' How silly could it have been if it forced Louisa to take off overseas?

Dot also told her that Louisa would be back. 'This is her home, darling. Besides, she loves Ollie and Emmy too much to leave them permanently.'

Six long years later, Louisa still hadn't stepped back onto Australian soil and Jesse wasn't a lot wiser about the reason why. Her parents didn't talk about it, and Louisa had never confided in her sister as to why she'd left the country so abruptly.

She glanced at the clock again. Eleven thirty. Steve still wasn't home. She got out of bed and wandered the house, trying to ignore her shaking left hand. Usually she'd check on the twins—watching them sleep always calmed her—but tonight they were at her parents' place. She made herself a cup of green tea, retreated back to bed and tried reading her book.

What if Steve had been in an accident and was lying in a ditch somewhere? For a moment, she wished it were true. But she knew it wasn't. He was at a sex party somewhere, snorting cocaine and possibly being infected right at this very second with an STD . . .

Stop it, Jesse!

She could barely control herself as the anger raged inside. What kind of man did this to his wife? His kids? She had loved him. Loved her family. And now? Well, now her life was in tattered ruins.

But she refused to let despair defeat her. Working hard to rein in her thoughts, she calmed her breathing, because once the dark side took hold . . .

I choose to be positive.

From the top drawer of her bedside cabinet, she pulled out a bottle of Blackmore's Valerian and gulped two tablets, then turned off the bedside light. *I choose to be positive.* It was just after midnight.

Steve crawled into bed at three thirty. Did he really think she was naive enough to believe he'd been working until then? His boldness astounded her. She was seething. He'd ruined the life they'd built together. She shuddered to think what her parents would say when they found out—because eventually they would. Everyone would! Jesse's life as she knew it was over. It had been built on a lie. And it wasn't just one lie or one indiscretion. This was a completely separate secret life.

What else had Steve kept hidden from her? Another family? She'd read about that kind of thing: a seemingly straight-up family man who, after being killed in a car accident, was found to have three other wives . . . or boyfriends. She'd also read stories about sex parties going wrong and family men being murdered. It could so easily be Steve. For starters, Jesse wanted to murder him! It took every bit of strength not to roll over and knee him in the groin.

Instead, she shifted to the other side of the bed and lay there thinking as the hours ticked by.

Wednesday morning, Jesse dragged herself out of bed on autopilot and, after her mother dropped the children off, got them dressed and organised for school. Despite what catastrophes might befall you, life went on . . . In another country, there might be a tsunami, a suicide bombing, war—but in Jesse's world, the kids still needed to be fed, their homework completed, their teeth brushed.

Last night, in between dozing, listening out for Steve and over-thinking her wretched life, Jesse had had another weird dream. This time about Louisa leaving. It had started with Louisa calling her name.

'Louisa?' Jesse had replied. 'Is that you? I'm so happy. It's so good to have you back home. I really missed you. Don't ever leave me again.'

Jesse was standing in the middle of the flower shop where she'd worked many years ago. Ollie and Emily were young, only three or so; they were tugging at pale pink tulips in a vase. 'Stop that,' Jesse told them. She handed them two rolls of ribbon and a balloon each to play with and they started rolling around on the filthy wet floor.

'I'm going,' Louisa said.

'But I don't want you to leave.'

'I have to. It's all blown up.'

'What has?'

But Louisa wouldn't explain. 'I can never come back here again.' She was crying, sobbing Jesse's name over and over.

Jesse reached out to put her arms around Louisa but she couldn't seem to touch her.

'I hate all these flowers,' Louisa had screamed.

Then *pop!* Emily's balloon burst, making Jesse jump. She looked around for Louisa, but she'd gone. She'd left Jesse again.

Jesse had woken up feeling startled and unsettled.

When she dropped the kids at school, she found herself lingering longer than usual at the gate.

'I love you,' she called as they raced off into the school yard. Emily didn't give her a backwards glance, but Ollie turned around and ambled back to where Jesse was leaning against the car.

'I hate seeing you so sad, Mummy,' he said, hugging her tight. 'Everything will be good, you'll see.'

She nodded through her tears. 'You have a good day, my darling. The best. I love you.'

'I love you too,' he said and kissed her cheek.

It took every bit of strength Jesse had to let him go. She wanted to hold him, to tell him he could take the day off so they could hang out together and go to the beach or the movies. But she didn't. What was she doing to that beautiful boy, she wondered as she drove away. She swore he could see into her heart, that he knew what she was thinking, how she was feeling.

Once home, she forced herself to eat half a banana and then dialled Steve's number. There was never going to be a good time for this. She didn't have all the facts but she had enough.

'Where were you last night?' she started. She was trying to remain calm but could feel her voice breaking.

'Working,' he replied, not missing a beat.

'And last Thursday night?'

'Working.'

'Liar!'

She was pacing like crazy and switching lights on and off. Flick, flick, flick. In her mind, she saw him with a range of nameless, faceless women, stroking and kissing them, having sex on leopard-skin rugs, revelling in his perversion.

'I don't know what you're talking about.' Steve's tone was measured, superior.

'People saw you.'

'Which people? What exactly was I supposed to have been doing?'

Jesse couldn't believe he was carrying on with the charade. He'd been caught, and he knew he'd been caught, yet he still acted like he was God.

'I'm not going to dignify those questions with a reply. You're a sick man.'

'I'm sick? That's funny. What about you with your pacing and other obsessions?'

'This isn't about me, Steve.'

Silence.

'Look,' Jesse stammered, trying to erase the filthy images from her mind. 'I don't want you here. I want you to move out.'

'Who are you to tell me I can't live in my own house?' he yelled. 'A house, I might add, that I paid for. If anyone should be leaving, it's you. You're not a fit mother. You're the one who's sick.'

'I don't want to argue with you, Steve,' she said, feeling faint. 'I just can't live with a man—'

'What? Go on. Say it!'

'I can't live with you now that I know it's all been a lie. You're not the man you claim to be.'

'You're talking nonsense. Besides, it's not me you should be interrogating. It's those sluts you call friends!'

'How can you say that?'

'And as for your sister—'

She hung up before he could say another word. Arsehole.

Jesse was shaking so hard she could barely breathe. She needed to take a long, brisk walk around the neighbourhood but she didn't think her legs would carry her that far. She was almost hyperventilating.

Steve was being a prick, acting like he was the wronged one, like he hadn't been caught out. What more could she do? Show him photographic evidence? An ugly thought flashed into her mind: she prayed there weren't any incriminating photos of him on somebody's hard drive.

She contemplated taking the kids to her parents and staying with them until she figured out what to do next, but why should she have to move out of her own house?

Nausea overwhelmed her. She only just made it to the bathroom in time, threw up in the toilet, then collapsed on the cool tiles, lying silently for several minutes. She could feel the distress eating away inside her. All she wanted to do was sleep. She closed her eyes.

Sometime later, she woke feeling marginally better and slowly stood up, walked into the kitchen and popped a couple of headache tablets.

Louisa? Where did she fit in all of this? Jesse felt a little jolt at the back of her throbbing head . . . some distant memory trying to break free.

She dialled Louisa's number.

'Tell me what you know,' she said when Louisa answered. 'About Steve.'

She heard Louisa suck in air like it was in short supply. 'Pardon?' she said.

'About the parties.'

Louisa hesitated. 'I wanted to tell you—'

'Oh God! You knew!'

Jesse's world collapsed. Because Steve hadn't admitted anything, she'd been hanging on to a hope that Stella and Carly had been mistaken. Stella had said it was dark at the party; they couldn't be sure it was Steve. But now, with Louisa's words, it all became horribly real.

'Jesse? Talk to me. It was a long time ago. I was a different person back then.' Louisa was speaking but Jesse couldn't comprehend what she was saying. 'And then six years ago—'

'When you left Australia?' Jesse said, trying to follow the conversation.

'Yeah. Dad's golf friend recognised me.'

'Hang on. What?'

'He told Dad that the last time he'd seen me, I'd been dressed in a black corset and suspenders and had been whipping his bare bum with a cane.'

'What's this got to do with Steve?'

'Everything. Isn't that what you're asking me?'

'I'm not sure.'

'Jesse, I knew years ago that Steve was into this crazy shit.'

The conversation was happening faster than Jesse could process it. Louisa and Steve? With the golf guy? It didn't make sense.

'You were in it together?' she asked.

'Not exactly,' said Louisa. 'I was being paid.'

'I'm confused. What are you telling me exactly?'

'I'm telling you that when I first met Steve fifteen years ago, he was into bondage and shit—'

'God! Fifteen years ago? But—'

'—then he met you and I recognised him and he promised me he wasn't into it any more—'

Jesse took a long breath. 'And Dad's friend?'

'He'd been a client years before. I never expected to see him again. Then when he saw me with Dad, he assumed—'

'Jesus, Louisa! What part of you decided it would be a good idea to keep this secret from me?'

'I was protecting you. Steve loved you, and I thought he was telling me the truth when he said he'd stopped living his fantasy double life.'

'You were protecting yourself more like it. So you were a . . . prostitute?'

'Never. It wasn't like that. Look, it was a long time ago. Tell me how you found out about Steve.'

'Friends saw him at a party.' Jesse paused, feeling her throat constrict. 'He was wearing a nappy.'

Louisa groaned but didn't say anything.

Jesse continued. 'As I thought about it more, I remembered a conversation we'd had just before you went away.'

'I'm so sorry. I really am. What are you going to do?'

Jesse couldn't answer. Her life was over. It was as simple as that. Soon everyone would know and she'd be the laughing stock of the North Shore.

'Jesse! You've got to believe me—I got out of it years ago and Steve promised me he'd done the same.'

'This is unbelievable. An unbelievable nightmare. You! Steve! I feel utterly betrayed. How could you have kept this from me? Allowed me to marry a man like that?'

Silence.

'Is that why you haven't been home all this time?'

'I couldn't trust myself not to tell you about Steve.'

'How could you think that something like this could be kept secret? I can't forgive you for this. Why didn't you tell me?'

How could her life ever return to normal after such a revelation? She felt stupid, alone and thoroughly humiliated.

'My life's over,' she shouted down the phone line.

Her body began to shake, to convulse . . . she felt as though she was shrinking . . . disappearing. Suddenly, it wasn't her body any more.

Jesse dropped the phone as her mind went blank.

14

*L*ouisa freaked out when she heard a thud—presumably Jesse falling. The rational part of her hoped she'd only fainted, but what if she'd hit her head on a table corner or had a heart attack? Ever worse scenarios clamoured for her attention as she dialled her mother's number. Jesse would hate her for getting Dot involved but she didn't know who else to call. She certainly wasn't going to ring Steve.

Dot called half an hour later to say that Jesse was okay. Thank God.

'I'd like to know what brought this on,' she said to Louisa. 'Jesse says she didn't eat much breakfast—'

'So, there's a simple explanation,' Louisa reassured her. 'Can I talk to her?'

Dot huffed before handing the phone over to Jesse.

'I'm sorry,' Louisa started, knowing how much she'd hurt her sister.

'We'll talk about this later,' Jesse replied, her voice barely audible.

'Are you okay?'

Dumb question. How could Jesse be okay given what she'd just found out? Plus, Louisa had involved their mother who'd no doubt interrogate Jesse for hours once Louisa was off the phone.

'I'm fine,' Jesse said gruffly and hung up.

So now Jesse knew. She knew about Louisa, about Steve . . . Louisa almost felt relieved. She'd meant what she said about telling Jesse anything she wanted to know. She'd be honest. It was time. What did she have to lose?

Louisa thought about that question some more. A lot, actually. She'd already lost her father, and was now on the brink of losing Jesse if she didn't deal with this situation carefully. Dot was oblivious and Louisa hoped that could continue. Eventually, Louisa would have to face her father again and that would be torture. Six years ago, she'd explained as little as she could get away with.

It had been an unfortunate coincidence that her dad's friend had seen Louisa with Tom. He'd assumed Louisa was on the job and had bowled up to them with a sly wink and nod. Tom, of course, had had no idea what was going on. When Louisa had been forced to explain it to him, he'd listened in a silent daze, not knowing where to look or what to say. Could it have been more embarrassing? Well, yes actually, but Louisa didn't want to think about that possible scenario. She never wanted to see her father look at her like that ever again. Humiliation, disappointment and despair in his face.

'Why, Louisa?' he'd said. 'We would have given you money.'

He'd begged her not to tell Dot and Jesse, and of course she didn't. Why would she choose to shame herself further? But not telling them had meant she continued to protect Steve. At least she wouldn't have to do that anymore.

Six years was a long time to be away from her family, but disappearing had seemed the only answer. Life in Sydney, the revelations . . . it had spun out of control. And Steve? He'd been beyond smug, telling Jesse that Louisa was a bad influence on the kids. Like he could talk!

'Promise me you aren't dabbling in these parties anymore and I'll go quietly,' Louisa had said to him just before she left Australia.

'I don't have to promise you a thing.'

And the bastard hadn't. Sometimes she could have kicked herself for not telling Jesse what she knew about him. But she hadn't believed it would have helped the situation. Ollie and Emily had been three years old when she left. There was no way she could have told Jesse about Steve's past without totally destroying her, and Jesse had been fragile enough at the time.

So she'd got the hell out of Sydney. Melbourne, Perth, even Hong Kong, weren't far enough away. She had connections in San Francisco, so it had seemed as good a place as any. She'd got a job at the University of San Francisco and an apartment in Nob Hill, and before she knew it, she was settled and life was good. Then she met the professor and life had skyrocketed to sublime.

Louisa gazed out of her apartment window to the harbour in the distance. The wind was howling. She'd always known the day would arrive when Jesse would discover the truth and she'd have to explain everything. She had imagined it would be earth-shattering, a ticking bomb finally exploding. But she felt strangely calm. Once Jesse was over the shock and saw Steve for the dirtbag he truly was, she'd come through the experience stronger.

Louisa wondered if Steve was still doing cocaine. Back in the day, he'd snorted any drugs he could get hold of. Man, he'd been a huge coke head. Soon after Jesse had started going out with him, she'd mentioned that Steve had offered her some. She'd been horrified. She'd only ever tried grass before—once—and hated it.

'I felt so out of control. Yuck. Do you think Steve might have an addiction?' she'd asked her sister.

It had been the perfect opportunity for Louisa to warn Jesse, or at least plant a seed of doubt in her mind. But she hadn't wanted to rock the boat, and certainly hadn't wanted to incriminate herself. So she'd said nothing. She'd reasoned that it was none of her business, and that as long as Jesse wasn't being hurt, it was okay.

The trouble was, Jesse was being hurt. She just hadn't realised it, and neither had Louisa, not really. Lots of people Louisa knew took drugs. They still had good jobs, led active lives. In hindsight, that decision was a cop-out. Another one of her fuck-ups she could have handled so much better.

She checked her phone for messages. Still no word from Philippe.

As much as she didn't want to admit it, she missed him. A lot. And it wasn't just the sex. She missed his laugh, his warmth, the way his top lip curled when he smiled. Where was he and what was he doing? An image of his naked body popped into her mind. Just the thought of him grinding against her, skin to skin, was enough to get her burning with desire.

She shook off the feeling and checked her university schedule. She would head out to Australia and see her family, for sure. But she couldn't possibly go until the spring break, after Easter. For one thing, she couldn't let her students down; and for another? In three or four months, the dust would have settled, Jesse would have moved on, Dot and Tom would be used to the idea that Jesse and Steve were finished . . . Yes, by then life would be a lot calmer. In fact, she might not need to go back to Sydney at all. They'd all be so busy . . .

When Jesse came to, her mum was shouting her name and pounding on the front door. She got to it just as Dot was letting herself in with the spare key.

After Dot had phoned Louisa, she fussed about the kitchen making tea while Jesse sat at the bench and looked on. Her mum reminded Jesse of a sparrow—short, petite and darting about the kitchen at a hundred miles an hour. She felt exhausted just watching her.

'Are you sure you don't need to lie down?' Dot said, eyeing her suspiciously.

Jesse shook her head. She felt sick and could barely keep her eyes open, but she wanted to stay upright while her mother was there.

'All right. But, Jesse,' Dot said, handing her a cup, 'I know what's been going on.'

Not her mother, too. Jesse felt her chest tighten as she tried to suck in air. Please don't tell me that Mum knows about Steve! It wasn't right. She was so wound up, she'd gone beyond feeling embarrassed. All she could think of were the horrors that lay ahead for her: explaining to her children why Mummy and Daddy weren't living together, the divorce, coping as a single parent, Steve and his . . . games.

'Don't look so surprised,' Dot continued.

'I . . . I don't know where to start,' Jess stammered before bursting into tears. She could feel herself sinking into the stool, wanting to close her eyes and to forget about everything . . . the conversation with Louisa, the last few days. To go back to a time when her world was still intact. Far from perfect but at least manageable.

'What made you think we wouldn't find out?' Dot said.

Jesse shook her head. 'I really hoped it wouldn't become public knowledge.'

Dot raised her eyebrows. 'Hence the name, I suppose.'

'Pardon?'

'The name—the Secret Women's Business Workshop. I know all about it, Jesse.' Dot pulled a pamphlet from her bag and read aloud: *'Don't leave it until you wake up one morning and realise you've lived your whole life for everyone else and you no longer know who you are or what makes you happy.'*

'Where did you get that?' Jesse said, jumping down from the stool.

'I found it.'

'In my handbag!'

And less than half an hour ago, thought Jesse, remembering the extra brochure she'd picked up at the meeting the other day.

Dot waved her hand dismissively. 'What is this? A cult?'

Jesse shook her head. 'Mum, really.'

'Wake up to yourself, Jesse. You have enough responsibilities. Secret women's business indeed.'

Jesse wasn't up for this conversation, but it was a hell of a lot better than talking about Steve's indiscretions. So her mother had been snooping. Jesse wondered what else she'd found.

'The group sounds interesting,' she said evenly.

'Interesting or not, you have enough going on in your life without adding this to the mix. Perhaps you should come to church with me? Bring the children.'

'Mum, you can't go snooping around in my belongings. And it's none of your concern if I want to go to a meeting and—'

'And what?'

'Better myself.'

'Jesse, love. Look at you. You don't need more stress.'

It took Jesse a moment to figure out what Dot was talking about. She was standing by a light switch, flipping it on and off, while tapping her right foot on the floorboards.

She really didn't want to have this conversation with her mother. She'd never understand. 'Mum, you don't need to be privy to every waking moment of my life—'

'Jesse, your mother's only trying to help. Aren't you, Dot?'

Jesse gasped and turned. Steve was standing barely two metres away, watching her.

'I called him on my way over,' Dot explained.

'There was no need,' Jesse said.

Dot raised her eyebrows. 'No need? I had no idea what I might find when I arrived. I was scared, Jesse.'

Steve had a fake smile plastered across his face. He kissed Jesse on the cheek. 'You okay now?'

She nodded and turned away from him. Had he asked her that a few days ago, she wouldn't have doubted his sincerity. But now? She wasn't buying it at all.

'I'll leave you to deal with her, Steve,' Dot said, picking up her handbag. 'Maybe you can talk some sense into her.'

'I'll do my best,' he replied, smiling broadly.

Jesse wanted to vomit. 'Mum, you don't have to leave. Stay and have another cup of tea.'

Dot shook her head. 'Your husband's home now, darling. He'll look after you.'

Steve beamed. 'I always do.'

Jesse took her mother's arm as they walked to the front door, more because she was shaking than for any other reason.

'Settle down,' Dot said sternly. 'Put this nonsense about secret women's business out of your head. Focus on your family. You don't need any more stress or distracting influences.'

'Mum!'

'Come to church with me, or do some yoga, but for goodness sake get your act together. Steve will take care of you, but Jesse, you have to be reasonable.'

With that, she waltzed out the front door and left Jesse alone with a monster.

'Smart woman,' said Steve, who was now standing beside her. 'Drives me crazy with her inane chatter, but she's all right. Knows when to leave.'

Jesse couldn't move or think. As long as the kids were with her, she could cope, but when it was just the two of them, like right now, she wasn't sure what Steve might be capable of doing.

'We need to talk this through,' he said calmly, as if reading her mind.

She shrugged him off as he tried putting his arm around her.

'Jesse, you're not well. You need to see someone.'

'I'm perfectly fine. You're trying to pin your sickness on me and make it my responsibility.'

'Sweetheart,' he said, moving towards her again. 'What are you talking about? I don't have an illness. You, on the other hand—'

'Stop it. Don't touch me. You're trying to make out that I'm crazy.'

Steve smiled. 'Why would I do that? You've had a bad fall. You need to see a doctor. At the very least, you need bed rest. Come on, I'll help you upstairs.'

'I don't want a bloody rest.' Jesse's head was spinning. Her stomach churned. She felt as if she was about to vomit, as she had earlier in the day. But there was no way she was admitting that to him. 'I spoke to Louisa.'

'Really?'

'She said she knew you years ago.'

'As if she'd remember!'

Jesse ignored him. 'So you were into this before we met?' She was determined to get him to admit it. 'I'm relieved it wasn't something I did, that I neglected you somehow so you sought comfort elsewhere. You've always had an addiction. You were always into those games.'

Steve took a pace back. 'So what if I was? What business is it of yours?'

First step.

'It's my business,' Jesse said calmly, 'because I'm your wife, your so-called life partner, and I deserve better.'

She didn't want to have this conversation; she just wanted him to admit the truth. She was twitching and it was his fault. She'd never used to tap her foot or flick light switches before she met Steve. She hadn't needed to triple-check that the iron or oven was switched off. She'd been happy, confident.

'And I deserve to be with someone who's not a nutter,' Steve said, pulling her back into their horrid conversation. 'Someone who doesn't switch lights on and off and retrace her steps over and over. That's what I deserve.'

Jesse hated him. How had she ever found him charming and handsome? He was a bully. He made her sick.

She grabbed her car keys from a side table. 'I'm picking up the kids.'

'Come on,' he said, his voice even. 'Let's discuss this rationally, before it gets out of hand. I've made some possible errors in judgement—'

'You've done way more than that, Steve.'

'Hang on! We've both contributed to this—'

Jesse shook her head and pushed past him. 'I'm leaving.'

He crossed his arms. 'You'll regret it.'

Jesse was over an hour early to pick up Ollie and Emmy, so she drove to a nearby cafe and ordered a skinny latte. She was all alone. There was no one she could ring who wouldn't judge her. Except maybe Stella. She'd support her. She always supported her, but was there anyone else who'd look out for her? Anyone else who had Jesse's best interests at heart? She wondered.

She'd never been good at making friends. At best she had acquaintances. There was nothing wrong with that as long as she only wanted to talk about teachers, the netball roster and the tuckshop menu, but right now Jesse needed more. That was one of the reasons she was so interested in the Secret Women's Business meetings. She was hoping to meet like-minded people—at a distance. She shook her head, remembering that her mother had taken the brochure with her when she left.

Jesse had always struggled to let people get close to her. When she married Steve, she'd let the few friendships she'd had slide, except for Louisa, of course. But when Louisa left, Jesse had felt let down, betrayed. Louisa was the person Jesse always turned to, so when she moved overseas, Jesse had had no one. Her best friend had suddenly disappeared.

Louisa's departure had affected her deeply, but Steve had been dismissive. 'She's gone. Deal with it.'

Now Jesse knew why. He'd had an ulterior motive for wanting Louisa to leave and never return.

After losing Louisa, Jesse had vowed she'd never allow herself to feel that vulnerable again. She had Steve and her children, whom she loved and trusted, but she began closing herself off from others, building a wall that seemed to stretch higher and higher as time went by. Now, apart from Stella, and occasionally Carly, Jesse rarely confided in anyone.

Even when she did see Stella and Carly, like the other night, she felt like she was somehow missing out. On what, she didn't know. A great joke, a funny exchange, life in general. Jesse couldn't pinpoint it, but it just felt like she was being left behind.

And now, faced with the unspeakable revelations about Steve, she knew her marriage was doomed. How could she ever trust him again?

She shook her head. The truth was, except for when she was with Oliver and Emily, Jesse felt heavy with loneliness and now, regret.

She lost count of how many times she'd stirred her coffee, but when she swallowed some, it was barely warm. Why couldn't she have had a simple life, one in which both she and her husband were normal? Happily in love and bringing up two adorable children? They'd got the adorable children right, just fucked up every other detail. Why did everything have to turn to mud?

The thought of spending another night in the same bed as Steve was abhorrent. She couldn't do it. But she also didn't want to run away and give him the satisfaction of knowing he'd triumphed. She'd rather walk barefoot over red-hot coals than admit defeat. Steve hadn't won, not by a long shot.

Tomorrow she'd be at the library. She could make it until then. Just. For now, she needed to play it smart.

15

First thing Wednesday morning, Carly rang Jesse to apologise. She knew she'd behaved badly last night, all that stuff she'd blurted out. It didn't matter that it was true, what mattered was her delivery. Appalling. She needed to talk to Jesse, square things off. But all she got was Jesse's voicemail. Maybe she was screening her calls.

Carly phoned Stella. 'Okay, so I'm an idiot and a shocking friend. I'm really sorry. I've already left a message on Jesse's phone.'

'You said what you needed to,' replied Stella, not unkindly.

'I could have said it better.'

'Agreed, but listen, Jesse rang me late last night. She knows we're telling her the truth.'

The news took Carly by surprise. 'How was she?'

'Calm. Too calm.'

'What should I do?'

'You've left an apology,' Stella said. 'That'll do for now. I'll call you when I know more.'

Carly hung up, still feeling dreadful. Poor Jesse. The phone rang again, almost instantly. Brett. Carly hadn't really spoken to him since the sex-talk fiasco yesterday afternoon.

'Steve rang me,' he said. 'He kept going on about you and Stella interfering in his life. What does he mean?'

Carly gave him the first excuse she could think of. 'He's just annoyed because Stella and I told Jesse she should stand up for herself more.'

'Carly, Steve's furious. You don't want to aggravate him. Sometimes you women—'

'We women what?'

'You get carried away with other people's lives. You need to try not to get caught up in suburban gossip.'

'Really? So you think encouraging Jesse to stick up for herself is gossip?'

'Whatever, Carly. Just don't take it on as a personal crusade. If Steve's in the wrong—'

'What do you mean, if?'

'I just mean, don't get involved. Let Steve and Jesse sort out their own domestics. I think it'd be in your best interests to give them some time alone.'

'But—'

'I don't have time to deal with this right now. I'm trying to run a company and keep you happy. I'd appreciate you pulling your head in.'

Carly wanted to argue, but Brett had a point. The last week had been an ongoing nightmare and Brett didn't even know half of it. Last night's behaviour at Stella's, the carry-on at the pub last week . . . Carly was beginning to wonder whether she might be in the grip of a mid-life crisis.

'If you and Stella keep interfering, Jesse's situation, whatever that may be, is only going to get worse,' Brett said. 'And, Carly,

I really don't need my wife's friends' husbands ringing me at work.'

'Okay,' she said meekly. 'Point taken.'

'Thanks. Steve sounded . . .' He hesitated.

'Steve sounded what?'

'To tell you the truth, he sounded a little unhinged. Not normal.'

'Oh.'

'Carly?'

'Yeah?'

'Never mind. Have a good day, okay?'

She mumbled 'Yeah' again and hung up. So even Brett thought Steve sounded crazy. She took it as a good sign that Brett had rung: it showed he cared about her safety.

All too quickly, she remembered her outrageous flirting with Toby and felt guilty. How could she do that to her husband? There was no way she could tell Brett why Steve was so furious with her. He would be horrified.

Carly watched as the clock ticked over past midday. She couldn't wait any longer for Jesse to phone back. She called her again.

Jesse's mum, Dot, answered. 'Jesse's not well. She's resting.'

'Is there anything I can do to help?'

'No, thanks,' she replied, short and clipped. 'I'm here. Jesse will call you when she's feeling better.'

And that was the end of that! Dot was one very tough nut. She hung up and Carly was left wondering why Jesse had taken ill. Maybe it was the business with Steve—her nerves had gotten the better of her.

Well, there was nothing else she could do about Jesse now. Carly wandered over to the computer to check her emails. She was feeling rather sick herself as she wondered if there was anything further about Nicholas and whatever debauchery and carry-on he was involved in on the other side of the world. She gulped as she saw another message from Nicholas's sports master.

Apologies if my previous email alarmed you. It appears that some locker room high jinks got out of hand and one of the younger students complained. I understand the Australian reputation for exuberance, but when it comes to flicking wet towels onto naked boys' backsides (Carly winced at the words 'naked boys' backsides' and had to force herself to continue reading), *action needs to be taken. Nicholas is not the only student involved, and all have been suspended pending an inquiry. As sports master, I need to take any complaints seriously. Rest assured, this matter will be thoroughly investigated. However, I do anticipate a speedy and satisfactory resolution. I will keep you informed.*

She re-read the email several times. Nicholas had been cavorting with naked boys in the showers. It did her head in thinking about it. There was no way around it: she had to tell Brett. Imagine if he tried keeping something like that from her? She'd kill him. But first she decided to ring Nick and get his side of the story. She felt sick with dread. She'd failed her son. She should have been more aware and more involved.

She took a few moments to compose herself before dialling Nicholas's number. Part of her hoped his mobile was switched off, but he answered after two rings.

'Hi, Mum. I was expecting your call.'

'So it's true,' Carly said, trying to keep her voice even.

'Which part?'

'The part about you being suspended for flicking towels in the locker room?'

'Yeah. Dumb, hey?'

'Nicholas, how could you?'

'It was a game. No big deal. But one kid went ballistic, overreacted and dobbed.'

'Do you need me to come over?'

'What? To Wales? Now you're overreacting . . . It was a towel. A bunch of guys in a locker room rumble. What's the big deal?'

Carly was verging on tears. The big deal was that he'd been harassed by his coach last year, or maybe he'd even had an affair with him; the big deal was that he'd been suspended for coercing other boys into inappropriate behaviour. The big deal was . . . Carly really needed a glass of wine. She checked herself. The last thing Carly needed was alcohol.

'Mum, are you okay?'

'Nicky, I'm just . . . You're so far away and I feel so useless. I want to help you.'

'I can look after myself.'

'Is there anything else you want to tell me?'

'What? No! You shouldn't even know about this.'

'But, Nick—'

'Seriously, Mum. It's cool.'

He hung up and Carly felt even worse if that was possible. She wanted to believe him. He was her son. But her mind immediately returned to Mr Busby and those letters.

She got on with the housework and then did some gardening, but she couldn't focus. Even though her head was still pounding from last night, every time she opened the fridge and caught sight of the chardonnay bottle, she wanted to pour herself a glass. Guilt was gnawing away at her. She had to speak to Jesse, to let her know how sorry she was.

God, I desperately want this day to be over, she thought as she dialled Jesse's number. She wanted to get all of this nasty stuff out of the way—with a little help from Ms Villa Maria—and then tomorrow would be a new and glorious beginning. A new, clean-living, happy Carly. But today? Well, today, she had a list of distressing activities to get through and Jesse was slap-bang at the top. Giving into temptation, she opened the fridge door, pulled out the wine and poured herself a glass.

'Jesse,' Carly said, relieved when her friend answered. 'It's Carly.' She reached for her wine glass and gulped. This was going to be an excruciating call, she could tell. 'I'm ringing to apologise for last night. I had no right—'

Jesse stopped her. 'Carly, I understand. You didn't want to be the bad guy, but you were.'

Carly didn't know how to respond to that.

'Look, Steve's here now,' Jesse whispered. 'I can't talk.'

'But, Jesse, I'm so sorry. And your mum said you were sick. Are you okay?'

'Fine, thanks.' She sounded weird. Preoccupied. 'Anyway, Steve and I are sorting everything out.'

Really? Carly didn't buy it. Jesse sounded anxious. She heard shuffling in the background. 'Is there anything I can do?' she ventured.

'You've already done more than enough.' It was Steve.

'Jesse?' Carly said. But the line was dead.

Carly quickly drank the rest of the wine and poured another glass. Her hands were trembling.. Should she ring back? Call Brett? She thought for a moment, then phoned Stella.

'What do you mean he eavesdropped on your conversation?' Stella asked after Carly had explained the situation.

'Exactly that, and then he said, "You've already done more than enough," and hung up.'

'And Jesse didn't say anything?'

'Not after that, no. I'm worried.'

'I'm sorry, Carly, but I'm going to have to go. Liz is eyeballing me—' Stella hung up.

Carly rinsed her empty glass. Nothing good could come from a third glass of wine. She already felt numb. Instead, she took two Nurofen Plus and went up to bed. She doubted she'd fall asleep but she needed to lie down and pull herself together. She was crawling under the sheets when her mobile rang. Now what?

'Instead of being so eager to gossip about my family, why don't you take a good long look around your own backyard.' Steve's voice was unmistakable.

'Pardon?'

'You heard me. I'm sure you've got a few of your own family secrets you'd prefer to remain secret.'

'Steve, I never meant . . . I mean—'

'I know what you mean, Carly, and all I'm saying is that before you go snooping about in my business, perhaps you should look more closely at your own family.'

'I have nothing to say to you. I think you need help.'

Steve laughed. 'I need help! That's rich coming from you. Why don't you ask your husband what he gets up to when he's away on business—on those nights when you're stumbling into bed alone after a few too many chardies?'

'What are you implying?'

'I'm simply saying,' said Steve calmly, 'that before you go gossiping about other people, you should make sure no one is gossiping about you. By the way, I can recommend the Oyster Bay Riesling this week. It's on special for a hundred and thirty bucks a dozen, and since you buy your liquor by the crate, you'll save a bundle. Or rather, Brett will.' Steve clicked off.

Carly was shaking. Did she really drink that much? Had it become common knowledge?

As for Brett . . . what did Steve mean? Yes, Brett travelled a lot and worked long hours—what banker didn't? There was no way she was going to let Steve make her feel paranoid about her marriage. This was about him and his wrongdoings, his debauched lifestyle, not about Carly and her husband. Fuck Steve!

On autopilot, she walked down to the kitchen, opened the fridge door, pulled out the half-empty bottle and poured herself another glass. She deserved it after what she'd just been through. Her mind was racing, darting in all directions. She needed the drink to calm her nerves.

Was Steve implying that Brett was having an affair? The thought had crossed Carly's mind, many times. But so far it had been pure speculation. Did Steve have proof? Brett was still attractive, he had a great sense of humour, he was intelligent. He got on well with Stella and Jesse, and whenever Carly had seen him with his work colleagues he'd seemed to get along well with them, too, especially the women. She continued gulping wine as her mind went into overdrive. The trips away, the late-night phone calls and texts . . . It all made perfect sense. And if Steve knew for sure that Brett was having an affair, that would explain why Brett had phoned her in such a flap this morning. He didn't want Steve revealing his secret to Carly.

She tried to compose herself. Perhaps if she sent Brett a text? Fumbling with her phone, she managed to type out *Spoke to Steve. Madman! Making all kinds of accusations about you. LOL! C xx*, before climbing into bed and passing out.

Moments later, or what felt like moments later, Brett was above her, shaking her awake.

'What's going on? What do you mean Steve's been making accusations? I told you not to talk to him.'

Carly took some time to figure out what he was talking about. 'Brett?' Her mouth felt dry and she had a throbbing headache. 'I don't—'

'Are you drunk?'

'No. I—'

Brett sat down on the side of the bed and Carly struggled to sit up and face him. 'What the hell is going on around here?' he demanded.

'Shhh. Keep your voice down,' Carly pleaded. 'Steve rang me. He's a lunatic, he was raving on about all sorts of things.'

'Like?'

'Like, I don't know. Telling me to look in my own backyard before snooping around in his. He's threatening me because of what Stella and I know about him.'

'And what is that, exactly?'

Carly hesitated. Her head was swirling. She felt heavy, almost nauseous. Then she started crying. Not huge, racking sobs, but a continuous stream of tears; she could feel them running down her cheeks.

'Carly? What's up? Tell me.'

She shook her head. 'Nothing.'

'Right. You don't normally cry over nothing.'

She looked at him. 'Is that right, Brett? Can you honestly say you know what I cry about?'

'I know you cry when you've had too much to drink.'

She waved him away with her hand.

'I know you cry over Nicholas, old movies, kittens in pet shops—'

'Stop it. You don't know anything.' She knew she should have stopped there, but she didn't. 'You don't know that Stella and I saw Steve at a sex party—'

'A what?' That had shocked him. 'When?'

'Last Thursday. You also don't know that I sat on a guy's lap and told him I wanted a fuck buddy—'

'Carly, that's enough. You really are drunk.'

Carly ignored him. 'You don't know the half of it.'

'Why are you telling me this?' he asked. 'Why do you do this to yourself? I saw the empty bottle in the kitchen.'

'Because I'm lonely.'

'You don't have to be lonely. I'm here. Will's here. Why don't you come to his basketball games occasionally, or watch TV with us?'

She shook her head. 'Why would you want me to? I'm old.'

'You're not old.'

'I will be soon, and it frightens the hell out of me—the wrinkles, the grey hair. My body . . . ugh. I'm ugly.'

'You're only ugly because you've consumed an entire bottle of wine. Stop it. Drink some water, take a couple of Panadol and you'll be as good as new in the morning.'

Out of the corner of her eye, Carly saw Will hovering at their bedroom door, deliberating whether or not to walk in. He watched for a moment, thought better of it and disappeared down the hallway.

Carly let out a huge sob. 'What am I going to do with the rest of my life? You have your work, Nick's left and William will be gone in less than two years. Where does that leave me? Alone and old, that's where.'

'So instead of alienating yourself from us, why don't you join in?' Brett suggested. 'It doesn't have to be all doom and gloom.'

He disappeared into the bathroom and returned with a huge tumbler of water. 'Drink this.'

She did as she was told, managing to stop crying.

'Feeling better?'

She nodded.

'Okay, start at the beginning. Last Thursday night, you, Stella and Jesse went to the pub where you cracked onto a group of guys—'

'I didn't crack on—'

'No? You told a complete stranger you were looking for a fuck buddy. Am I right?'

'Maybe.' Carly started tearing up again. 'I didn't mean it. I was being stupid.'

Brett rolled his eyes. 'Understatement. Then what? You went to a party where you saw Steve . . .?'

'It wasn't just any party; it was one of those swingers things, a sex party—'

'Go on.'

'We were standing there, totally gobsmacked, when we saw Steve—'

'Where was Jesse?'

'She'd left the pub ages before. Meanwhile, Steve was sucking on a dummy, wearing a nappy and being dragged about by a dominatrix.'

Brett shook his head. 'Excuse me?'

'He was also wearing a studded black dog collar.'

'Sounds unreal.'

'It was. We tried to leave, but he saw us. Since then he's been bombarding me and Stella with text messages and emails, saying that if we tell Jesse—'

'He's been threatening you?' Brett's voice was ice. 'Now it's all starting to make sense. Why didn't you tell me this before?'

'I was ashamed.'

Brett put his arms around her and kissed her forehead. 'Carly . . .' he was shaking his head, 'you really know how to get into trouble, don't you?'

She couldn't answer. She was suddenly very tired. 'That's not the worst of it,' she said.

Brett sighed. 'There's more?'

'Last night at Stella's, I told Jesse about Steve.'

'Carly! What was her reaction?'

'She ran off, but not before screaming that Stella and I had always hated Steve and now we were making up stories to cause trouble. I should never have blurted it out, even though I wanted her to know. It was wrong.'

Brett stood up. 'I've heard enough for one session. We'll talk more about this in the morning when you're feeling better.' He paused. 'And, honey, you really should think about taking a break from the wine for a while.'

'Mmm,' she mumbled.

'Stay in bed and get some rest. I'll sort out dinner for Will. Do you have a busy day tomorrow?'

'Nup.'

'Glad to hear it, because I don't think you'll be up for much. I'll bring you up some Panadol.'

'Don't need them,' she replied.

'You might think you don't, but trust me, you do. They'll make you feel better.'

'Nothing could make me feel better,' she said sadly.

'That's what I don't understand,' he said, serious again. 'I'm really angry with you, Carly. We've built a life together and sometimes I think you go out of your way to try to piss it all up against a wall.'

'It's not that,' said Carly, finding some clarity in her voice. 'It's just that we're so . . . comfortable.'

'And that's a bad thing?' He shook his head.

'I thought it was,' she said, flopping back down on the bed. 'We used to be so wild. But now I don't know any more.'

Carly woke hours later and stared around the pitch blackness of the room until her eyes adjusted. Brett was asleep beside her, and on the bedside table sat two headache tablets and a full glass of water. She swallowed the tablets and turned to Brett, nudging him in the side with her finger.

'Brett?' she stage-whispered. 'Are you asleep?'

He rolled towards her. 'Not any more.'

'Do you ever feel the urge to dress up?'

'Carly!'

'Do you?'

'No. Go to sleep.'

'And group sex doesn't appeal to you?'

'Why?' Brett asked, now fully awake and propped up on his elbow. 'Does it appeal to you? Is this the kind of wild you think you've been missing out on?'

'No, just asking. Brett?'

'Yes?'

'Did I mention the fuck buddy thing to you tonight?'

'Yes, love. I'm afraid you did.'

'I'm going to be in big trouble tomorrow, aren't I?'

'No,' he said, kissing her shoulder. 'I was angry but now I'm just sad. We have a good life together, Carls. You're not in trouble, but you're going to be sick and embarrassed.'

'I want to be a better wife.'

'I know you do, my love,' he said, rubbing her arm. 'But for now, just try being a quiet one.'

16

Against a backdrop of a beautifully bright full moon, Jesse held her newborn, marvelling at how perfect she was, how effortlessly her tiny fingers gripped Jesse's forefinger. She watched, mesmerised, as her baby gurgled contentedly. She was in love, so in love, and so happy. Her life was complete.

Suddenly, the baby was ripped from her arms. Steve was beside her, berating her for wanting another baby. He was adamant. No more kids. 'I'll never allow it.'

'But having another baby would be good for us,' Jesse pleaded. 'Maybe it's the answer to our problems.'

'And what problems would they be, Jesse?'

'We hardly see each other any more. A new baby—'

'You can't handle another child. You can barely manage the two we've got. It's out of the question. End of discussion.'

'Maybe you'll love me again if we have another baby.'

'I'm not going to take that risk. You need to look after the twins, especially Ollie.'

'What do you mean?'

'Do I really need to spell it out for you? What happened to the shrink you were seeing?'

'That was years ago.'

'Well, maybe it's time you went back. And take Ollie with you. He's heading down the same path as you.' Steve's lips weren't moving but Jesse could still hear his voice berating her. 'Why would I want another child with you, another retard to deal with?'

'Is that really what you think of me? Steve? Steve!'

Jesse woke up. It took her a moment to adjust, to realise that she'd been dreaming. Holding the baby in her arms had felt so real, so right. Typical that Steve had come along to ruin it. Retard was such a harsh word.

She glanced at the clock: 3 am. On the other side of the bed, Ollie and Emily slept peacefully. Jesse sighed, rubbed her belly and drifted back to sleep.

'I wish we could sleep in your bed every night, Mummy,' said Emmy when she woke on Thursday morning.

Jesse wished so, too. She had been awake for a good fifteen minutes, just staring at them both, aware of their warm little bodies breathing contentedly next to her. She felt at peace, loved and strong when she was with them. Despite what she and Steve had become, they had created two perfect children.

'Where's Daddy?' asked Ollie, rubbing his eyes and sitting up.

'At work, darling,' Jesse said, very aware that Steve hadn't come home last night.

While the kids got ready for school, she showered and thought back to her dream. It had felt so real, she'd felt so connected to the baby. As she dried herself, she looked at her naked form in the mirror, her flat stomach. She thought back to her pregnancy with the twins. She had loved it, right up until the twenty-eighth week when she'd become so heavy and tired she could barely move. Those babies sure knew how to kick. She remembered the sensation as if it were yesterday.

'You look pretty, Mummy,' Ollie said when she walked into the kitchen.

That was all the encouragement she needed to guarantee a fantastic day. She didn't want to think too much about the future, about tomorrow or the day after that. Isness was the business. She needed to live in the now. It was all about keeping her head above water, putting one foot in front of the other and moving forward, no matter how slowly. If she thought about Steve, she started to twitch, so she needed to put him out of her mind, at least while she was at the library. After work, she'd have the children to distract her and dinner to prepare. Maybe they could have another movie night like last night, when they'd watched *Shrek* and eaten popcorn.

I choose to be positive, she kept repeating over and over . . . Anything to keep her thoughts optimistic and her mind off Steve. As long as her outlook remained upbeat, she could get through this nightmare.

My phone rang. I checked the caller ID: Mike.

'You're up bright and early. I haven't even eaten breakfast,' I said, trying for nonchalance.

'Early shift, taking a break. Thinking of you. Thought I'd call. Too keen?'

I smiled. 'Nah. So what's up?'

'What's up is that I want to see you. I finish at noon. Any chance you could meet up for coffee? Or lunch?'

I hesitated. Yes, I wanted to see him again. But . . . I was sure there were buts; I was just having trouble remembering them.

'Your silence isn't encouraging, Stella.'

'Sorry. It's just that—'

'You think too much. Look, I'm not asking you to move in with me. I'm just offering to buy you a caesar salad in your lunch break, okay?'

I took a deep breath. I was getting way ahead of myself. 'Okay. Sounds great. Where will I meet you?'

'Cafe 42? Twelve thirty?'

'Good. See you there.'

I hung up feeling nervous. Excited as well, but nervous. I had a date with Mike! I silently danced a little jig.

I glanced at the time. Arrrgh! Late! I dressed, hurriedly splashed on some make-up and bolted downstairs for breakfast.

'June,' I said, noticing her elaborate turban, 'what have I told you about wrapping your own turbans? Let me help.'

'I can do it. I've been on this earth seventy years—you adapt.' She paused. 'If you don't mind, I'll stay here for the day. Your garden, dog and cat are looking decidedly neglected. They could do with some attention.'

I hugged her. Great! I wouldn't be late for work, after all. I glanced at the animals. 'They'd love the company, and yes, the garden could do with some TLC. Just don't overdo it.'

I glanced outside. It had started raining. Maybe June wouldn't need to water the garden or take the dog for a walk. Enforced rest! I liked the sound of that.

June regarded the cat currently making a meal of the dog's ears. 'At least they have each other. Better hope they die together.'

I shrugged. 'You do look rather regal in your crimson turban and silver sequined blouse.'

'Thank you,' she beamed. 'I can still rise to the occasion of dressing myself and applying make-up. It's just a pity that the chemically laden dishwashing liquid you insist on buying is drying my good hand out and making my nails brittle.'

June! God love her.

'Mum, who are you meeting up with?' Hannah asked. She was staring into the open fridge, clearly hoping some new and previously hidden food delight would magically appear.

I took an imaginary step back. 'Pardon?'

'On the phone before? You were giggling and acting stupid.'

'I wasn't being stupid, Hannah. Anyway, he's just a friend.'

'A he?' said June. 'One of your doctor friends?'

Sharp as a tack! 'Yes, as a matter of a fact.' I couldn't prevent myself from grinning like a fool.

June's and Hannah's faces dropped.

'My God! You've only just thrown Daddy out,' Hannah squawked, slamming the fridge door shut.

June nodded. 'Exactly! How are you supposed to win Terry back when you're cavorting around with other men?'

'I'm not cavorting, and I didn't throw your father out, Hannah. He left of his own accord.'

'Because you pushed him,' she shrieked.

'Nonsense. So what's happening at school today?' I asked, attempting to change the topic. 'How's Sara?'

'Ugh! Don't ask! I'm not speaking to her. She stole my look.'

Ben walked into the kitchen. 'Is this about the feud with Sara Hewson? For God's sake, Hans, build a friggin' bridge.'

Now it was Ben's turn to stand and stare into the open fridge.

'I didn't realise you had a look,' I said to Hannah, watching as she buttered toast on the kitchen bench, getting crumbs and butter everywhere.

Her hair hung untidily over one eye, her uniform was a good ten centimetres too short, and her cherry lip gloss looked a lot like red lipstick. Definitely a school no-no. But she wouldn't listen to me. I'd have to let her teachers deal with her . . . and then listen to her outraged complaints about the shocking unfairness of school rules. Ben wasn't looking any tidier. His fringe was too long, his pants barely covered his backside, his white shirt wasn't tucked in, his tie was skewiff, and his black shoes were scuffed and unlaced.

Hannah glared at me and flicked her hair. 'The left side part, sweeping over the right eye and ear? Sara totally stole it from me.'

'Noob!' shouted Ben. 'Justin Bieber did that years ago. You're such a loser.'

And Farrah Fawcett before that, I thought.

'What is a noob, exactly?' asked June, sipping her tea.

'You know, Nanna, a noob, a douche,' Ben replied.

Hannah started screaming at him, he screamed back, and June, ignoring the teenage hysteria, struck up a conversation about laundry items with the dog. I left them to it and walked out of the house into the pouring rain. People always went a little crazy in wet weather . . . or was it windy weather? No matter. The people I lived with skated close to the mark pretty much all the time.

On the drive to the library, I thought about June's comment about winning Terry back. I definitely didn't want him back, but was I ready for him to marry someone else? I was stunned that I could be replaced with such ease and so quickly. Wife number one to wife number two in the space of a couple of months. Not that Terry was keen on the marriage idea, but it was only a matter of time. With a cleavage like that, Amanda would wear him down eventually.

Then I thought about Mike and my stomach started doing backflips. Why was I so resistant to taking things further with him? Despite agreeing to lunch today, I didn't want to get involved in all that relationship stuff again, at least not so soon. I couldn't imagine introducing Hannah and Ben to my . . . what? Friend? Boyfriend? Lover? No, the more I thought about it, the more I realised I wasn't up for anything serious right now. But still, I couldn't help smiling whenever I thought about Mike, especially when that tingling sensation took over . . .

As I turned into the library car park, my mind returned to more pressing matters. What was I doing thinking about myself when Jesse's troubles were so much more serious? I'd called her again last night and she'd seemed calm, but she'd only known about Steve's dalliances for twenty-four hours; surely that wasn't long enough to process the information fully? I doubted she'd formulated an action plan yet. On the one hand, it was a no-brainer that she should leave Steve. But on the other, her kids were much younger than mine and still at primary school. They'd be confused, devastated . . . And, as I'd already surmised, Steve wouldn't leave quietly.

During our conversations, Jesse had mentioned a couple of times that she intended applying for the full-time librarian position. I needed to warn her about Liz. Now definitely wasn't the time for Jesse to badger her about more hours. The problem was, I agreed with Liz that Jesse wasn't up to working full-time, at least not at the moment. Maybe in a few months, when things had settled with Steve, she'd be in a stronger emotional state to take on greater responsibility and longer hours at the library. But now? I honestly didn't think so. But I was concerned about having that talk with her, given everything else that was going on in her life.

Liz was hovering by the entrance when I walked into the library.

'I don't think it's going to stop,' I said, shaking my wet umbrella.

She grimaced. 'I'm off to a meeting up the road. I've left a pile of paperwork for you to go through. And could you make up some signs saying the computers will be turned off fifteen minutes before library closing time? Otherwise, we'll continue getting idiots like last night who won't get off even as we're turning the lights out and rattling our car keys in our hands.'

'Sure,' I replied. 'Have a good time.'

Liz was off and running to her car in the rain, seemingly stepping into every deep puddle along the way.

Even though Jesse had left plenty of time to drop the twins off at school and drive to the library, she was late and she couldn't understand why. Maybe it was the rain. People always drove erratically in the rain. Then there were the roadworks. One lane was blocked and the others were moving torturously slowly. Even so, she should have been on time. She banged her hands on the steering wheel, willing the traffic to move faster. The last thing she needed was for Liz to catch her coming in late. She didn't want to provide her with any more ammunition about her work habits. As the traffic crawled along, she got increasingly agitated, so much so that she couldn't keep her foot still on the brake or the accelerator and the car started kangaroo hopping. It took all of her concentration to coordinate her feet and get the speed right.

In an effort to calm herself, Jesse thought back to the Secret Women's Business meeting and how uplifted she'd felt afterwards. 'I choose to be positive,' she whispered to herself, remembering her mantra and reminding herself to stay focused on the present, the here and now. Isness IS the business!

Yesterday, Rebecca had left a phone message asking for feedback. When she finally got around to returning the call, Jesse knew she'd only have good things to report. She was very much looking forward to the next meeting.

She also liked the fact that no one there knew her or her husband or was likely to hear their humiliating secret that was about to become public knowledge. She was anonymous. This was one tiny part of her life that Jesse could nurture quietly alone. Some women chose Pilates or vodka; Jesse chose these meetings. She hoped they'd give her the strength she'd need to hold down a full-time job once she separated from Steve.

Separated. The word rolled around inside her head. She'd be like Stella. Amazing how quickly a person's life could change. Last week, Jesse couldn't have imagined walking in Stella's shoes. This week? Well, they were practically treading the same path. It was reassuring knowing Stella was on her side. Maybe she'd tell Stella about the Secret Women's Business meetings, once she'd become comfortable with the women there and could hold her own. Stella might even attend meetings with her. A distinct possibility.

The recent hiccups at the library had been just that—hiccups. The worst had been a couple of weeks ago when Liz had pulled her off the loans desk because Jesse's nervous habits had resulted in a line of borrowers that extended beyond the periodicals section. Jesse had been truly shocked to discover so many witnesses to her silly behaviour. She needed to check herself and make sure it didn't happen again. She needed to concentrate, to focus on her career as a progressive, caring and efficient librarian. Positive thoughts. When the timing was right and Liz was in a charitable mood, she'd ask her about the full-time position. It wasn't as if she didn't have the qualifications. If Liz gave her a chance, Jesse was confident she could handle the responsibility.

Jesse pulled into the library car park twenty minutes late. She forced herself to breathe deeply several times before she entered the building. She was determined to have a successful day no matter what obstacles she faced.

I'd been at the library an hour when Jesse rushed in.

'Sorry I'm late. Bad traffic, roadworks, wet weather, the lot,' she said as she locked her handbag in the staff cupboard. 'Where is she?'

'Relax. At a meeting up the road with the other library heads.'

Jesse nodded and disappeared into the bathroom. When she came out, I handed her a coffee. 'Tell me what's been happening?'

She sipped her drink. 'Where to start? But first tell me what I should be doing.'

'There's a bit of printing and filing to be done and a load of shelving. Are you up for it?'

I didn't want to sound patronising but I also wanted to protect her. If she wasn't up to shelving the books correctly, I'd prefer she didn't do it at all. There were plenty of other tasks that needed doing.

'No problem,' she said. 'Have you spoken to Liz about my idea for a monthly book club?'

I shook my head. I'd completely forgotten. 'Not yet.'

'Maybe we could talk to her later today?'

'Sure.'

A monthly book club was a great idea, but the staff were already overstretched.

I left Jesse to get on with it while I continued organising author week, which was less than a month away. Liz had left me phone numbers for a dozen publishers' publicists but I hadn't made much of a dent in the list by the time she returned.

'How's it going?' she asked, her eyes veering towards Jesse.

'Great.' But I didn't have any idea. I'd been so busy I hadn't checked on Jesse since she'd begun shelving.

'I've got a pile of reports to fill out by this afternoon,' Liz continued. She sighed. 'I don't know why I'm surprised. It's the same after every meeting.'

She disappeared into her office. A good sign. She was too busy to pull Jesse aside and ask her twenty questions.

Jesse and I crossed paths in the periodicals section later in the morning.

'Fill me in,' I whispered.

'Steve didn't come home last night. He knows I'm serious about him leaving.'

'And?'

'And I think it's going to be really hard. I had no idea what he was up to . . . I mean, when I force myself to think about it, I can vaguely recall snippets that might have suggested . . .' She shook her head. 'And then all the stuff with Louisa.'

'Like what?' I said, keeping my voice low and pretending to tidy *Marie Claire* magazines.

Jesse shook her head again. 'Louisa knew about Steve.'

'What?'

'I don't know the full story, but Louisa used to . . . she used to be professionally involved in those parties.'

'No way!' I knew Louisa had been a wild child, but still.

'She was a dominatrix apparently. She knew Steve before I did.'

Liz's voice interrupted us. 'Are you two actually doing any work?' She checked her watch. 'Stella, you can go on your lunch break.'

I glanced up at one of the wall clocks. It was almost time to meet Mike. I felt uneasy about leaving Jesse with Liz but the way Liz was glaring at me, I had no choice.

'Fine,' I said, squeezing Jesse's hand. 'We'll talk more later.'

17

I was still processing the extraordinary information about Louisa as I walked to Cafe 42. A revelation like that would have knocked Jesse out. Louisa and Steve? I would never have guessed it. Had they ever . . .? I couldn't even finish the thought. Bizarre. It just went to show what people were capable of hiding from their family and friends. Perhaps that had something to do with why Louisa had left Sydney.

Mike was already seated at a table when I arrived. He smiled, stood up and kissed me on the cheek. Part of me was disappointed he didn't go straight for the lips. He smelled like freshly cut grass. Swoon.

'Nice to see you,' he said, stepping back self-consciously and taking his seat again.

I nodded shyly. 'You too. Short shift today?'

'Probably not. I'm on call. No doubt there'll be an emergency. There usually is.'

It occurred to me how demanding Mike's job would be, never being able to relax and completely switch off.

'It must be incredible doing the work you do,' I said. 'Saving lives.'

He nodded, raking a hand through his hair. 'I don't always win.'

We ordered lunch and made small talk while we waited for it to arrive: kids, travel and, of course, the other night.

He had a way of looking me direct in the eyes when he spoke, and also when he listened to my replies, that made me nervous but was also very attractive. I wondered why on earth his wife had ever let him go. I could feel myself wanting to touch him and wondered if it was just physical attraction or if it went beyond that, perhaps hoping that this might be the start of something deeper.

Deeper? No! What was I thinking? I'd only just ended a marriage to a man I'd loved very much and who happened to be the father of my teenage children. I needed to take a huge step back.

Still, when Mike reached out and took hold of my hand across the table, I didn't pull away.

'What are you thinking?' he asked.

I glanced at my watch. 'That I should be getting back to work.'

'How disappointing.'

'No, I meant . . . this has been nice.'

He raised his eyebrows. 'Nice in that it was totally boring and awkward and you can't wait to escape? Or nice in that you wish your lunch break wasn't so short and perhaps if this was dinner . . .?'

I shifted in my chair. 'The second option, I think.'

'You think?'

'Stop it, Mike.' I grinned feeling heat rush through me, warming my face. 'You know what I mean.'

'I think we need to have dinner to find out what you really mean.' He reached out, pushing the hair back from my face. It had been a long time since anyone made me feel like this.

I couldn't wipe the smile off my face on the walk back to the library. Was this really happening? Mike and me? Maybe I was getting ahead of myself but I couldn't deny the attraction between us. I felt like I was floating on air.

I was locking my bag away when Jesse appeared looking visibly upset.

'Liz thinks I'm too slow stacking books and cataloguing DVDs,' she said.

'I'm sure it's not that bad. You're meticulous, organised and thorough. The customers love you. I'll talk to Liz—'

'That's not the issue and you know it,' Liz said behind me.

I wheeled around to face her.

'What is it then?' Jesse asked.

'It's about Stella covering for you when she should be doing her own job.'

'I—' I started, but Liz cut me off.

'Here's the thing, Jesse. I understand you like to have everything in order, and I'm not suggesting that you stack the books by height, colour and width. But you're too slow most of the time and, well, we're not running a charity.'

'I'm not slow all the time.'

'No, you're not,' I agreed.

'But you are when you're tired or having a bad day, like today,' said Liz, gesturing to where Jesse had been stacking shelves. She'd barely made a dent in the trolleys.

'Maybe you just need a break,' I said calmly, knowing Jesse was about to have a full meltdown and that Liz was looking for any excuse to ask her to take unpaid leave for a month.

Jesse turned to me. 'A break from the library is the last thing I need.'

'Good thinking, Stella,' said Liz at the same time. 'A holiday is exactly what Jesse needs.'

'No, I don't.' Jesse was practically screaming.

I felt ill. I'd totally put my foot in it. 'I meant a break as in a walk outside,' I back-pedalled. 'To take you out of the situation so you can walk back inside feeling fresh.'

Liz rolled her eyes. 'I think Jesse knows the job is getting too much for her. She also knows we're trying to run a business.' She looked at Jesse and attempted a smile. 'Sometimes it's like you're living in a different world . . .'

Jesse twirled her hair, becoming more agitated.

'That's not fair,' I said, but Liz stopped me.

'Stella, Skyla needs relieving on the customer relations desk.'

'But—'

'Now.'

Not wanting to create a bigger scene, I did as I was instructed, but I felt I'd let Jesse down. God knows what Liz was about to say but I had a bad feeling and now I wasn't there to support her.

Minutes later, Jesse rushed past me in floods of tears. I went after her.

'Jesse?'

'I've been made redundant. Effective immediately.'

'No!' This was much worse than I'd expected. I felt responsible. I'd never wanted this to happen. Yes, maybe Jesse needed a rest and to see a counsellor, but to lose her job? This would kill her. Jesse loved the library.

'Why didn't you back me up, Stella? I needed your support.'

'I do support you—all the time. I'm so sorry this is such a mess. I'll sort it out with Liz. We'll work something out.'

'The library's the only thing I have that's mine, that makes me feel good about myself,' she said. 'Now, I have nothing.'

'Jesse,' I said, putting my hand on her shoulder. 'We'll get through this.'

I didn't want her hurrying out upset and angry. And I meant what I'd said. I was going to talk to Liz and sort this out if I could. What did I mean 'if'? I had to, for Jesse's sake.

Her expression changed from despair to resignation. 'You might, but . . .' She shook her head. 'It's okay. I mean it's not the end of the world. There are plenty more libraries, hey?'

I nodded, but didn't trust myself to look at her. I should have had her back and I hadn't.

'I've got to get out of here,' she continued, swinging her bag over her shoulder. 'If I've forgotten anything, can you keep it for me?'

'Sure,' I said. 'I'm so sorry.'

'It's all right,' she said, drying her eyes. 'Maybe a rest is exactly what I need. You never know, Liz might be doing me a huge favour.'

I started to walk with her to the door but she stopped me.

'You have a job to do. Besides, it's raining.'

'I'll call you tonight,' I said, and watched her run to her car.

Jesse sped out of the car park and onto the main road. Her mind was racing, leapfrogging from one thought to the next as the rain lashed her car and the windscreen wipers whooshed furiously. With the tears that were streaming down her face, the visibility ahead was practically zero. Jesse kept her eyes on the road as she mulled over the day's events. She'd been made redundant! The one thing that had been keeping her going, keeping her strong and focused, had been her job. Now Liz had ripped it from her.

Perhaps if it was just a matter of losing her job alone, Jesse could have coped, but coming on top of Steve's betrayal and infidelity . . .

What could she have done differently to hold her marriage together? To go back to how it used to be? To make Steve love her again? Where had that love gone? Had it simply vanished one day while he was drinking his morning latte and reading the *Financial Review*? Or had it slowly eroded over time, chipping away until there was nothing left?

The more she thought about his double life, the more furious and upset she became. She'd been patient and kind. She'd loved him . . . and for what? Reality felt like a sharp dagger slicing open her heart. What had made him go to those parties? Was it boredom? With her, with their marriage? When Steve was at those parties, did he consider Jesse at all? How she might feel about what he was doing?

Then there was Louisa. Her own sister had been lying to her for years. How could she have let Jesse marry Steve, knowing what she did? Why hadn't Louisa warned her? Protected her from the hideous revelation that lay ahead?

Carly and her big mouth. If only she hadn't blurted it all out, Jesse would be none the wiser. And Stella! Jesse had practically begged her to talk to Liz and convince her that she'd be a valuable full-time employee, but Stella had chosen not to support her.

She couldn't control her thoughts or tears . . . jumping from Steve to Louisa to losing her job, the Secret Women's Business meetings. Jesse wanted her old life back. Damn it! Why was this happening to her?

The rain was coming down in thick sheets. Yellow hazard lights flashed at the side of the road, warning of the ditches that were prone to flash flooding. Jesse's foot tapped wildly on the accelerator and her hands clenched the steering wheel so hard they were a ghostly white. She needed to stop the car, calm down and get a grip. And she would, just as soon as she could see well enough to pull over.

18

I marched straight into Liz's office and slammed the door
closed. 'How could you?'

Liz looked up from her computer. 'How could I what?'

'Retrench her? She's devastated.'

'What choice did I have, Stella? If anything, I should have
done it months ago.'

'But you have no idea about her family situation. This couldn't
have come at a worse time.'

'I'm sorry if Jesse's personal life is problematic, but she's a
liability. It was only a matter of time before we had real problems.'

'So you're saying we don't have real problems with her now?
That this situation could have been avoided?'

'Stella, you're being deliberately difficult. We don't have the
funds or the resources to keep up with Jesse patrol.'

'But on her good days, she positively beams and she's always
up-to-date with new releases. Jesse lives and breathes the library
and the patrons love her for it.'

'I'm sorry, Stella. My mind's made up.'

We stared at each other a few moments before Liz said, 'Anything else?'

'You can't do this.'

'I can. It's done. End of story.' She shook her head and went back to reading her computer monitor. I stood my ground until she looked up again. 'Seriously, Stella. I don't have time for this.'

'Neither do I,' I said. 'I quit.'

I grabbed my bag and marched out of the library.

I shook my head as I walked to my car. What had I just done? My job! Fuck. I couldn't afford to quit. Besides, I loved the library. Yes, Liz was a pain, but she was a manageable pain most of the time. Nevertheless, I had to stick up for Jesse. Support her, go after her and talk her down, which was exactly what I intended to do.

I swung out onto the road, still furious with Liz. The woman had no compassion. She was a cyborg, no doubt about it.

It was hard to hear my phone ringing over the downpour but eventually I did. I fumbled through my bag and reached for it. 'Yes?' I said distractedly.

'Stella, it's Toby. I've got June's test results. She doesn't—'

I was having trouble concentrating, not to mention that visibility was almost nil. 'Sorry. Could you repeat that?'

'June doesn't appear to have Alzheimer's,' said Toby calmly. 'Doctor Gordon's only conducted preliminary memory tests, as you know, but it doesn't look sinister.'

Relief washed over me. 'Thank goodness.'

'We'll schedule her for further appointments so we can absolutely rule it out, but I'm confident . . .'

I could barely hear Toby over the rain, and the cars in front of me had come to a standstill. There was some sort of commotion up ahead. Looked like a car accident. Smoke was billowing everywhere.

'Stella?' Toby said. 'Stella, are you there?'

'There's been an accident,' I said, pulling up on the side of the road. 'Oh my God. It's Jesse,' I screamed, as I saw her car mangled up against a huge gum tree. The front part was totally wrecked.

'Stella?'

'We . . . we need an ambulance,' I cried, dropping my mobile and tripping over my feet in my frantic attempt to get out of my car.

Two men were trying to break open the front doors of Jesse's car.

'What happened?' I shrieked to the few bystanders who were watching.

'She drove into a tree,' said one.

I walked closer to the wreckage.

'Don't,' said a man, grabbing me by the arm. 'Don't go any closer.'

'I have to. She's my best friend.' I was shaking, doing my best to remain upright.

The stranger continued holding me. 'We've called an ambulance. Shouldn't be too much longer.'

I could see Jesse slumped back against the driver's seat, bloodied, unconscious. There were sirens in the distance, getting closer.

'I have to talk to her,' I begged the man. 'She needs to know I'm here.'

He looked at me kindly. 'Let's wait for the paramedics. Sam, come here.'

A Labrador that had been barking at the wreck fell silent and obediently came over to us.

'I've got to help her,' I sobbed, but did as the man suggested.

An ambulance parked near Jesse's car and two women climbed out. A third ambo, a man, directed everyone to take several steps back. It all seemed to be happening in slow motion.

The police arrived and the man with the dog walked over to them. In a daze, I followed.

'Did you actually witness the accident?' one of the officers asked the man.

He hesitated. 'Yes.'

'And what did you see?'

'I was walking Sam, my dog, on the other side of the road. The driver was travelling in the opposite direction. She pulled her car over and slowed right down. Maybe even stopped. And then barely a minute later . . .' He paused.

'Go on,' said the officer, looking up from his notes.

'Well, this is the unbelievable part. She seemed to accelerate straight into the tree.'

'No!' I screamed, feeling suddenly dizzy. Not Jesse.

Someone led me away. 'Is there anyone we can call? Family? Your friend's husband maybe?'

I shook my head, sobbing into my hands. Poor Jesse. This couldn't be happening. It just couldn't. Her car was completely mangled. It would be a miracle if she . . .

I couldn't think like that. Jesse needed me to be strong. I wiped my eyes and stood up. 'Yes, of course. Her family. I need to phone her family.'

Somehow I made it to my car, opened the door and retrieved the phone I'd flung on the floor in my haste to get out. I dialled Steve's number.

The ambulance's siren started up again as it sped away.

'Where are they taking her?' I heard the man with the dog ask the police.

'Royal,' one of them said.

Mike, I thought, just as Steve answered the phone.

'What do you want?'

'Steve?' My voice quavered. 'Jesse's been in a terrible accident.' The words tumbled out of my mouth. 'Car accident. They're taking her to the Royal.'

'If this is some kind of joke—'

'Please hurry.'

Before he could say anything else, I hung up and dialled Carly's number.

'Hey, Stella.'

'Carly!' I sobbed. 'It's Jesse. She's been in a car accident. They've taken her to the Royal. I'll see you there.'

'But—'

'Carly, I don't know any more. Just hurry up and get there.'

As soon as I hung up, my phone rang. It was Toby.

'Stella, Mike's on his way in. He's had word to expect a patient who's been in a car smash near your work. Is it—'

'Jesse. God, yes. She looks bad. Really bad. I don't know what to do.'

'At this stage there's probably not much you can do. Are you coming in?'

My mind went blank.

'Stella, are you there?' Toby's voice was firm and clear. 'We're getting ready to receive her. I'll talk to you when I can.'

I dropped the phone to my side. Over at Jesse's car, the police were taking photos, removing personal items and interviewing witnesses.

The man with the dog reappeared next to me. 'I'll drive you to the hospital,' he said gently.

'No, I couldn't.'

'It's no trouble, as long as you don't mind Sam joining us.'

I motioned towards the police. 'Don't you have to stay?'

'I've told them everything I can remember. They have my details. They'll be in touch if they need me. Come on, it's a ten-minute drive. Let me take you.'

I burst into tears again. I needed to be with Jesse but I was a mess. I wiped my eyes and nodded. 'Thanks.'

'Sorry, I introduced Sam but not myself,' he said as he helped me into my car. 'I'm Robert. Rob. And you are?'

I sat in the passenger seat in a daze, staring at the throng around Jesse's car. It still didn't seem real. 'Stella,' I said vaguely.

Rob pulled out onto the road. He was driving at the speed limit but we seemed to be moving in slow motion.

'Excuse me,' I said. 'I need to ring my husband, ex-husband actually. But we're still good friends. He should know.'

'Can you remember his number?'

I nodded. 'Speed dial.'

Terry answered after one ring.

'Jesse's been in a car accident,' I told him, sobbing again. 'They're taking her to the Royal. Meet me there?'

'Of course, love. On my way.'

Rob and I arrived at the hospital seven minutes later. He tied Sam to a pole just near the emergency entrance. It was wet and cold outside.

'Will he be okay?' I asked.

'The smokers will keep him company,' said Rob, guiding me through the hospital's automatic doors.

I was in shock, unable to focus, so Rob asked for directions to the emergency waiting room. Around us, doctors and nurses flew by in a blur. Finally, we made it to the waiting room. I looked around hoping to see a familiar face. No one else was there yet.

'Can I get you anything?' Rob asked. 'Water? Coffee?'

I shook my head.

'At least take a seat,' he said, signalling to a row of chairs near the windows.

I sat, wringing my clammy hands together. 'I don't know what to do. What do you think's happening? Where is she? Why isn't anyone else here?'

'I don't know.'

'My God,' I said, my voice sounding strangled and foreign. 'I don't know what to do.'

'I don't want to leave you here alone,' said Rob, 'but I feel like an intruder. I shouldn't stay.'

'Please do, at least until someone else gets here.'

'I'm really sorry about your friend.'

I looked at him and seemed to see him for the first time. 'Yeah.' I started crying again. 'How did it happen? The roads were wet and slippery, but Jesse's driven that road hundreds of times. Hundreds.'

Rob was silent.

'You told the police that Jesse slowed down and pulled over to the side of the road,' I said.

'That's what I saw.'

'Then what happened?'

'Look, Stella, maybe I didn't see things clearly. I'm not sure.'

'But you said she accelerated into the tree?'

Rob took a deep breath and sighed. 'Yes. To be honest, it

203

looked like she slowed down almost to a stop and then sped into the gum tree. I'm sorry.'

I was sobbing again, shaking my head. 'That can't be true.'

Rob nodded. 'I hope you're right.'

The seconds ticked by as if they were hours. I distracted myself by thinking about the kids, the roast I was cooking for dinner, the storm and the flash flooding in the area. But there was only so much distraction I could manage before other thoughts started hijacking my brain. The last time I'd been in a hospital waiting room—other than for June's sprained arm—was after Dad's car accident. Images of him in intensive care filled my mind: tubes everywhere, the burns . . . Once the swelling and bruising had faded, it had looked like he'd had a facelift. His legs had borne the brunt of the impact and had required numerous skin grafts . . . I shuddered at the memory, wishing Mum and Dad lived closer, not in Melbourne, a thousand kilometres away.

Carly came rushing into the room. 'I got here as quickly as I could. What happened?'

I stood up. 'Jesse's been in a terrible accident.'

Carly hugged me. 'I hope they've got the other bloke in custody.'

I stood back from her and wiped my eyes. 'That's just it. There wasn't anyone else involved.'

I looked around for Rob but he'd gone. My car keys were on the seat next to me. I hadn't even thanked him.

Carly gasped. 'But how did it happen?'

'Yes, how?' It was Steve.

It was the first time I'd seen him since last Thursday night. I went to hug him, but he backed away.

'Don't touch me. Just tell me what happened to my wife.'

'She was in an accident,' I started.

'You were there?'

'No. I arrived a few minutes later. It happened just after she left the library.'

'That goddamn library! I told her I didn't want her working there.'

It's a little too late for that, I thought as the three of us stood there awkwardly.

'I'm so sorry,' ventured Carly.

Steve didn't acknowledge her. He walked over to the unoccupied nurses' station and rang the bell. 'Hello? Anybody here?'

I couldn't believe his attitude. It was as if he'd been greatly inconvenienced and was doing everyone a favour just by gracing us with his presence.

A minute later, Mike appeared. It was odd seeing him again so soon. Then again, lunch seemed like years ago. Carly and I rushed over to him.

'I wish we were meeting under better circumstances,' he said. 'Stella, I'm so sorry. How are you bearing—'

'Ahem, Doctor? I'm Steve Foster, Jesse's husband.'

'Yes, I know who you are,' said Mike calmly.

Steve seemed taken aback. 'Can I see my wife?'

'I'm afraid Jesse's had a severe head trauma,' Mike started. 'It appears—'

Both Carly and I gasped. My whole body was shaking.

'Is she alive?' Steve jumped in.

'Yes, Jesse's alive,' Mike said. 'But you can't see her. She's being examined for injuries.'

'But Mike,' I said, my voice rising, 'she's okay, isn't she?'

Steve looked at me. 'How do you know his name?'

'Doctor Mike Thompson,' said Mike, not missing a beat as

he stuck out his hand to shake Steve's. 'I have some papers for you to sign, Mr Foster. This way, if you will.'

He led Steve out of the waiting room and down the corridor.

Carly and I had been sitting there for what seemed like hours when Terry showed up.

'How is she?' he asked after hugging us both.

'We don't know,' I said, shaking my head.

'What happened?' He wrapped his arms around me in a gesture of comfort.

Briefly, I thought about the oddness of Terry and Mike both being here, but I was too worried to care about social niceties.

'It all happened so quickly,' I sobbed. 'Jesse ran out of the library crying, I confronted Liz—'

'Why was she crying?' Carly asked.

'Liz retrenched her. Claimed Jesse's quirks had become too much of a distraction for her to continue working properly.'

'Poor Jesse,' said Carly. 'She would have been devastated.'

I nodded. 'After my argument with Liz, I quit—'

'You what?' said Terry. 'It must have been quite a disagreement.'

'I got in the car and headed home. I'd only been driving a couple of minutes before I came across the accident.'

'Jesus!' said Terry. 'How did it happen?'

'I'm not sure,' I stammered. 'A witness says she deliberately accelerated into a tree, but Jesse would never do anything so reckless. She loves her kids.'

Terry shook his head. 'Nightmare.'

'A nightmare we're having to live through.' Steve was back again.

'Steve, mate,' said Terry, 'I'm so sorry about this. But Jesse's one strong woman. She'll pull through, you'll see.'

'I wish I had your blind confidence,' Steve said dismissively.

'Do you want me to call Jesse's parents?' I asked him.

'I've already rung them,' he said.

It felt like I'd been at the hospital forever but only fifty-five minutes had lapsed. At this stage, we couldn't do more than wait. I phoned Hannah and Ben to fill them in on the situation, and asked Steve if he wanted me to ask a friend to pick up Ollie and Emily from school.

He declined, telling me, 'It's all under control.'

A little while later, Toby walked into the room. Both Carly and I swooped down on him.

'How is she?' I asked.

'Early days,' he replied, then saw Steve and went over to him. 'Mr Foster?'

Steve jumped slightly. 'Do I know you?'

'I don't think so. My name's Toby Mitchell. Together with Doctor Thompson, I'm attending to your wife.'

'What are you doing here then?'

'Keeping you up-to-date and informed,' Toby said calmly. 'At the moment, Jesse's undergoing a series of X-rays to assess for fractures of the skull and spinal instability.'

'Oh God,' Carly said, clutching at my shoulder.

'Her brain has sustained significant swelling and bruising due to the trauma of the accident.'

Steve considered Toby's words for a moment. 'Right. So, when will she be better?'

'I'm afraid that's like asking how long a piece of string is. The truth is, we really don't know. As long as it takes, I'm afraid.'

'As long as it takes? Really? That's your professional opinion?'

Toby nodded. 'I'll let you know more as and when we have news.'

He pulled me aside and spoke briefly about June's test results before disappearing through the doors to attend to Jesse. I had to hand it to Toby: he had grace under pressure. If I'd been him, I would have belted Steve.

Terry walked over to me. 'Stella, I'm sorry about Jesse, but if there's nothing I can do here, why don't I go home, check on Mum, see the kids after school and organise dinner? Looks like you're in for a long night and I think I can be more helpful doing something practical.'

I hugged him, tears rolling down my cheeks. 'Thanks, I appreciate it.'

'It'll give me some time to spend with Mum alone.'

'She doesn't have Alzheimer's. I know you were worried so I had Toby—'

'The doctor here? The one from last Sunday?'

'Yeah. I had him organise some preliminary tests and just now he spoke to me about them. He said that once people get to a certain age and start forgetting things and becoming increasingly absent-minded, their children assume they have dementia, but it's often not the case.'

'That's a relief.'

'Yeah. It's more likely a combination of old age, grief over Jimmy—'

'Still?'

'Still. And stress.'

'About?'

'Our separation, getting older, not being able to do what she wants when she wants. The fall the other day wouldn't have helped.'

'I guess I should have trimmed the hedges like she asked.'

I nodded. 'And maybe you could also take a more softly-softly approach with her regarding Amanda, too.'

Terry rolled his eyes. 'Amanda! I need to tell her I'll be home late.'

He kissed me, then walked over to Steve and shook his hand. Terry was a good bloke. I was so glad he was the father of my children.

Just after he'd left, Jesse's parents arrived and made a beeline for Steve.

'My baby,' cried Dot. 'Where is she? What happened? Somebody tell me what happened!'

'Jesse's been in a car accident,' Steve said. 'She's being attended to now.'

'Is it bad?'

'We don't know yet,' he said, and for the first time since he'd walked in, I sensed a vulnerability about him. His confident veneer was slipping.

'Dot,' I said, walking over and hugging her. 'I'm so sorry.'

'Stella, what happened? Were you with her?'

I shook my head. 'No, but I do know she's in the best hands possible. These doctors are miracle workers. Jesse's going to be fine.' I was saying it for my own peace of mind as much as for Dot's.

Jesse's dad, Tom, had hugged Steve but hadn't said a word. I felt incredibly sad for him as he walked towards the windows and stared down into the car park. Dot joined him and took his hand.

'What should we do?' Carly whispered to me. 'I feel useless sitting here.'

I nodded. 'Let's wait until we hear more and then decide.'

19

$\mathcal{I}$t seemed like forever before Toby and Mike reappeared.

Mike was carrying a clipboard with several pages of notes attached. He cleared his throat. 'Because little can be done to reverse the initial traumatic brain damage, our primary focus is on stabilising Jesse to prevent further injury.'

Brain damage? The words pulsed through my mind and I barely heard the rest of what Mike was saying.

'We've been able to stabilise her and we're now ensuring proper oxygen supply to her brain and body. We're also maintaining sufficient and adequate blood flow while controlling her blood pressure.'

'But how is she?' asked Dot. 'When can I see her?'

'Not yet, I'm afraid,' Mike replied. 'We've done X-rays and a CT scan to assess damage to the brain. What we do know is that Jesse has suffered a severe blunt head trauma, but the good news is that, despite swelling and bruising of the brain, we've ruled out any other mass lesion or compression of the brain stem.' He paused. 'However, Jesse is unconscious and has broken her right foot. She's being prepped for surgery now.'

'Unconscious?' said Steve, speaking for the first time. 'But that means she's in a coma?'

Mike nodded. 'That's correct. I'm sorry I don't have better news for you.'

Carly and I turned to each other, unable to speak.

Tom stepped forward. 'Tom Buckland, Jesse's father. When do you think you'll have a prognosis?' he asked in a choked voice.

'It's hard to tell,' Mike replied. 'But we're doing everything we can to make sure she's comfortable. We'll be giving her medications like steroids for swelling as well as anti-epileptic drugs in case of seizures. In the meantime, we have to wait until the brain recovers from the initial trauma.'

'Jesse fainted the other day,' Dot blurted out. 'Could that have had anything to do with the accident? Did she black out? I told her she needed to slow down, that she was taking on too much stress and wasn't taking care of herself or her family. But she doesn't listen to me. No one listens to me.'

Tom rubbed her arm tenderly.

'It's true,' she continued, shaking him off. 'She didn't listen to me. I knew something like this would happen. It was a matter of time.'

'Do you have anything you can give her?' Steve asked, clearly agitated by Dot's ramblings.

Everyone turned to look at him.

'Well?' he said impatiently, staring at Toby and Mike. 'Do you?'

What was he suggesting? A quick shot to the temples?

Tom took Dot to sit down nearby, but she continued babbling at a hundred miles an hour. Everyone had different coping mechanisms. Talking was Dot's.

I closed my eyes briefly as I leaned against a wall for support, wishing the day would come to an end. Toby and Mike were talking in hushed tones to Steve, and Carly was pacing up and down the waiting room. I called her over to join me.

'This is my fault,' I said. 'If I'd supported Jesse more at the library, none of this would have happened.'

'That's not true,' said Carly, tears trickling down her cheeks. 'It's my fault. Me and my big mouth.'

I shook my head. 'It's not you. I should have helped her more at work. I knew Liz was angling to sack her.'

We took seats at a table and stared over at Steve and the doctors.

'How do you think he is?' Carly asked.

I shrugged. Who knew with Steve?

A few minutes later, Brett arrived. He came straight over to Carly and hugged her tight and stroked her hair. 'It'll be all right,' he soothed. For all of Carly's complaints about Brett, he certainly seemed loving and caring towards her.

Turning to me, he said, 'How are you holding up? Carly said you were the first on the scene.'

'Okay,' I whispered, then shook my head. 'It's like a bad dream. I keep pinching myself, hoping I'll wake up.'

'And Steve?' he asked.

We turned to look at Steve again, who was now standing alone by the water dispenser. Brett walked over to him and tried to hug him. Steve resisted, then shook his head and started talking. I couldn't hear their conversation.

Toby came back into the room. As Carly and I made our way towards him, I heard Steve say to Brett, 'Those women.' Brett glanced at us briefly before turning back to Steve.

'How is she really?' Carly was asking Toby.

'The next twenty-four to forty-eight hours will be critical.'

'And?'

'And if she pulls through, we'll hold our breath for the next day and then the one after that. I'm sorry I can't tell you more.'

Carly sniffed back tears. 'It's okay. You're doing your best.'

He put his arms around her and hugged her.

'Hey! You guys are looking a bit too familiar,' I said.

Carly broke free and shot a glance at Brett. He was staring straight at her. Steve looked over at us, too, and I saw his eyes widen before he let out an audible gasp. No doubt the pieces were rapidly falling into place in his mind.

'I think he knows,' I whispered to Carly and Toby.

Toby glanced towards Steve who was still staring straight at us. 'You could be right. I'll see you both soon,' he said, and left the room.

Moments later, Brett was beside Carly. 'Who was that guy you were all over?'

'Pardon?'

'It doesn't matter. I'm just curious.'

'He's just a doctor, Brett. I'm upset. He was comforting me.'

Brett raised his eyebrows. 'Okay. It's a tough time for everyone.'

'How's Steve doing?' I asked.

Brett paused. 'Not good. Having a hard time. It's to be expected.'

Doubly so, I thought, given that the two attending doctors had already met him under dubious circumstances.

'Maybe if he'd treated Jesse better, none of this would have happened,' Carly said.

'Keep your voice down,' Brett told her.

'Why? It's what everyone thinks.'

Brett glanced around the room. 'I'm going in search of a coffee. Can I get either of you anything?'

Carly shook her head.

'No, thanks,' I said. 'I should go and speak to Dot.'

Brett kissed Carly lightly on the forehead. 'I'll be back soon.'

I went over to Dot and Tom at their table by the window. 'How are you?' I asked.

'How do you think I am?' said Dot. 'Distraught. I'm not even allowed to see my own daughter. It's not right.'

'Come on, love,' said Tom, reaching across the table to hold her hand.

'Is there anything I can do?' I asked. 'Phone Louisa for you?'

Dot wiped her eyes. 'Tom's already called her.'

Tom nodded. 'She'll be on the next flight out of San Francisco.'

'Did I hear right?' It was Steve. 'Louisa's coming here?'

'Yes,' said Tom, taking a deep breath. 'Our Louisa is finally coming home.'

I glanced at Steve. The can of Coke in his hand was shaking. He seemed stricken by the news of Louisa's return.

When I got home late Thursday night, June was sound asleep but Hannah and Ben were waiting up for me. I explained to them exactly what had happened.

'But what's a coma?' Hannah asked, pale with worry.

'It's like a deep sleep where the person can't be woken up and doesn't respond normally to pain, light or sound,' I said, having memorised Mike's spiel. 'When Jesse hit her head on the steering wheel, her brain had a severe traumatic injury and she went into a coma straight away.'

'But she'll be okay, won't she?' Ben said.

'I don't know,' I whispered. 'I just don't know.'

I said goodnight to the kids and made myself a cup of peppermint tea before stretching out on the lounge. I tried closing my eyes but kept opening them to stare at a photo of Jesse, Carly and me on the side table. It had been taken at a Robbie Williams concert last year. We all looked so animated, joyful . . . alive.

After a restless night's sleep, I spent most of Friday at the hospital. Not that I knew what to do. Mostly I just sat with Jesse when her mum, dad and Steve took a break.

In the afternoon I had a longer chat with Mike over coffee in the hospital cafeteria. He told me that although Jesse was stable, it was still touch and go.

'It might be days, weeks, maybe even months, before she recovers,' he said.

'So you don't even have an approximate time line for her improvement?'

'I wish it was that simple,' he replied.

'Can't you do something? Anything? We're all just waiting around. Aren't there any drugs you can give her to make her better?'

'Stella, do you think if there was a magic bullet we wouldn't have tried it? I'm sorry but we're doing the best we can.'

I started tearing up. 'Well, your best isn't good enough.'

Mike sighed. 'Do you know how often I hear that? For all the good we do, when a patient dies—'

'Are you saying—'

'No, but it always comes down to the ones who don't make it, the ones we can't fix.'

'But Jesse's my best friend.'

He held my shoulders, forcing me to look at him. I noticed the dark circles under his eyes. 'Do you believe in prayer?' he asked.

I shrugged him off. 'Not really.'

'Well, do you believe Jesse can hear when you talk to her?'

I nodded.

'Good. Then that's what you should do. Talk to her.'

'I'm sorry,' I said, wiping my eyes. 'I know you're doing everything you can. You must be exhausted.'

He placed his hand over mine. 'I could say the same about you.'

It was at that moment that Steve walked up to us. 'You two disgust me. I don't want you seeing my wife,' he said, glaring at me. 'And as for you—'

Mike stood up. 'As for me, Mr Foster,' he said firmly, 'I am your wife's primary doctor and I will thank you to respect that.'

Go, Mike!

Steve looked taken aback. 'Whatever,' he muttered before walking away.

Mike resumed his seat. 'That went well.'

'He's such a charmer.'

'Clearly not pleased Toby and I are on the job.'

'Yeah, he thought he'd never see you again.'

Later, I went and saw Jesse, despite Steve's directive. Still, I was careful to keep out of his way. She didn't look like Jesse; so many bandages and tubes. It was frightening. Her poor kids. Dot told me that when they'd eventually been allowed to see her this morning, Emily had been calm, very reserved and quiet, but Oliver had been beside himself, in floods of tears, not wanting to leave his mum's side when visiting time was up. Heartbreaking.

As banged up as Jesse looked, now that she had made it through those crucial first twenty-four hours, I was confident she'd pull through. She had to. She was surrounded by the best medical care in the country. And as for the ridiculous talk that she'd somehow deliberately done this to herself, it was cruel. I knew Jesse well enough to know that even though Steve was a prick, she'd never leave her children voluntarily.

20

'How are we ever going to get through this?' Louisa's dad, Tom, had asked her when he'd rung with the news about Jesse's accident.

Louisa had been over the question herself dozens of times since he'd called. Now, she was slouched in a smelly hot taxi on her way from Sydney airport to the hospital where Jesse was lying in a coma.

The taxi wound its way through streets clogged with peak-hour traffic. The place felt more familiar than Louisa had expected, as though it had been months not years since she'd left. There were a few more buildings, and certainly more pedestrians and cyclists weaving their way along the roads. Sydney was a clean city, a sunny city, she'd give it that.

She looked down at her nails, which were bleeding and sore. She had chewed them to the quick. She felt numb. What if Jesse died and Louisa never got to say goodbye? They had been close once, best friends, but Louisa hadn't been part of her sister's life for a long time. There were phone calls, sure, but that wasn't the same, was it? Louisa had left family life behind when she bought her ticket to freedom.

What if she hadn't told her all those things? What if she'd continued to keep them secret? Would Jesse be in this state now?

The guilt was agonising. Louisa could barely face herself, let alone her parents and Jesse. If only she hadn't had that horrible conversation with Jesse. If only . . .

'Here do?' the taxi driver asked.

'I guess.'

Louisa stood outside the main hospital entrance. To her right, a mix of orderlies and nurses crowded together, smoking, laughing. She inhaled deeply before walking towards the enormous glass doors. When they silently slid open, she hesitated. The anticipation of seeing Jesse in a coma was frightening. She could feel the perspiration trickling down her forehead. It felt like thirty degrees even though it wasn't yet 9 am.

The antiseptic smell hit her as soon as she walked in. She suppressed the urge to vomit. Standing in the entrance area, she stared at the dull grey carpet, cream walls and a huge painting of an Australian landscape on the wall, with white lilies in a glass vase on a white marble table below it. The flowers were on the turn, their scent more like odour than fragrance.

Louisa was wasting time and she knew it. Avoidance therapy, her analyst called it. But she wasn't in a hurry to move. Besides, her feet seemed incapable of carrying her towards the reception desk.

'Louisa?'

She turned to see a tall, slim woman walking towards her. Pretty face.

'Stella. Stella Sparks, remember?' the woman said, extending her hand to shake Louisa's.

Louisa remembered Stella as having dark hair, cut in a neat bob. Now it was much blonder and longer, kind of messy and easy. She still had the same generous smile, though.

'I'll take you upstairs if you like,' she went on. 'Your mum and dad are waiting. How was your flight?'

'Long.'

'How are you feeling?'

'I'm not quite sure,' Louisa replied. 'How's Jesse?'

'No change, I'm afraid.' Tears trickled down Stella's cheeks. 'But she's hanging in there.'

Louisa followed her along a corridor lined with breakfast carts and linen trolleys. *Hanging in there*: she repeated Stella's words in her mind. It had been four days now since the accident. She'd hoped her father had been exaggerating the extent of Jesse's injuries, but it didn't seem so.

'At least she's been moved to a private room,' said Stella, as they took the elevator up to the third floor.

When they arrived at Jesse's door, Stella spoke again. 'I have to warn you, she's pretty messed up. I'll be downstairs at the cafe if you need me.'

She hugged Louisa and walked back in the direction they'd just come. Louisa flinched. Her heart was pounding. Blinking away tears, she took a deep breath, knocked and opened the door. She saw her dad first and fixed her eyes on him. She didn't want to look beyond. Didn't want to see her sister. To face reality.

Tom walked over, arms outstretched. 'It's been too long,' he whispered, enfolding her in his arms, his eyes wet with tears.

Louisa had only seen her father cry once. It was beyond painful. He looked so much greyer than when she'd last seen him. And older. Much older.

Dot was sitting in a grey hospital chair leaning against a grey steel hospital bed. A bed that Louisa quickly turned away from. Dot was holding something in her left hand; her right hand extended towards Louisa. Louisa walked over, took it and squeezed hard.

'You're here now, thank God.' Dot took a deep breath. 'I feel so weak, like He might take me at any moment.'

'Who, Mum? Who might take you?'

'You know,' she replied, looking heavenward. 'God.'

'She's not good,' said Tom, looking down at Jesse.

Louisa forced herself to look at her sister, too. Once she did, she found she couldn't turn away. This was real. Jesse was lying in a bed barely a metre from where Louisa stood. Her head was bandaged and her cheeks were bruised and discoloured beyond recognition. Tubes ran from her mouth and nose. The rest of her body was covered with white bedcovers, hidden from view. In addition to the IV pole, there were various machines that beeped and whistled at short intervals. Louisa only knew it was Jesse because her name was printed in large black type on a white cardboard sign stuck to the bedhead.

She closed her eyes. 'What happened?'

'Freak car accident,' started Tom, 'resulting in—'

'Severe blunt head injury,' finished Dot.

'How?' Louisa asked.

'I know what you're thinking,' Dot said. 'You're wondering what we could have done to stop her. Why didn't we do more to help her?'

Louisa hadn't been thinking that at all. 'Mum, it was an accident. It was no one's fault.'

Tears slid down Dot's face. 'Jesse was . . . is . . . troubled. You know that. It's always been there, of course, but lately it's been getting worse.'

'Don't, Dot!' said Tom. 'This was an accident, nothing more. Jesse's a good girl.'

'Tell me more about the accident,' Louisa prompted.

'It seems Jesse pulled over to the side of the road. Stopped her car and then . . .' Tom wiped away his tears with a damp blue handkerchief. 'A witness said she accelerated into a gum tree.'

'What sane person does that?' Dot asked.

'Her foot must have slipped,' Louisa said.

'That's what I think happened, too,' agreed Tom. 'The way she's been tapping her foot of late, it makes sense.'

'So she's stressed?' Louisa asked.

This was her fault, no doubt about it. Jesse had found out about Steve, then, on top of that, Louisa had dropped her bombshell. It had been too much for Jesse to cope with.

'The accident looked suspicious,' Dot said.

'For Christ's sake, you weren't there, woman.'

'But the police, Tom—'

'The police?' Louisa said. 'Why are they involved?'

'The police are investigating,' Dot said quietly. 'There were no skid marks . . .'

Tom shook his head. 'It's not true.'

This was unbelievable. There was no way Jesse would have deliberately driven into a tree. She loved her kids too much to do something that reckless. Louisa just didn't buy it.

'What were you talking about the other day when she collapsed?' Dot asked.

'I can't remember,' Louisa lied.

'Think, Louisa,' encouraged Tom. 'It could provide an important clue. Maybe she fainted again behind the wheel.'

'What with her fainting and foot tapping,' said Dot. 'I told you she wasn't well, Tom.'

Louisa looked at Jesse again. 'This is the worst thing that could have happened. Jesse, of all people. How are Steve and the kids taking it?'

She was relieved Steve wasn't here. It was going to be hard facing him, knowing what she did about him and how he'd treated Jesse.

'You know Steve; stoic, as usual,' said Tom.

Yeah, right, thought Louisa.

She took a seat on the other side of Jesse's bed. Wake up, she willed her. For God's sake, just wake up.

Carly was running through the streets, listening to her iPod and trying not to think about anything except the moment, the pretty gardens, the barking dogs, the other early morning joggers. All she wanted to do was run and keep running, to forget about the last couple of days . . . weeks. Tears streamed down her face as she repeatedly told herself to focus, to push through the sadness and pain. Though she kept running, not even slowing for the many hills in the area, the image of Jesse in her hospital bed, helpless, unconscious, covered in bandages, tubes sticking out of her, filled her mind.

It was all Carly's fault. That much she knew. The last few days she'd operated on autopilot, not really knowing what to do with herself. She'd burst into tears in the supermarket, composed herself enough to buy bananas, bread and milk, then burst into tears again at the chemist buying Panadol and Vitamin B12. She'd been a mess all weekend and was no better today.

Somehow, she made it back home. She didn't even realise she was on her street until she was practically at her front door.

Will was eating breakfast. He looked up when she walked into the kitchen. 'Hey.'

Carly smiled. She was exhausted, but at least she'd run five kilometres. That had to be more productive than lying curled up in bed crying. She flipped on the kettle. 'How's my boy?'

'Okay. Can I have some money? We're going to the Rocks today.'

She nodded. 'Of course. I'd almost forgotten.' She could feel herself tearing up again.

Will looked away, choosing to watch the cat destroying his chicken wing instead of his mother's distress. She knew he didn't know what to say to make her feel better.

'You know how I've got my learners,' he said, still staring at Norman.

Carly sighed. 'I'm sorry, Will. I haven't been taking you out as much as I should have been.'

'No, that's okay,' he said. 'We've been watching road-safety videos at school, seeing crash sites and stuff. Anyway, with Jesse's accident, we're all thinking that maybe sixteen is too young to drive.'

'I understand what you're saying, Will, but you'll be okay. We'll take it slowly and by the time you're ready to take your test, you'll do brilliantly, I'm sure.'

He smiled. She could tell that was exactly what he'd wanted to hear.

Carly had showered and was figuring out what to wear to the hospital when Brett phoned.

'How are you doing this morning?' he asked.

'Okay. I managed a run.'

'That's encouraging,' he said brightly. 'Will and I have been worried. You've been so exhausted and shaken the last few nights.'

'I'm doing okay,' Carly replied. 'It's Jesse who's in trouble.'

With Carly, it was one thing or the other: exercise or alcohol. As much as she'd wanted a glass of wine last night and the night before, she knew she couldn't. If she had one, she'd end up drinking twenty-one and that scenario was too depressing to contemplate. Instead, she'd focused on sleep and running the last few days, when she wasn't visiting Jesse.

Last night was the first night she'd been home for dinner since the accident. She, Brett and Will had sat in silence in front of the TV, eating takeaway Thai curries, and she'd fallen asleep soon after *Modern Family*. They made it look so easy on television: even when the characters were facing mayhem, they still managed clean, blow-dried hair, immaculate make-up and, most importantly of all, a happy ending. But at least the show had taken her mind off Jesse for twenty-two minutes.

After she'd hung up, Carly realised she still hadn't spoken to Brett about Nick. In fact, she'd barely thought about his situation since Jesse's accident. Not only was she a shocking friend, she was a terrible mother. Guilt swamped her; she could feel it eating away at her insides.

She was reassured to see Stella as soon as she arrived at the hospital.

'Any news?' she asked after they'd hugged and were seated in the sunshine near the hospital cafe.

'Louisa's arrived. She's in with Jesse now.'

Carly smiled. 'Thank God! Her parents will be relieved.'

'Yeah,' said Stella. 'Look, before the accident Jesse told me something about Louisa and Steve.' Stella proceeded to tell Carly everything she knew.

'Wow! I didn't see that coming.'

'Me either.'

Carly thought for a moment. 'I was aware that Louisa had left Sydney suddenly, but I had no idea . . . And now she's back.'

Stella nodded. 'That'll make for an interesting showdown with Steve. I haven't seen him yet this morning.'

'Count your blessings. Have you seen Jesse?'

Stella shook her head. 'No, but Tom was saying she's had a couple of mild seizures—'

'What?'

'It's okay. I've spoken to Mike about them but . . .' Stella hesitated.

'But what?'

'I get the feeling he's not telling me everything. I feel like there's more we could be doing.'

'But what?'

Stella frowned. 'Look who's here.'

Carly followed Stella's gaze. It was Pete from the pub. An image of him nude and cavorting on a sofa with several other naked people popped into her head.

He saw them and walked over. 'Ladies,' he said, 'I'm sorry we're not meeting again in better circumstances.'

Carly couldn't help herself: she giggled nervously.

He glanced at her. 'Not those circumstances.' He indicated their bench. 'Do you mind?'

Stella and Carly shuffled along a little to make room.

'I want to apologise for taking you to that party,' Pete said. 'I knew what was going on, but Mike and Toby had no idea. I'm sorry for dragging you both along.'

'No one dragged us,' Carly said. 'We went freely.'

'Speak for yourself,' said Stella.

Carly nodded. 'Okay, I dragged Stella, but Pete, you didn't drag me anywhere.'

'Still, you weren't expecting that sort of party, and then seeing your friend's husband . . . It's not good.'

'Do you have any updates on Jesse?' Carly asked.

'I'm not her doctor. I think she's stable, though.'

Stable was better than unstable, Carly thought.

He stood up. 'Nice seeing you both again.' And walked away.

'That must have been hard for him,' said Stella.

'I guess. I keep wondering where we'd be today if we hadn't gone to that party. If we'd gone home like you wanted to.'

'I doubt we'd be here,' Stella said, 'but you can't change what's happened. Should we go up and see her?'

Carly glanced through the cafe window and noticed that Tom and Dot were at the counter. 'I don't want to intrude, but yeah, I would like to see her. And then I might go into the city. Walk in Hyde Park. Meet Brett for lunch.'

'Sounds nice,' said Stella.

It did sound nice. Carly couldn't remember the last time she'd been into Brett's office. A few hours in the city might be just the boost she needed. Brett was always telling her that she took no interest in his work, so she'd surprise him. Show him that she could be an involved and interested wife.

21

*J*esse shifted uncomfortably in her sleep, pictures and thoughts racing through her mind. It dawned on her that she could hear her father crying. He never cried.

'Dad, what's wrong? What's the matter? Are you hurt? What's happened?'

He didn't answer.

Dot was there, too: she called out Jesse's name.

'I'm right here,' Jesse said.

'How did this happen?' her mother was asking, her voice shaking with anger.

Her dad replied that he didn't know.

Jesse could see herself: it was weird. She was seven years old and lying beside the river in the spot where her family used to go on camping holidays. Gradually, the picture became sharper. It was very dark and the trees, gums, towered above her. There was a heavy mist and a cool breeze. Jesse was wet, her clothes were soaking. Her parents were hunched over her, both crying.

Louisa and Jesse had been playing a silly game. Their father was supposed to be keeping his eye on them but he'd fallen asleep under his newspaper. They were daring each other. *Higher*, they screeched as each took it in turn to jump from tree branches into the water below. Higher and higher they climbed, taking greater risks each time.

Jesse jumped and missed her mark, hitting her head on a submerged rock. The current dragged her downstream, pulling her under the water. Her head hurt; it was bleeding when her dad eventually pulled her out of the water. Jesse could see herself lying very still. Then she started coughing, vomiting, shivering . . .

'She's going to be okay,' her dad was saying. 'She's fine. Our little girl is going to be just fine.'

'I knew she'd be all right,' said Louisa, her voice little more than a whisper.

Louisa was beside her and Jesse felt comforted. Her big sister was back and everything would be okay. Jesse smiled to herself. She just needed to rest a little longer.

'I thought they'd never leave,' Louisa said to Jesse. Tom had taken Dot off for a walk and some fresh air. She sat down in her mother's vacated chair and took Jesse's hand in hers. It was limp and warm. 'If you wanted me to visit, you could have asked. You didn't need to go to such extremes.'

Four years. It had been four years since Louisa had seen her sister.

'I've been thinking about that time you, Ollie and Emily came to visit me in San Francisco,' she went on, deliberately keeping her voice cheerful. 'Remember how we hired that red convertible Mustang and drove down the coast to Los Angeles and Disneyland? Magic.' She stroked Jesse's arm before holding her hand again. 'We had so much fun. Ollie and Em didn't want to leave Disneyland, even though it was almost ten o'clock at night and they could barely keep their eyes open.'

Louisa thought back to how the holiday had ended . . . waving them goodbye at the airport. She remembered Jesse saying, 'Come home soon, darling. We miss you.' And she'd blown Louisa a kiss before the three of them had disappeared behind the departure gates.

'I loved that holiday,' Louisa said, tearing up. 'Come on, Jesse. Say something. Anything.' She kissed her sister's hand as tears streamed down her cheeks. 'I'm so sorry I haven't been here for you. That I left you. I'll make it up to you, really I will. Just wake up, okay?'

It was strangely calm and quiet in the room, apart from the whistling and beeping of the machines. Louisa felt powerless. There was nothing she could do to help. She let go of Jesse's hand and it lay where she'd left it, red and creased from Louisa's vice-like grip. She stood up and walked around the room, looking at the flowers, reading the dozen or more cards that had been sent. November lilies mostly, a bunch of cream lisianthus and a box of colourful gerberas with a bright pink helium balloon encouraging Jesse to *Get Well Soon*.

Louisa sat back down again. 'Jesse, it's really strange being back. Mum and Dad . . . well, they don't look like our parents. They're so sad. It's like they've given up. We need you, Jess. Come back to us. We all love you, darling girl. Wake up! Tell me you're okay. I won't neglect you again.'

A noise came from behind her and Louisa looked up to see Steve in the doorway. It was the first time she'd seen him in six years. She stood up, fighting to control her feelings, resisting the urge to physically attack him. He was responsible for this tragedy.

Steve didn't look too pleased to see Louisa either. 'Ollie, say hello to your Auntie Louisa,' he said, rather than greeting her himself. He turned back to the corridor. 'Where's he gone?'

'It's okay,' Louisa said. 'I'll find him.' She rushed past Steve into the corridor.

It didn't take her long to spot her nephew hiding behind a trolley of dirty linen. 'Hi, Ollie,' she said brightly. 'Look at you! You're so tall now.' She gave him a hug, even though he resisted. It was awkward and her arms felt heavy around his slight frame. 'I'm so sad about your mum. Will you come in to see her?'

He shrugged. Louisa was taken aback by how much he looked like Jesse: her olive skin and green eyes. The same sandy hair, too.

'Come on, I'll hold your hand,' she said.

He hesitated for a moment before allowing her to lead him inside, towards Jesse's bed.

'It's like she's sleeping,' Louisa said.

'Mum doesn't sleep with hoses coming out of her mouth and nose.'

'Oliver!' Steve barked.

'No, he's right. It was a silly thing for me to say. Where's Emily?'

'Downstairs with her grandparents.' He shook his head and continued, 'Ollie wanted to kiss his mum good morning before he goes to school.'

'She's getting better, isn't she, Dad?'

'I hope so.'

Louisa thought it odd that this brave little boy, with his perfectly ironed grey shirt and shorts and navy and red striped tie, had to go to school and spend the day mastering fractions and comprehension while his mother lay here in a coma.

Ollie kissed Jesse hesitantly on her bruised, puffy cheek and then ran out of the room.

'Should we go after him?' Louisa asked.

Steve sighed. 'He and Emily are doing it tough.'

'Steve, I'm so sorry,' Louisa said, forgetting her anger and focusing on the children.

'I bet this isn't the homecoming you had in mind.'

'No, but Jesse's going to be okay. I know it.'

'It doesn't seem real. Four days ago she was fine . . . and now this.' He seemed bemused. 'Why?'

Louisa shook her head. 'Accidents happen. I guess she also had a lot on her mind.'

'Like what?'

She couldn't believe what she was hearing. Hello?

'Are you forgetting any special parties you've been to lately?' she said.

'One lousy party. Anyway, this isn't about me. It's about Jesse. We need her to get better so we can move on from all of this,' he waved his arms in the air, 'and start over fresh.' He shook his head and stared at Jesse's still body. 'Why did she do it?'

'It wasn't on purpose.'

Steve didn't respond.

'Mum mentioned something about—'

'God, your mother! She hasn't shut up since she got here.'

Louisa wanted to tell him to leave her family alone, but she couldn't be that hypocritical. She preferred to live in another country and rarely spoke to her parents. Then again, she hadn't married Jesse and chosen to live in the same city as her in-laws. Still, she took another tack.

'Before all of this happened, Jesse told me she wanted to have another baby and you said—'

'It's none of your business what I said.'

'She's wanted another baby for a long time.'

'I don't have to listen to this.'

'You told her that it was "fiscally irresponsible to bring another child into this unpredictable world".'

'So what if I did?'

'Jeez, Steve, you're unbelievable! No wonder she's been nervous.'

Steve stared at Jesse. 'So you're saying she did this to punish me?'

'I can think of better ways to punish you than by slamming into a tree.'

Why had she said that? This was too awful. She couldn't face Steve any more. She needed to get out of the room and breathe in some fresh air. She turned to leave, and almost bumped into a man in a white doctor's coat who was hovering in the doorway. He moved closer and Louisa read his name tag: *Dr Mike Thompson*.

'How's she doing?' Steve asked him.

'She's not responding as well as we had hoped.'

'But she's all right, isn't she? I mean, it might take a while, but she'll be okay?' Louisa said.

'This is Louisa, Jesse's sister,' said Steve.

Doctor Thompson nodded in her direction. 'It's taking longer than is ideal.'

'What does that mean?' Louisa asked.

Another doctor strode into the room as she spoke. 'Doctor Phillips,' she offered as she went straight to Jesse.

'Louisa, Jesse's sister,' Louisa replied.

It was Doctor Phillips who answered Louisa's question. 'No two coma patients are the same. Some are displaying movement and making sounds by this stage; some, like Jesse, aren't. The hard truth about coma is that we don't know how well, or even if, the patient will recover. Recovery from any brain injury, especially one as significant as Jesse's, takes time.'

'Can we do anything to help her?' Louisa asked.

'You're doing all you can by being here and talking to her. You could also try playing her favourite music and maybe even reading stories. It all helps. But right now, we need to continue our tests.' She turned to Steve. 'We're going to raise Jesse's temperature to see how her brain responds.'

Steve nodded and Doctor Thompson ushered him and Louisa from the room. As they walked away, the 'Do not disturb' light outside Jesse's door flashed in red neon.

Doctor Phillips' words played through Louisa's mind: *The hard truth about coma is that we don't know how well, or even if, the patient will recover.* Any scenario other than Jesse waking up and walking out of the hospital unaided didn't bear thinking about. She was going to be fine. Any minute now, she would wake up and wonder what all the fuss was about. Louisa could imagine how horrified Jesse would be that her family and friends had spent days grieving around her.

The last thing Louisa wanted to do was hang out with Steve, but he was heading to the cafeteria to meet up with her parents, who were looking after Ollie and Emmy. And, strangely, Louisa wanted to be near her family right now.

Louisa, Dot and Tom were sitting by the window, watching Ollie and Emily, who were outside in the playground.

'Coffee?' Tom asked Louisa.

'Thanks. Strong. Black.'

'Two sugars, right?'

'No sugar, thanks.'

'Of course,' said Tom.

'We'll go home soon, Louisa, so you can rest,' Dot said.

'I'm okay,' Louisa said.

Emily came inside. She was the image of Steve: dark brown eyes, straight brown hair, thickset, almost the complete opposite of Oliver's build and complexion.

'Hi, Emily,' Louisa said. 'Remember me?'

Emily ran behind her father's back. Half an arm reached out to snatch the remains of a muffin Dot had been pulling apart. Dot didn't notice; she was staring out the window at a man sitting in a wheelchair in the morning sunshine.

Tom returned with a coffee, which he placed in front of Louisa. He watched while she took a sip. 'Okay?' he asked.

Louisa nodded. 'Perfect.'

Everyone was tired. Worn out. Trying to make sense of the last four days. But still, Louisa was itching to have a go at Steve. How he could stand there like he'd done nothing wrong was incomprehensible to her. She glared at him but he took no notice.

'Go and play on the swings with Ollie,' he told Emily, 'while I have a word with Nanna and Pop.' She obeyed him and he turned to his in-laws. 'The doctors say Jesse's not doing as well as they'd expected.'

'She has internal injuries,' Dot said. 'It was only the airbag that saved her. She drove so fast into that tree. Why?' She banged her fist on the table.

'Easy, love,' said Tom, grabbing her hand and pulling it towards him.

'She's going to be fine, Mum. You'll see,' said Louisa, struggling to keep her voice calm. The last thing they needed was her mother's theatrics taking centrestage.

'I knew something was up with her, Louisa. I knew it. She hasn't been herself.'

'Leave it, Dot,' Tom said, glancing over at Steve.

Louisa closed her eyes as her mother continued talking.

'I could see it. Whenever she dropped a pen on the floor she had to tap her right foot three times before she bent down to pick it up. And what about her checking all the locks on the house before she went out? She was stressed. I should have stepped in and done something. I should have known it would end like this.' Dot started crying. 'Goodness knows how she got on at the library.'

'Come on, Mum,' Louisa said, putting her arm around her. 'From what Jesse told me, she loves working at the library.'

Steve snorted. 'How would you know? I told her the job was too stressful.'

'It wasn't the job causing her stress,' Louisa said pointedly. 'She wanted to be at the library. She looked forward to it.'

'True,' agreed Dot.

'Whatever,' said Steve.

Dot turned to him. 'What about you? Did you notice her habits getting worse?'

Steve puffed out his chest. 'Of course. Even Ollie's picked up a few of them.'

'And did you do anything to help her?' Louisa asked, unable to stop herself. She'd had enough of her brother-in-law, and was more than ready to reveal some significant truths about him.

'Of course I tried to help her,' said Steve, indignant.

'Did you really?' Dot said. 'Because I never saw it.'

'Dot,' Tom cautioned.

'You must have seen she wasn't herself—or were you too busy to notice?' Dot's tone had a sharp edge to it.

'I noticed, Dot. I told her to get help. Just the other afternoon, actually, when she had the fall.'

'And where were you then, Steve? I was the first to reach Jesse even though I called you straight after Louisa phoned me. I was at your house for a good thirty minutes before you turned up and your office is only fifteen minutes away.'

'Thank you, Dot, but I can't leave work mid-meeting. Our company is involved in some highly secretive and strategic movements right now. It's non-stop. I can't just up and leave every time there's a crisis at home. My staff rely on me. And, yes, I did notice something was up with her. That's why I told her to get help. I can't watch over her twenty-four seven.'

'Told her, yes. But did you actually help?'

'What are you implying? And, by the way, what did you do to help?' Steve was glaring at Dot. 'Jesse always seems particularly stressed after talking to you.'

'Let's stop right there,' said Tom. 'This isn't helping anyone.'

Steve looked towards the playground. The kids, oblivious to the adults' conversation, were playing on the seesaw.

'I'm sorry,' he said. 'But her behaviour was affecting the children, Ollie in particular.'

'So you agree it's gotten worse in recent months?' Dot said. Steve nodded.

'There you go,' Dot said. 'There has to be a reason. Once we find the source of her worries, we'll have the answer to why she's been so stressed over the past few months.'

Tom nodded.

'I don't understand why she didn't talk to me about it,' Dot went on. 'I'm her mother.'

'Maybe she tried,' Louisa said.

'I know what you're all thinking,' said Steve. 'It's my fault. I'm the bastard responsible!'

Louisa couldn't have put it better herself.

'I can hear you lot from inside the chapel,' said Milly, Louisa's elderly grandmother, as she walked towards their table.

Louisa got out of her chair to hug her. 'Grandma!' She kissed her on the cheek. 'I'm so happy to see you.'

Louisa loved Milly. Her fondest memories of growing up involved her grandma: Christmas drinks at which Milly got slaughtered after two tumblers of sherry; Jesse's seventh birthday party where she'd given a pink piglet piñata such a ferocious beating all the other parents had looked alarmed.

'Despite the metre in height I've lost?' Milly said.

Louisa smiled. 'You're just as I remember you.'

'Don't give me that nonsense, Louisa. I wasn't born yesterday. When did you fly in?'

'A little while ago.'

'Seen your poor sister then?'

Louisa nodded.

'And your niece and nephew?'

She nodded again.

Milly looked around the table at everyone. 'Couldn't spare a few moments to pray to our Lord? Even short prayers find their way to heaven. You're all too busy for that I see.'

Dot rolled her eyes. Tom squirmed in his seat. Steve half-smiled.

'But you've got time for coffee and cake!' Milly was on a roll. 'Am I the only believer here? I'm in the chapel, praying, asking for guidance, and I walk out and what do I find? You lot huddled together, caterwauling and sipping cappuccinos. The Lord should be our caffeine at this time.'

'Okay, Mum, that's enough,' said Dot, helping Milly into an uncomfortable plastic cafe chair. 'I'm surprised you'd pray in a chapel anyway, given your newfangled ways. Would you like a tea?'

Milly nodded. 'Yes, I think I would.'

'Well,' said Steve, getting up, 'I'd better take the kids to school.'

'But what about Jesse and the doctors?' asked Dot.

'I'll go up now before I leave.'

'I'll come with you,' Louisa said.

Steve glared at her but said nothing.

'Steve,' Doctor Thompson said as soon as he saw them, 'I'm afraid I have bad news.'

Louisa covered her mouth with her hand. Please let her be okay, she thought. Everything appeared to be moving in slow motion. She wanted the doctor to get on with it and tell them the news, but when he started speaking again his words were fuzzy. Louisa stumbled and the doctor caught her.

'Are you okay?' he asked.

She closed her eyes in an effort to compose herself. 'Of course. Go on.' But she was still having trouble focusing. Jet lag. Her mouth tasted funny and the room was spinning. Maybe if she sat down . . .

'Pregnant?' Steve spat out the word.

That got Louisa's attention. Jesse, pregnant? Man, that sister of hers was good at keeping secrets—rather like Louisa herself.

'There must be some mistake,' Steve went on. 'Jesse can't possibly be pregnant.'

'I'm sorry, but whatever the case, unfortunately your wife has miscarried.'

Steve didn't seem to hear. 'We had this talk only last week. She's not pregnant. It's impossible.' He sounded livid.

'Calm down,' Louisa said, regaining some strength. 'Maybe she didn't get the memo.' She turned to the doctor, feeling light-headed but focused. 'How pregnant?'

'Approximately six weeks,' he said.

'Six weeks!' Steve fumed. 'This just keeps getting better. I don't—'

'Is she okay?' Louisa asked. 'How will this affect her recovery?'

'The miscarriage won't affect Jesse's physical recovery. But any time a woman suffers a miscarriage there's the inevitable emotional trauma.' He looked at Steve. 'I'm sorry. If you'll excuse me.'

'She must have known she was pregnant all this time,' Steve said after the doctor had left the room. 'Did you know as well?'

'Me?' said Louisa. 'I knew she wanted another baby, but no, I didn't know she was pregnant. Maybe Jesse didn't know either.'

'Ha! She would have known! And just when the hell was she going to tell me? On the way to the delivery room? Despite everything we talked about, she went and got herself pregnant. Again.'

Louisa sat down beside Jesse. 'Under the circumstances, it doesn't really matter.' Steve went to say something else, but Louisa pointedly ignored him and took Jesse's hand. 'Jesse, can you hear me? It's Louisa. I'm here with you. Can you hear me, sweetheart?'

'As if she can bloody well hear you,' said Steve. 'Look at her.'

'We're supposed to talk to her,' Louisa started.

'Oh yeah?'

'Yes, actually. We need to let her know we're here. Talk to her about what's happening in our lives. Ask her questions, include her.' She stroked Jesse's hand. 'We're not going to leave until you get better, Jess.'

'Great,' said Steve. 'When she starts talking back and tells you why she got pregnant, let me know.'

'She's not pregnant any more, Steve.'

'No . . . Well, when she wakes up—'

'What? You're going to yell at her for not obeying your orders?'

Steve rolled his eyes. 'Jesse knows she's in the wrong. I just want her to admit it. Then we can put all of this nonsense behind us.'

Louisa glared at him, unable to speak.

'It's late,' he said, glancing at his watch. 'I've got to drop the children at school and get to work.'

'Aren't you forgetting something?' she said as he moved past her towards the door.

He stopped and turned around, looking puzzled. He checked his pockets for his wallet and keys. 'No, I don't—'

'Don't you want to kiss your wife before you leave?'

Steve did a for-fuck's-sake eye roll and walked over to the bed. He bent and kissed Jesse's bandaged forehead. 'See you soon, darling.' He straightened and glared at Louisa. 'Happy? It's not as if she knows I'm kissing her.'

'I can see this is really tearing you up.'

'Don't you dare talk to me about compassion, Louisa. You waltz in here, holier than thou, after an absence of six years, expecting everyone to fall at your feet. Don't you dare think you're better than me. If Jesse wasn't in this state, you'd still be on the other side of the world basking in your debauched lifestyle.'

'How can you say that?'

'You've never had any intention of coming back.'

'What would you know? I love Jesse.'

'Yeah, of course you do, Louisa. She's got all of your letters to prove it.' And he pushed past her and out into the corridor.

22

arly and I were about to enter the hospital cafeteria when
Liz phoned. She sounded distraught. I turned and walked
outside to our familiar bench in the sunshine. Carly followed me
and sat down. I paced as Liz talked.

'Skyla told me the news. I've been trying to get hold of you
for days. I can't believe it. How's Jesse? Is it bad?'

I filled her in as best I could.

'You don't think I caused this, do you?' she said.

What was I supposed to say? Yes, Jesse was so upset over losing
her job, she got distracted by the rain and her tears and drove
into a tree. I wasn't that heartless. Liz was suffering enough.

'No, Liz,' I said after a pause. 'I think it was probably a
combination of bad weather and bad luck.'

'I've sent flowers.'

'She'll appreciate that.'

'Stella, you're not really quitting, are you? We need you.'

'Thanks, but I can't really think about the library right now.
My priority is Jesse. At the moment I can't think beyond the
next hour, let alone the next day or week.'

'Of course. Take your time. We've got a couple of casuals filling in.'

'How did that go?' Carly asked after I'd ended the call.

I shrugged. 'Liz feels responsible.'

'We all do.'

'Yeah. And I know Jesse wouldn't want me quitting. But I'm still furious with Liz. Eventually, life will have to return to some kind of normalcy. I mean, we can't wait at the hospital all day and night for weeks on end.'

Carly nodded. 'But I feel so guilty getting on with the everyday while Jesse's here. It all seems so pointless.'

'I know. Every time I think about leaving the hospital, I panic. I don't want to leave Jesse alone. She needs us, especially when she first opens her eyes.'

The last few days had passed in a blur. All the waiting . . . and then, when we were allowed to see her, the reality that this wasn't some minor bump to the head. The woman lying in intensive care, all battered and bandaged, hooked up to tubes and machines, didn't look like Jesse.

'At least Louisa's here now,' Carly said. 'That'll make Jesse happy. Coffee?'

I nodded.

Inside the cafe, we walked over to where Dot and Tom were sitting.

'Great news that Louisa's arrived,' I said.

Dot nodded.

'Any other news?' asked Carly.

'There's never any news,' said Dot sadly.

'She's . . .' Tom faltered. 'She's had another seizure, but they've given her medication.'

'The doctors say that's not out of the ordinary,' I said, trying to sound encouraging.

Tom nodded. 'You're right. For now, there's essentially nothing we can do except wait, but it's so frustrating.'

That's what we were all doing. Waiting. And I'd never been good at that.

Carly and I left Tom and Dot and went to the counter.

'You know what? I don't think I can face another coffee,' Carly said.

'Me either,' I agreed. 'So now what?'

'I feel like I'm in the way. I might—'

'Look,' I whispered. Louisa and Steve were standing just outside the cafeteria, glaring at each other.

We went to join them. 'How is she?' I asked.

'In a coma,' replied Steve.

I stood there appalled, not knowing where to look, afraid of bursting into tears at any moment.

'Hi,' said Carly, extending her hand to Louisa. 'You must be Jesse's sister. I'm Carly.'

Steve rolled his eyes and pushed past us.

Louisa shook her head, then smiled at Carly as she blinked back tears. 'Nice to finally meet you.'

I put my arm around her. 'Jesse'll be okay.'

'I know,' Louisa sniffed. 'She has to be. Now, if you'll excuse me . . . ' She went to join her parents.

'Stella, I think I'll get going and come back later,' Carly said, glancing at her watch.

I spotted Mike down the corridor. 'I won't be far behind you,' I said. 'I'll just have a quick word with Mike.'

'Okay,' said Carly. 'Let me know if there's any news.'

'Will do,' I said, dashing away down the hall. 'Mike!'

He turned and waited for me to catch up.

'How is she?'

'I wish I had better news,' he said, giving my arm a gentle rub.

'Have the seizures been bad?'

'No. Still . . .'

'Still, what?' I pressed.

'Our biggest concern is that she's still unconscious; she hasn't opened her eyes once since the accident.' He paused and I could almost hear him deliberating over what to say next. 'Stella, I'm afraid it's up to Jesse now whether or not she wakes up. The best thing you can do is talk to her—tell her what's going on in your life, your friends' lives. I know how hard this must be for you, but at the moment it's a waiting game.'

'And the odds?'

Mike grimaced. 'I don't give odds.'

'Even? Sixty-forty? What?' I hesitated for a moment. 'What about her brain?'

He glanced down at his hands before answering. 'We're hoping for a one hundred per cent recovery, Stella, but there's no way to tell what her brain is going to do. I'm sorry, but there's no magic shot and no surgery option. Only time will tell.'

I shook my head. It was hard to take in.

'Talk to her,' he said again. 'Tell her how you feel. And, Stella, whatever happens, don't neglect your own family. It's easy to get caught up with what's happened to Jesse, but, as harsh as it sounds, life goes on, and your children need you as much as ever. Don't forget that.'

I nodded.

'Stella . . . ' He hesitated.

'What?'

'Nothing. I need to check on other patients, but I promise I'll let you know if there are any changes to Jesse's condition.'

After Mike had disappeared into an elevator, I stood rigid for a few moments, deciding what to do. I wanted to see Jesse, but I didn't want to intrude on Jesse's family; I was starting to feel I'd outstayed my welcome. Maybe if I just peered in on her? I wouldn't stay long. I just needed to check in and say hello.

Arriving at Jesse's room, I peeked in and was relieved to see only Louisa there.

'Sorry, I don't want to interrupt,' I started.

'Not at all. Come in.'

I pulled up a chair and sat on the other side of Jesse's bed. Together, we stared at her.

'Any change?' I asked.

Louisa shook her head. 'Did you know she was pregnant?'

'Pregnant? She'll be so happy.' Then I realised what Louisa had said. 'Wait. *Was* pregnant?'

Louisa nodded. 'She miscarried.'

'No!'

'Yeah. She was about six weeks along. You didn't know?'

I shook my head. 'Maybe Jesse didn't know either.'

'Maybe.' Louisa gripped her sister's hand tighter. 'Are you in there, Jess? I'm sorry about the fight with Steve. Despite what that prick says, I do love you, darling.'

We sat in silence until Louisa spoke again. 'I've got so much to tell her, but it feels weird talking to her when she can't respond.'

'I know the feeling,' I said quietly. 'Would you prefer me to leave?'

'No, stay. We can both talk to her.' Louisa took a deep breath. 'I'm sorry I called your husband a prick, Jess. But fuck! He's a massive prick. And to think you had sex with him not once but twice. Really. You're a braver woman than I could ever be.'

'She's brave all right.' I smiled at Jesse, then looked at Louisa. 'Just before the accident, Jesse told me you'd known Steve a long time?'

'Back in the dark days, yeah. You must think I'm . . .' She trailed off.

'I don't think anything. Truly.'

'I know it hurt Jesse, finding out about me and what I used to do. I should have told her sooner. Not kept it hidden.'

'I can understand why you didn't tell her.'

'Yeah, part of me didn't want to acknowledge it. If I'd told her about Steve's involvement, it would have meant telling her what I'd been up to as well and I couldn't bear the thought of disappointing her. So I chose to believe I was doing the right thing by not interfering in Jesse's life.'

We sat silently for a few moments, both gazing at Jesse. Two clear plastic prongs extended from her nose and I watched as she breathed oxygen in and out through them. A bank of machines monitored her vital signs, flashing red and green on a digital display. The tube to Jesse's mouth had been removed and her facial swelling had subsided.

Louisa started talking again. 'So, Jess, after you get out of here, you've got to stick to your guns and leave him. I might even stay in Sydney for a while. You can teach me how to cook because I suck big time. I'll let you in on a secret: I've always been jealous of your culinary abilities. Remember Mrs Beetle's home science class and the end-of-year bake-off? She was so pissed off when your double chocolate mud cake beat her saggy sponge. Remember? I'm sorry I've missed out on so much. The kids . . . So much time has passed by.'

She stroked Jesse's hand then looked over at me. 'How do you really think she's doing?'

I shook my head. 'Who knows? It's hard to take in, isn't it?'

'Impossible. Jesse's always been so full of energy.'

'Yeah, she's always so on. So alive.'

'But she was struggling before the accident, right?'

'Yeah, even before the Steve bombshell, she wasn't doing great, dealing with her anxiety issues. She'd been working hard to keep them in check. Steve's controlling behaviour didn't help. And on top of that, she'd just lost her job.'

'No! She didn't tell me.'

'It happened right before the accident.'

'Poor Jesse.'

'The manager at the library didn't want to put up with Jesse's quirks any longer so she made her redundant. I was furious. Still am.'

'How does the anxiety manifest itself?' Louisa asked.

'She's got a thing about threes. She'll stamp her foot three times if she drops a pencil or if she's stressed. It's a coping mechanism. Not many people notice. I only do because I see her all the time.'

Louisa looked stricken. 'And there I was on the other side of the world, completely preoccupied with my own life. Too busy to fly back to Sydney to see her. And for what? I wish things could be . . . different.'

'You're here now, Louisa. That's what's important.'

'But it shouldn't have taken something like this for me to come back and see her and the twins. She's going to be devastated about losing the baby. Do you think she knew she was pregnant?'

I shook my head. 'I really don't know. She talked about wanting another baby, but whether she knew or not she was expecting, I have no idea. I do know that a pregnancy would have symbolised a new beginning for her. New life, new hope.'

'And now that's been taken away from her.' Louisa leaned over Jesse and whispered, 'Jesse, are you there? Wake up, sweetie. Stella and I are here, waiting to talk to you.'

We sat in silence for a long time, watching Jesse and listening. Outside the room, staff wheeled trolleys and medical equipment up and down the corridor, and I could hear the muffled conversations of people making their way to visit friends and relatives.

'Jesse mentioned you were seeing someone?' I said, wanting to break the silence.

'Philippe, yeah. He's great but it's nothing serious.'

'Do you want it to be?'

'Nah. I have a tendency to move on when things get too cosy. I mean, marriage and commitment is fine—they're just not for me.'

Even though my marriage hadn't worked out, I thought what Louisa was saying was sad. Okay, so I didn't want a commitment with anyone right now, either, but I knew what it felt like to be in a long-term, loving relationship, and when it worked it was heaven.

Of course, thinking about long-term relationships led me on to Mike . . . and how the idea of taking our friendship any further frightened me. The proper thing to do was have some time on my own and grieve over the end of my marriage. But what if the feelings I was developing for Mike were real? An intense connection like that didn't come along often. I'd been with Terry seventeen years, and Mike was the first person I'd met since Terry who'd made me stop and think, what if?

Just then, the man himself walked in with two other hospital staff I hadn't seen before.

'We're going to run more tests now,' he said gently.

'Of course,' said Louisa.

'We'll keep you posted,' Mike added, holding my gaze for longer than he needed to.

Filled with warmth, I turned to Jesse. 'We'll be back soon, hon.'

Louisa and I caught the elevator to the ground floor, along with a heavily pregnant woman and her partner, who was flustered and fussing over her. We let them out first and I watched as she waddled towards the gift shop. Then I thought about Jesse and her miscarriage. It was too sad.

'Stella, can I ask you something?' Louisa said.

I turned to look at her. 'Shoot.'

'Mum said there'd been talk that Jesse might have deliberately . . .' She didn't finish.

'One of the witnesses said he thinks that's what happened,' I told her. 'But I can't believe Jesse would do that. Not with Ollie and Emily to look after. She would have needed to be deeply depressed to do that, no longer in control of her actions. I saw her practically every day and I don't think she was in that kind of state.'

The more I considered the idea, the more resolute I became. There was no way Jesse would have deliberately driven into a tree. And if she'd had the slightest inkling she was pregnant, I was doubly sure that self-harm would have been the last thing on her mind.

23

To tell the truth, Carly couldn't wait to leave the hospital. It was depressing seeing the devastated looks on the faces of Jesse's parents; watching Ollie and Emmy play on the seesaw, knowing something was terribly wrong with their mother but not quite understanding the gravity of the situation. Not to mention the fact that it was hard being around Steve.

Also, regardless of how many times Stella argued otherwise, Carly felt responsible for what had happened to Jesse. If she hadn't blurted out what they'd seen at the party last week, none of this might have happened.

And then there was Toby. Every time she saw him at the hospital, it was an ugly reminder of her ridiculous behaviour. Carly was embarrassed she'd flirted with him so madly. She really was a different person when drunk.

She dropped her car at home, caught a train to Town Hall station and started walking up towards Hyde Park. The last time she'd popped into Brett's office was three years ago. Both boys had come along and they'd all had lunch at the revolving Summit Restaurant, forty-seven floors above the city with breathtaking

360-degree uninterrupted views of Sydney and beyond. Then they'd climbed the Harbour Bridge. It was a great day. It was hard to believe it had been three years. Time flew.

Over the past few days Carly had made the decision to give her marriage another go. Jesse's accident had made her realise how precious life was; it could be snatched away in seconds. Will and Nick deserved her full attention and a strong commitment to their father and she was going to do her best to deliver.

As she walked down Elizabeth Street towards Brett's office, she wondered what was happening with Nicholas. She still hadn't heard back from Peter Sinclair, the sports master who'd been in contact with her. Nick hadn't called or emailed either. If Brett was in a relaxed mood today, she'd definitely bring it up.

She glanced at her watch. Almost midday. She was hungry and totally coffeed out. An image of Jesse lying in that horrid hospital bed, machinery whirring around her, flashed through her mind and she shuddered, silently praying that this afternoon there'd be news about an improvement in her condition.

When she arrived at Brett's building, Carly momentarily forgot which floor he was on. Ninth, that was it. Inside the elevator, she checked her reflection in the mirrored walls and watched the numbers change as they ascended. She was a little nervous, it had been a long time. At the ninth floor, the elevator pinged and the doors opened. She took a right towards his office. As she approached, she saw him leaning against the wall and talking to someone, a woman. Colleague? Secretary? He was animated. It was good to see him smiling, enjoying some office banter. She felt her heart skip a little. She really did love him.

'Carly,' he said when he saw her. 'What a nice surprise.' He kissed her on the lips, then introduced her to his colleague, Jane, before she walked off. As he led Carly inside his office, he said, 'Is everything okay?'

She nodded. 'It's been a while, hasn't it?'

'Better late than never. I'm happy to see you. Any change with Jesse?'

Carly shook her head and stared out the window. 'It's so sad and I feel useless.' She turned back to face him. 'Then there's us. I'm sorry for everything.'

'Carls, it's not just you. I haven't been doing my bit either. I need to pull back on my work commitments and spend more time with you and Will, especially now with Nicholas away.'

'About that,' Carly said, feeling tears well in her eyes. 'Nick's in a bit of trouble.'

'What kind of trouble?'

'He's been suspended from his coaching job because he and some other boys were fighting in the locker room.'

'That doesn't sound too bad. I'm sure—'

'Wait. There's more. Nick . . . the boys were naked, flicking towels around.'

Brett raised his eyebrows. 'So? They were in a locker room. It's not like they were streaking through the school grounds. I'm sure it'll all be sorted.'

'But the suspension?'

'It's an English school—I'm not surprised. But if it makes you feel better, I'll ring and see what I can find out.'

Carly nodded, fresh tears coming. They were already talking about Nicholas so now was the time to bring up the matter of the letters. 'There's something else . . .'

Brett half-smiled and motioned for her to sit down. 'This is certainly the week for it.' He pulled up a chair up beside her. 'Okay, I'm listening.'

'It's about Nick, but I don't know where to start. I found some letters . . . I think he might have been having a friendship with a teacher, a male—'

Brett sighed and put his hand on her knee, stroking it gently. 'I'm going to stop you there.'

'No, I need to tell you this. I'm not making it up.'

'I know you're not. But I already know about the letters.'

Carly blinked. 'What?'

'Mr Busby. Nick spoke to me about him. I went to the school and we sorted it out.'

'You kept this a secret from me?'

'Nick didn't want a fuss. We were both worried you'd blow it out of proportion. Anyway, I fixed the problem.'

'But why didn't you tell me?' Carly said, brushing away his hand and standing up. 'He's my son.'

'Carly, calm down,' Brett said, rising, too. 'Everything's okay. You're creating a drama out of nothing.'

She had to get out. Take herself for a long walk so she could think. On the one hand, she was relieved Brett already knew about the letters and the matter had been dealt with, but on the other, she was furious with him for not telling her. So furious she could barely look at him.

'I need to go,' she said, walking towards the door.

'Stop. Calm down. Let's have lunch and talk about this rationally.'

'Don't tell me to calm down.' She kept walking, only stopping when she reached the elevator. She jabbed the button with her finger. 'Hurry the fuck up.'

'I can explain,' said Brett, trying to step between her and the elevator.

Carly put her hand up in front of his face to stop him. 'Please don't.' The elevator doors opened. Several suits moved to the side to let her in. 'I don't want to know.'

The doors closed on Brett, a look of resignation on his face. As they descended, her phone started ringing. An older woman standing beside her touched her on the arm. 'Don't answer, love. Give it time.'

She nodded and turned the phone off without bothering to check the caller identification.

Once out of the elevator, Carly put her sunnies on and fled down the street, not looking back. She walked all the way down to the Opera House, along the foreshore and into the Botanic Gardens, tears flowing. Finally, she took a seat on a park bench and, in a daze, watched the ferries bobbing along the harbour.

By the time she checked her watch again, it was nearly three o'clock. She had no idea how it had got to that time but didn't really care. She turned on her phone to find several messages—all from Brett. The rational part of her knew he must have believed he had good reason to keep the matter from her, but she was hurt. All these years, she'd believed that she and Nick were close. Why couldn't he have confided in her?

She caught the train home and walked straight to the fridge in search of wine. It had been four days since her last glass. She'd give up drinking again, tomorrow.

As she drank the chardonnay, everything started falling into place: the devastation and betrayal she felt at Brett not confiding in her about the problems Nick was having at school; his assertion that he'd preferred to fix it himself rather than discuss it with her; his belief that she'd overreact and turn it into a huge drama.

Who was she kidding? This wasn't a marriage. She couldn't lie to herself or to Brett any more.

She thought back to when she'd told Brett about her desire for a fuck buddy and he hadn't seemed fazed. Oh, he'd said he was angry, but he wasn't. Not really. Carly gulped more wine as thoughts dashed in and out of her head. And what was the story with his colleague, Jane? They'd certainly seemed very chatty and friendly when she'd arrived unexpectedly at the office today. He was having an affair, she just knew it.

Carly heard the key in the door turn as she reached for the bottle. It was empty. She'd drained it in less than an hour.

'Carly, I've been so worried,' Brett said when he found her propped up at the kitchen bench. 'Are you okay?'

'Couldn't be better,' she trilled. 'But Brett, our marriage is over. Finito. Done and dusted.'

'What are you saying?'

'I'm saying that Blind Freddy could see that we haven't been getting along for a very long time. Why can't you?'

'Carly, stop.'

'No, it's over. You and I don't fit together any more. We don't do anything together. We're a joke. You have your business and golf and that's it. When you're not working, you're playing golf—'

'I haven't played in months.'

'Or fucking your lady friend. Who knows?'

'You've been drinking. You're not making any sense.'

'I'm making perfect sense. Besides, I don't have a problem with any of this. It's great you've got other activities to distract you.'

He shook his head. 'Distract me from what exactly?'

'Haven't you been listening? Our marriage, Brett!'

He reached out to hold her but she pulled away. 'How could you? How could you not tell me about Nicky? I feel so hurt and betrayed.' She shook her head. 'The fact that you couldn't even confide in me tells me everything I need to know about the state of our relationship.'

'That's not true, darling. We were trying to protect you—'

'Protect me? Please!'

'I'm sorry,' he said, looking sad and beaten. 'I am truly sorry.'

'Can't you see?' Carly said, struggling to compose herself. 'We've ended up like Stella and Terry.'

'No, we haven't.'

She took a step back. 'How can you say that? Anyway, I've been thinking that with Nicholas overseas it might be good to take a break.'

'Take a break?'

'Yes, as in you and me taking a break from each other, exploring other paths.'

'But I don't want to explore other paths. I'm happy on this path.'

'You aren't.' Carly burst into fresh tears.

'Carls, this is a passing phase, trust me. You're upset because you're missing Nicholas. That's what the problem is. Why don't you call him? You'll feel better once you've spoken to him. Then, tonight, we can go out to dinner, just the two of us, or see a movie. Why don't we do that?'

'Brett,' she groaned.

'You're being emotional because of all this talk about Nick. I'll never leave you, ever. This is my home, my life. This is where my family is.'

'But I don't even know if I love you any more. We've had a good run—'

'We're still having a good run.' Brett's eyes began to well up, too. 'I love you. I love my boys. I can fix this, really.'

•

Carly went upstairs and took a shower. When she came back downstairs half an hour later, Brett had marinated steaks for dinner, prepared a salad and was fixing a leaking tap in the laundry.

'On the weekend, we'll have a clean-up,' he told her. 'Time to get stuck into some odd jobs around the house and garden that I've been neglecting for months. Just make a list and I'll get on with them.'

'Brett,' she said, but couldn't think what to say next. The fight had completely gone out of her. She nodded. 'Okay, sure. Sounds like a good plan.'

24

*S*tella insisted on driving Louisa to her parents' house, but despite Louisa's invitation to come in, Stella just dropped her off. Louisa stood at the front gate, looking around, seeking out familiar sights. Where once there had been paddocks and horses grazing across the road, there were now five blond-brick monstrosities. Ugh! The gravel street of her childhood was a bitumen road with cement guttering, and there was even a cement pathway for pedestrians.

Overgrown camellia trees lined the fence of her parents' home, and the huge liquid amber she and Jesse used to climb as kids was losing its leaves. Ancient agapanthus plants crept along the driveway. The house itself was still as Louisa remembered, just more weathered and badly in need of a paint job. The once dark green woodwork was pale and flaky and the window frames looked dated and worn.

'Come on, Louisa. I've made a pot of tea,' Dot called impatiently from the front door.

Of course she had. Louisa nodded and walked towards her.

Dot's arms were outstretched to capture Louisa as soon as she made it up the steps to the veranda. 'Welcome home.'

A cursory glance around inside revealed that most of the furnishings remained the same, but the framed photos had changed. They'd used to feature Jesse and Louisa at various ages; now they were mostly of Oliver and Emily. Then there were all of Dot's churchy ornaments: a crucifix, the Madonna—no change there.

Louisa followed Dot into the lounge room, where her father and Grandma Milly were sitting. Louisa saw that Tom's favourite chair had survived, even though it now looked worn and tattered. Dot had given it to him as an anniversary gift many moons ago and no one else had dared sit in it, ever.

'Ah, Louisa, you're home,' said Tom, folding his newspaper and putting it down on the side table.

'About time,' said Grandma Milly.

'Any news?' Tom asked, standing up.

'The doctors were doing more tests when Stella and I left.' Louisa wasn't ready to talk about Jesse's pregnancy. 'I hardly recognised the street. It's changed.'

'A lot of things have changed since you lived here, Louisa,' said Dot, handing her a cup of tea.

'I'm surprised Steve didn't stay longer at the hospital this morning,' Louisa said, turning the subject away from her prolonged absence.

'Steve's Steve. He works hard and expects everyone else to fall in line,' said Dot.

'But given the circumstances . . .'

'Everyone copes in their own way,' added Tom.

'Well, he's an arrogant prick, if you ask me,' Louisa said.

Grandma giggled into her tea. 'No change there, then.'

'Louisa, really,' said Dot. 'What about you? How's university life?'

'Busy,' she answered truthfully. 'There are always new courses to teach, assessments, student dramas . . . never a dull moment.'

'Seeing anyone?' Grandma asked.

'I am, actually. His name is Philippe and he's . . . at uni with me.'

'Do I hear wedding bells?' Grandma probed.

'I don't think so.'

Dot clicked her tongue. 'You're not getting any younger, Louisa. Maybe this Philippe character is your Prince Charming. It's high time you settled down, don't you think?'

Great. She'd been home all of five minutes and her mother had already given her the settling-down lecture. Following Grandma's lead, Louisa pretended Dot hadn't spoken. 'What about you, Grandma?'

'Don't be ridiculous. No more weddings for me.'

'I didn't mean that. How are you?'

'You know me, love. Fit as a fiddle.'

'Why don't you tell Louisa about the newfangled church you're going to, Mum,' said Dot, raising her eyebrows.

Milly sighed. 'Dotty, the traditional church doesn't work for me any more. Simple as that.'

'Doesn't work?' Louisa asked. She just wanted to talk about something other than Jesse's plight for a few minutes . . . Her grandma's new church was as good as any other topic.

'I've been at it for eighty years, Lulu-Bell—kneeling in pews and praying to the Almighty. Still not getting any answers, so I've moved onward and upward. It's wonderful. We sing songs and have outings to bowling clubs.'

'Sounds like fun.'

'It is fun, Louisa! Jolly good fun. We sing, we clap—'

'It's a cult,' said Dot. 'Last week, she brought home an evangelical Christian surfer from Cronulla. He was all of twenty-five—'

'I'll have you know he's a delightful young man,' said Milly. 'A delightful young man who's teaching me the guitar, by the way. Imagine learning to play an instrument at my age. It's wonderful. Perhaps some day, I'll be the one playing the music at song time.'

If I had to put up with this on a regular basis, I'd go mad, Louisa thought. Aloud, she said, 'I'm sure you'll both be saved.'

'That's not the point,' Dot said. 'We should be united, praying as a family, especially at this time, not running off joining cults and chanting and clapping.'

'I'd hardly call it a cult,' said Milly, sipping her tea. 'Besides, I go to the old-fashioned church if there's no alternative, like I did this morning. I didn't see you praying there, Dot.'

Tom folded his paper and stood up. 'Might do some gardening before we head back to the hospital,' he said and disappeared through the kitchen door. Louisa's gaze followed him outside, where he stopped and deadheaded several agapanthus.

'Is he okay?' she asked. Because to her, he definitely didn't look well.

'Of course he's not okay, Louisa. Your sister is in a coma. He can't bear the thought that she might have . . . that we could have done more to help her and we didn't. That she's been suffering all this time.' Her mother took a deep breath before continuing. 'Whenever I asked Jesse how she was managing, she always said she was fine, even though recently she's been fussing—all that foot tapping, turning light switches on and off. It was breaking my heart. And when I think that she might have driven into that tree on purpose . . .'

'You don't know that,' Louisa said. 'Everyone I've spoken to thinks it was an accident. And if she did do it deliberately, then she was likely very depressed and not able to reason properly.'

'But no other cars were involved.'

'Dot, stop talking nonsense!' said Milly. 'I think I'll do a turn of the garden with Tom.'

Dot watched her elderly mother slowly make her way outside, then turned back to Louisa. 'She's completely lost now that Oprah's finished. How often did you say you speak with Jesse? You rarely call us.'

'I'm sorry,' Louisa said. She wasn't proud of her lack of contact with her parents, but being at home again made her feel seven years old.

'We manage. I wanted to talk to you about something else— something your sister's been up to. I caught her out just days ago. Have a look at this.' Dot reached inside her handbag and pulled out a brochure, which she thrust into Louisa's hand.

'Secret Women's Business Workshop,' Louisa read out loud. 'And . . .?'

'Louisa, this is serious. Jesse was getting involved in all manner of things that aren't normal or healthy for a woman like her. A mother. A married mother.'

'Says who?'

'Don't keep asking me questions like that. I just know it's not healthy. These clubs are known fronts for brainwashing cults. They make people do strange things and take them away from their families.'

'You and your obsession with cults, Mum. I don't think Jesse was about to join one.'

'I wouldn't be too sure of that.'

'How do you know?'

'Because I confronted her about it. Told her to wake up to herself, that she had responsibilities and just who did she think she was kidding? Secret women's business indeed.'

'How did she take it?'

'Told me to mind my own business.'

Louisa grinned. 'Fair enough, too.'

'Don't look at me like that, Louisa. I was shocked. She said the group sounded interesting. I said to her, interesting or not, she had enough on her plate without getting messed up in that kind of thing. I suggested she come to church with me—'

'She would have loved that.'

'Would you stop sneering for one second?'

Louisa tried to assume a neutral expression. 'How did you find out about this anyway?'

'I found the leaflet in her handbag.'

'You were snooping?'

'I was not. I didn't have to look very hard to find it. We had a terrible fight—Jesse said I was invading her privacy. I thought we shared everything, but she went crazy. Told me it was none of my business if she wanted to go to meetings and better herself. I said she could better herself by getting her tics under control. That girl is a walking convulsion sometimes. I told her she didn't need any more demands placed on her.'

'No, of course not. Not after you've just told her she's a walking bloody convulsion—'

'Louisa! Please don't use language like that.'

'This family has more pressing issues than the misuse of language, Mum.'

'It makes me wonder. If she was hiding this from me, what else was she keeping secret?'

'She's entitled to secrets. We all are. I can't believe you were prying—'

'I was looking for Panadol and happened to come across it.'

'I think Jesse might have a different take on the situation. When did you talk to her about it?'

'The day I went around to her house after the fall.'

'After she'd been on the phone to me?'

'That's right. She didn't seem herself. And now . . .' Dot started to cry. 'And now my little girl's in a coma in hospital.'

Louisa looked at how devastated her mother was and suddenly felt ashamed. Ashamed she hadn't been there to support her, sad that she'd missed out on six long years. When she'd left Australia, her father was still working full-time, her grandmother resided in her own home . . . And now? Well, now, they were all so much older. No one lived for ever, Louisa was starting to realise.

'Mum,' she said. 'I'm sorry. I never meant to let you down.'

'Hey,' Dot said, drawing Louisa in close and hugging her. 'Where's all this coming from?'

Louisa blinked back tears. She was so incredibly tired.

'You turned out all right,' said Dot, patting her affectionately on the arm. 'More than all right, Louisa. Why do you think I was so hard on you and Jesse? I didn't want you making the same mistakes I did. I didn't want either of you to go through the pain.'

Louisa immediately wondered what mistakes her mother had made, but was secretly pleased she was admitting to being hard on her daughters.

'Now that I'm older, I realise everyone has to travel through life on their own path,' Dot said. 'For all my instinctive nagging and interference in yours and Jesse's lives and my bickering with Mum, I realise that people need to make their own mistakes and find their own way home. Don't think for one moment I'm happy about it. I'm not. But I know that's the way it has to be.'

With that, Louisa burst into tears. 'I'm so sorry. I never wanted to stay away so long. It's just that . . .'

'You didn't want to talk to an old fogey like me about your troubles?'

Louisa nodded through her tears.

'Fair enough,' said Dot. 'I'd have wanted to clip you around the ears and lock you in your bedroom for ten years. Instead, you flew away. Don't ever do that again. Your father and I are old.'

Louisa followed Dot's gaze as it rested on a collection of family portraits hanging on the wall. 'As for Mum,' she said, focusing on a photo taken of Milly and her more than thirty years ago, 'God in His wisdom has deemed that she live with us. Divine punishment, if ever there was one.'

'Grandma's cool,' Louisa said, 'And she keeps you on your toes.'

'I guess.' Dot turned back to Louisa. 'You're home now, Lou. Please stay. We've missed you.'

Dot and Louisa hugged for a very long time before Dot finally pulled away. 'Come on then, dear. Upstairs and shower while I make peace with my mother.' She glanced outside to where Milly and Tom were talking animatedly beside an azalea bush. 'You know, the young man from Cronulla she brought home the other week was a thorough gentleman, and to tell you the truth, I don't actually mind the songs they sing.' She rolled her eyes. 'But if you tell Grandma I said that, I'll deny it.'

Louisa smiled. Families. 'Love you, Mum,' she said, kissing her on the cheek.

'You, too, darling.'

Louisa picked up her bags and walked upstairs, still holding the pamphlet that promised to change women's lives by helping them to *let go of guilt and fear and grow into our authentic selves*. She thought about Jesse's doomed pregnancy and wondered what other secrets her sister might have.

Grandma Milly had taken possession of Louisa's old room so she made her way into Jesse's room instead, which now housed bunk beds for Ollie and Emily. Louisa had always thought Jesse had the better room because hers overlooked the paddocks and the horses. You could see for miles out the window, almost to the ocean. Although Louisa's room was slightly bigger and had a built-in wardrobe, it overlooked the garage. Jesse's was definitely the pick: it was so much lighter and further away from their parents' room. Even now, she could see why, growing up, they'd fought about it.

Louisa unzipped her bag and peered inside. Just as she'd thought: she'd packed with her eyes closed. There weren't many clothes, and nothing suitable for a Sydney summer. But she'd make do. There was no way she was borrowing any of her mother's clothes. Or her grandmother's, for that matter.

She flopped down on the bottom bunk and closed her eyes for five minutes before she had a shower. She wondered what Philippe was doing. He'd been so understanding when she'd called him, frantic after her father's phone call about Jesse. He'd come straight over, calmed her down, arranged the flight to Sydney, and promised he'd take extra special care of Ziggy and her plants.

'You'd do all that for me?' she'd sobbed.

'Of course,' he'd replied. 'I love you, babe.'

He'd stayed with her the next couple of days and nights, feeding her, loving her, until the time came to drive her to the airport. Any fool could see he was a keeper, but their age difference worried her. How could she fall in love with someone eleven years younger?

266

To her complete surprise, lying there on the bunk, Louisa began to cry again. Who was she kidding? She was in love with Philippe and had been since that crazy, frantic afternoon in her office. This wasn't just an affair. She thought about him all the time. She loved him. He loved her.

She texted him. *Home. Jesse hanging on. Too sad. Miss you.*

'Could we drive past the accident site?' Louisa asked her father half an hour later as they were getting ready to go back to the hospital.

'I don't know, Louisa. I'm not sure your mother and grandmother—'

'We'll have to face it sooner or later, Tom,' said Dot. 'It might as well be now.'

Tom shook his head. 'It's a bit grisly, don't you think?'

Louisa completely understood her father's reluctance. If you'd asked her two hours ago, she wouldn't have wanted to go to the accident site either. But she felt she needed to see the place for herself to try to piece the jigsaw together.

'It might give us some insight into what really happened,' she said gently.

'Louisa's right, Tom,' said Dot. 'It's time we looked for ourselves, rather than relying on second- and third-hand reports.'

'But we promised the kids we'd stop in at Jesse's and pick up some music for her,' said Tom. 'We'll be late picking them up from school.'

'We will not,' said Dot irritably. 'We'll have plenty of time if we leave right now.'

It was a silent five-kilometre ride.

'I don't know why you want to do this,' Tom grumbled as he parked near the crash site.

'Just to see,' Louisa said.

She got out and walked towards the gum tree. It was on a straight stretch of bitumen road, a single carriageway with a 70-kilometre per hour speed limit. No blind spots, and the tree itself was huge. Huge and in plain view. There was bush scrub and long grass all around, but no other trees. You could clearly see where the front of Jesse's car had smashed into the trunk. The bark had been ripped away and there was broken glass and metal lying underneath and nearby.

Last week, when Jesse had had the accident, it was stormy, wet and windy, but today the sky was a brilliant blue, there was no wind and it was a pleasant twenty-five degrees. It didn't seem real.

'It's impossible to tell if she braked,' said Tom, after closely examining the grass for several minutes. He stood up and wiped his eyes.

'I'm sure she did, Dad,' Louisa reassured him. 'I'm sure Jesse braked. It was just a terrible accident.'

Dot and Grandma Milly watched silently. Dot made the sign of the cross over her chest. It was the first time Louisa had ever experienced both of them being quiet for longer than five minutes.

'I don't understand,' said Tom as they climbed back into the car. 'Why had she stopped here in the first place? For her to accelerate into the tree, she had to be well off to the side of the road, on the grass.'

'Jesse drives this road most days,' said Dot. 'She knows it blindfolded.'

'When she wakes up, she'll tell us everything we need to know,' soothed Louisa. She had a thought. 'What about a car malfunction? Brakes? There has to be a reason why she pulled over.'

'We won't know about the car until the police examiner gets back to us, and Steve said that could take a week or more,' Tom said.

Jesse's house looked so normal, suburban. The garden was messy and green; a couple of bikes lay haphazardly on the veranda. Staring at the bikes, it struck Louisa how much she'd missed in the last few years—birthdays, Christmases, school plays . . . The truth was, she didn't know her own niece and nephew. They'd been scared of her when she'd seen them at the hospital. It was beyond sad.

As for Jesse, Louisa prayed it wasn't too late to prove that they could be best friends again.

'What are you waiting for?' said Dot as Louisa hovered just inside the front door. 'Come on.'

Louisa followed her mother down the hall into the kitchen. There was an open packet of bread, a tub of margarine and a jar of Vegemite sitting on the bench. She put them all in the fridge while Dot put dirty plates and cutlery into the dishwasher.

Louisa did a quick scan of the area. 'Where do they keep the CDs?'

'In the TV room,' Dot replied, pointing to a room off to the side.

The top of the entertainment unit was covered with framed photographs of Jesse and the kids at various ages: Ollie in soccer garb, kicking a ball; Em in a black and white netball uniform lunging at the hoop. Jesse's kids were so adorable . . . and far too young to lose their mother.

Outside, Tom beeped the car horn. Shaking off her fear, Louisa opened the cabinet doors and grabbed an armful of CDs.

Five minutes later, they were waiting at the school pick-up zone.

'Let's try to be happy for Ollie and Emily's sake,' Dot said when they saw the twins appear.

'Are we going to see Mum now?' Ollie asked as he and Emmy clambered into the back seat.

'Sure are,' Louisa said, putting on an exaggerated happy face. 'And I picked up her favourite music, too.'

Dot attempted some chat about how the twins' day had been, but neither was interested. Like the rest of them, they were anxious to get to the hospital and see Jesse.

As they drove, Louisa watched people going about their usual daily business: walking in and out of the butcher's shop, the chemist, the newsagency. It seemed weird that for everyone else, life went on as normal. Meanwhile, their world had fallen to pieces. And they had questions . . . so many questions . . .

'Nanna, what happens when you die?' Emily asked as they walked through the hospital doors. 'The kids at school say it's like a big black hole that goes on forever.'

'Who said that? What a load of rubbish. Heaven is a beautiful place, full of gardens and nature.'

'What about hell?' Ollie said as they rode the elevator to the third floor.

'Hell's only for bad people.'

'Mum, how can you say that?' Louisa said.

'What? Hell is for bad people,' Dot said, indignant. 'I mean really bad people, Oliver. Like murderers, like Hitler—'

'Not Mum?'

'Of course not.'

'Ollie,' Louisa said, 'I don't think there is such a place as hell.'

'Neither do I,' Grandma Milly chimed in. 'The afterlife is like one big holiday with lots of happy, smiling friends, lots of singing and everyone eating lollies and cake.'

'Mother, really,' said Dot.

'What do you think, Auntie Louisa?'

Before she could answer, they'd reached Jesse's room and everyone went quiet. The afternoon sun had made the room brighter and warmer than it had been this morning. Ollie was the first to approach Jesse. He took her hand and put his head down on the bed beside her. After a few moments, he turned around to Louisa. 'Are you thinking about heaven?'

'Oh,' she said, choking back tears. 'Yes . . . I think heaven must be a happy place where people who've died watch over and guide us.'

'Like angels?'

'Yes, just like angels.'

'Do you think Mummy will be an angel soon?'

'Goodness, I hope not. Maybe far, far in the future.'

'What if you have a really bad person guiding you?' Ollie continued.

'There aren't any bad people when you die,' Louisa said.

'Then where do all the bad people go?' asked Emily.

'Yeah,' Ollie said. 'We don't want them hurting Mum.'

'No one's going to hurt your mum, Ollie. Besides, she's not going to die.'

'Do you know that for sure?'

Before Louisa could answer, Dot rushed in with, 'Of course we do. Now, come on. Why don't you tell your mum about your day at school? She'd love to hear all about that. Emily, you start.'

'My class said prayers for Mummy . . . and I read a book. My teacher said I didn't have to do any work today, but I wanted to.'

'I drew Mummy some pictures,' said Ollie. 'But I left them in the car.' He stroked Jesse's hand and whispered, 'Don't be lonely, Mummy. I love you always. I do.'

Louisa could see the kids' talk was upsetting her parents. Dot was sniffing back tears while Tom was blinking furiously in an effort to stem his.

'Who wants to come with me down to the chapel?' said Dot suddenly.

No one responded.

'Emily? Ollie?' Dot asked.

'I want to stay with Mummy,' said Ollie.

'You come then, Emily,' Dot said. 'Grandma will come, too, won't you?'

'If I must,' Milly replied.

'Then we'll put some fresh water in those vases, okay?' Dot said to Emily as they walked out of the room together.

'How about you put some music on, Louisa,' said Tom moments later.

'I was just thinking the same thing. Oliver, do you want to help me set up the CD player? Then you can choose some music you think Mum would like to listen to.'

Ollie's eyes stayed firmly on Jesse.

'I've got lots of CDs,' Louisa went on. 'Your mum sure likes Robbie Williams. She's got a zillion of his CDs.'

'Yeah, she loves him,' he agreed distractedly.

Louisa showed him the plastic bag full of CDs. 'Any one in particular?'

'She likes them all. Maybe this one,' he said, pulling it out. 'I gave her this for her birthday. She says it's her favourite.'

'Great choice.'

She helped Ollie put the CD player on the table and popped the music in. 'Your mum will love this,' she said as Robbie Williams's voice kicked in with 'Better Man'.

Louisa and Tom sat in silence and listened to the music while Ollie rubbed his mother's hand.

'Mum wouldn't leave me, not if she didn't have to,' Ollie said. 'She loves me.'

'Of course she does,' said Louisa. 'She loves you and Emily more than anything in the world.'

'And you don't leave somebody if you love them, right? You just don't.' Ollie stamped his right foot three times on the carpet.

Louisa and her dad glanced at each other.

'You just . . . hey, did you see that? Mum just squeezed my hand. She squeezed my hand! She's waking up!' shouted Ollie, tears streaming down his red cheeks.

'Quick. Call the doctor,' Louisa said to Tom, but he was already out the door.

Within moments, Doctor Thompson and several other doctors and nurses appeared in the room and began examining the monitors around Jesse. Steve followed close behind. Louisa assumed he must have just arrived.

'We'll run some tests,' Doctor Thompson said, 'but before you get too excited, you need to know that sometimes a patient in a coma may exhibit behaviour that mimics conscious behaviour. For instance, they may turn their head towards a sound or squeeze someone's hand. But it doesn't necessarily mean it's a purposeful movement.'

Louisa could see that Ollie was looking more and more distressed as the reality dawned on him that Jesse wasn't going to leap out of bed any time soon.

Steve saw it, too. 'Ollie, let's go and have a milkshake,' he said.

The little boy's eyes remained fixed on Jesse. 'I want to stay here with Mum.'

'Come on, let's leave the doctors to check on Mummy and go for a walk. You can tell me about your day.'

Steve looked tired and, Louisa hated to admit it, sad.

'Okay,' Ollie said. He turned to Louisa. 'You'll look after her, Auntie Louisa?'

Louisa nodded. 'Yes, Pop and I will.'

Ollie took Steve's hand and they left together. Tom waited until they were out out of earshot before speaking.

'So what exactly are you saying?' he asked the doctor.

'It's certainly encouraging,' Doctor Thompson said, 'but I don't want to give you false hope. Maybe her hand squeeze was purposeful, but it could also have been an involuntary movement that she had no control over.'

Louisa's heart sank. 'You'll run more tests?' she asked.

Doctor Thompson nodded. 'Now, if you'll excuse me.' He left the room, the other doctors and nurses trailing behind him.

Tom shook his head and banged his fist on the table next to the CD player. 'There must be something more we can do.'

Louisa reached out to hug him and he collapsed, sobbing, into her arms. She felt useless. This was so unfair.

'Dad, I'm really sorry about everything,' she said. 'What I mean is—'

'I know what you mean, Lou. I'm sorry, too. I could have handled the situation better.'

'No—'

'Yes, I could have. I'm your father. I treated you unfairly and I'm sorry.'

This was the longest conversation she'd had alone with her father in years. It made her feel sad for all the time they'd lost.

'Am I the reason you haven't been back?' he asked.

She could see how hurt he was, the tragedy of Jesse's accident compounding his grief and sadness. She didn't want to add to that.

'No.'

'Then why, Louisa? Why did you stay away so long?'

'I'm sorry,' she said, her voice breaking. 'I thought you wouldn't want to see me. I was ashamed . . . I'm still ashamed. My own father knowing . . .'

Tom hugged her. 'I don't care about that. It's all in the past. I care about my family. You are my daughter and I love you. Have always loved you, no matter what.'

Louisa felt hot tears falling down her cheeks.

'I'm glad you finally made it back to us, Looey-boo. I'm just sad it's under these circumstances.'

They both turned to look at Jesse again, and Louisa thought she saw a brief flicker of movement.

'Dad, I think her eyes just fluttered!'

25

After dropping Louisa home, I spent the afternoon dithering, picking up groceries, running errands, doing anything I could to distract myself from thinking about Jesse. I drove halfway to the mountains with the radio turned up full volume just so I wouldn't have to think. But of course none of it worked. Jesse was always on my mind. I felt so bloody guilty that she was lying in hospital in a coma. It was my fault. If only I'd stayed with Jesse after Liz sacked her.

By the time I got home, it was well after five. June was out the front, raking leaves.

'June!' I walked over and took the rake from her. 'Give me that! It's blazing hot out here. You should be resting.'

'All I do is rest. I like to keep busy.'

'At least come inside and have a cold drink or a cup of tea.'

'Good idea,' she said. 'How's Jesse?'

'No change, I'm afraid. The doctors were running more tests as I was leaving. The good news is that her sister's arrived from the States.'

June nodded and took a seat at the kitchen bench. I busied myself filling the kettle with water.

'It's just so tragic. I keep thinking about Oliver and Emily.'

'You never know what's around the corner,' she said.

I shook my head. 'No, you don't. So how are you feeling? You're looking bright.'

'Stella, I'm not an invalid. I'm feeling fine. And I'm not going crazy either.'

'I never said you were crazy.'

'Really? Then why all the memory tests with your doctor friend?'

'I don't know what you're talking about.'

'Don't give me that. Those tests weren't run-of-the-mill. They were specific tests for Alzheimer's. I know. I've done them before. It's not as if I haven't been worried about it myself.'

'June, I'm sorry. I thought you might fly off the handle or get embarrassed. Or worse, not know what I was talking about. It was wrong of me.'

June raised her eyebrows. 'I'll say.'

I poured boiling water into the teapot and took a couple of cups from the cupboard. 'Come and sit out on the deck.'

'I know I can be absent-minded and forgetful,' she said once we were settled, 'but I'm old. I can't be bothered remembering every specific detail of all the thousands of things I've done or am doing. Not to mention keeping up with everyone else's dramas. And I still think Terry was a fool to leave you.'

'It was mutual.'

'I know, but I don't think it's ideal.'

We sat in companionable silence for a while.

'I can't bear the thought of Jesse lying in hospital, lifeless,' I told her.

'Then don't,' she said. 'Imagine her doing something she loves, like being with her children or working at the library. Thinking about her lying in some God-awful hospital room isn't going to help anyone, least of all Jesse. You need to stay positive; it's your only hope of getting through this.'

'You're right,' I said, just as my mobile started ringing. I checked the caller identification. 'Terry,' I mouthed to June as I pressed the answer button. 'Hey, what's up?'

'Just checking in.'

'That's nice.'

'How's Jesse?'

'No change. The doctors are running more tests. How are things with you?'

'Not so good, I'm afraid.'

June started clearing the cups away. 'Leave those,' I whispered. 'Just sit down and read the paper.'

'Is that Mum? How is she?'

'Very good.' I smiled. 'Excellent. Now, about you not being so good: why?'

'Things aren't working out with Amanda.'

'But you've only been living with her a couple of weeks.'

June rolled her eyes and walked into the kitchen taking empty tea cups with her.

'And she wants to marry you,' I whispered so that June wouldn't hear.

'Exactly. Too much pressure. Can I come home?'

'Which home? This home? My home?'

'Yes.'

'The short answer is no. I'm sorry, Terry.'

'But why? I don't want to live with Amanda.'

'Then don't. Live by yourself.'

'I can't do that,' he said, sounding bemused by the notion. 'I'd be alone. I don't want to be alone, Stella.'

'What's the alternative? Find a replacement and move in with her?'

'Funny. No. After everything that's happened, I thought that maybe you and I could try again?'

Oh, Terry. I loved him. I truly did. He was the father of my children and a damn fine father at that. As much as the kids went on about him, they loved him, too. But as for us resuming our marriage? Not a chance. Terry was one of my closest, dearest friends and I hoped he'd always remain so, but the idea of having sex with him again? Well, that wasn't going to happen, no matter how many tequilas I slammed down.

'Tempting as that is, I'm afraid my answer is still no,' I said. 'Regardless of any problems you're having with Amanda, running back to me isn't going to solve anything.'

'Really, Stella, you can be so hard. Can I speak to Mum, please?'

'Sure . . . and Terry, everything will work out. Okay?'

'Thanks.'

I found June hovering by the kitchen sink, handed her the phone and left them to talk in private.

Terry was a good bloke. He'd always be in my life, but I didn't tingle any more when I thought about him. Not the way I tingled when I thought about Mike. Maybe, just maybe, I could give it a go with him. The timing was rotten, the kids would object, but if we kept it quiet for a while until we were both really sure, then maybe. All I knew was that I wanted to keep an open mind, and if Mike wanted to take me out to dinner, that wouldn't be such a bad thing.

•·

I was in bed reading that night when Mike called. Date call, I thought, then checked the bedside clock. Ten thirty. A bit late for chit-chat. He was really pushing the boundaries of good manners. But the thought vanished instantly at his first words after 'hello'.

'I think I might have good news for you.'

'What? Really?'

'Yes, really. Jesse's eyes fluttered open three times this evening. She's definitely showing signs of emerging from the coma.'

'I'm coming straight in.'

'Hang on,' he said. 'I'm not saying she'll wake up in the next hour or two. She's still not responding to requests to squeeze her hand or blink. But the signs are encouraging.'

'That's good enough for me.'

I hung up, threw on a pair of jeans and a T-shirt and raced over to Carly's. I had to knock several times before Brett finally answered.

'What's up?' he said, looking dazed.

'It's Jesse,' I said breathlessly. 'She might be waking up.'

'Waking up?' said Carly, emerging from the guest room. 'What are we waiting for, then?'

She and Brett were obviously having problems, but now wasn't the time to ask. We needed to focus on Jesse and, hopefully, some good news.

Within twenty minutes, Carly and I had arrived at hospital and were treading the familiar path up to the third floor. Louisa and Dot were sitting by Jesse's bed. They waved us in, and we hugged before turning to look at Jesse.

'It's going to be okay,' Dot said, sighing with relief.

The four of us crowded around the bed, willing Jesse to make some further sign, but she looked just as she had the past few days—all bandages, bruises and tubes. My heart felt like it was breaking all over again. It wasn't as if I was expecting her to jump up and dance the macarena, but I'd hoped for some confirmation, no matter how small, that she was on the mend.

'Where are Ollie and Emily?' I asked.

'At home with Tom,' said Dot. 'After what Ollie went through earlier today, we don't want the children seeing Jesse again until we've got firm news about her recovery.'

'And Steve?' Surely he should have been rearing his ugly head by now.

'No one's been able to contact him,' said Louisa. 'He came in briefly this afternoon, but left just before Jesse started responding. He asked Mum and Dad to take Em and Ollie for the night. We've called his mobile and left a couple of messages but he seems to have disappeared.'

Good.

My expression must have revealed what I was thinking because Dot said, 'Perhaps it's for the best at this stage. It certainly feels calmer when Steve's not here.'

'If my partner was lying here, I'd never leave, not if I could help it,' Louisa said.

Dot looked at Jesse and then at Louisa. 'He has to give the kids some sense of normality and continuity. And who knows why people behave the way they do. Perhaps seeing Jesse lying here is too much for him to handle.'

'Too bad, she's his wife.'

'I agree, but when the going gets tough, sometimes people run away rather than face their responsibilities.'

I tried to catch Carly's eye, thinking that we should leave Dot and Louisa to their private conversation, but she was in a daze, staring at Jesse.

'Steve has the twins to consider,' said Louisa. 'He should be thinking of them instead of about himself.'

'Some people never learn, never grow up,' Dot said. 'Maybe Steve . . . ' She trailed off, then added, 'How many of us do silly things when we're young, never thinking about the consequences?'

'And when we're not so young,' said Carly. 'Never thinking about how our stupid actions and their repercussions will haunt us later in life.'

'I suppose I'd do some things differently if I had my time over again,' said Louisa thoughtfully.

Mike arrived at the door. He looked shocking—pale and exhausted. He motioned for me to come outside.

'What's up?' I said. 'Please don't tell me it's Jesse. We're all so hopeful. She's—'

'Stella, Jesse's going to be fine. Her physical recovery will take time but the signs are definitely positive. I believe we're through the worst. There's something else, though . . .'

'What?' I could barely contain myself. 'Mike, what is it?'

'It's Steve.'

I raised my eyebrows. Steve was the least of my concerns. If he wanted me to leave Jesse's room, he'd have to come in and personally frogmarch me out. I was staying where I was until she regained consciousness. Carly, me, Jesse's mother and father, even Louisa—we'd all been a hell of a lot more attentive than Steve had been the past few days.

'Okay,' I said. 'What about him?'

'He's in emergency . . . an overdose.'

'Pardon?'

'Cardiac arrest. Looks like he's been on a bender. Most probably cocaine and—'

'Jesus! Will he be okay?'

'Yeah, but it was touch and go for a while.'

'Shit, shit, shit.' I shook my head. 'Does he have a dodgy heart?'

'Maybe. We'll run some tests over the next couple of days. Then again, maybe he just overdid it tonight.'

'You're kidding me,' said Louisa, who had appeared beside me. 'Talk about karma.'

Dot and Carly joined us, and the four of us listened to Mike's summary of the situation, all dumbstruck. Then Carly began to laugh. We all stared at her, horrified.

'I don't mean anything by it,' she said, but she'd set Louisa off now, too.

'But Steve,' said Dot. 'He's had a heart attack?'

I rubbed her back. 'It seems so.'

Louisa was shaking her head. 'What an idiot. I mean . . . why?'

'Maybe the pressure,' I said. 'And tonight he finally flipped.'

'We've all certainly been under a lot of strain in the last few days, that's for sure,' Dot agreed.

Carly nodded. 'It's been a difficult week,' and within seconds her and Louisa's laughter had turned to sobs.

Dot shook her head sadly and sniffed back her own tears. 'Those poor children,' she kept saying.

I was still too shocked to make a sound.

Mike did his best to calm us down, while a nurse organised cups of tea. By the time we had composed ourselves enough to walk back into Jesse's room, it was well after two in the morning. We gathered around her bed, Louisa holding her hand. Fittingly, Robbie Williams's 'Angels' was playing as we sat there quietly, not knowing what to say or where to look.

Dot broke the silence, reminiscing about the birth of Jesse's twins. 'They were big babies. Huge.'

'That would have been the last time Jesse was in a hospital,' said Louisa.

'Cracked rib,' Jesse croaked, barely audible. 'Two years ago.'

I felt as if I'd stopped breathing.

'Jesse?' Louisa said.

Jesse's mouth moved. 'I'm here,' she whispered. 'Always have been.'

I wanted to jump on the bed and hug her, but instead I ran out into the hallway. 'Jesse's awake,' I shouted towards the nurses' station.

26

*J*esse was alone in her room, resting after yet another team of doctors had done numerous checks and tests, when Mike walked in.

'Remember me?'

She smiled weakly. 'Mike?'

He nodded. 'Yeah, Mike. How are you feeling?'

'Groggy, tired, sore.'

'That's to be expected.' Mike pulled up a chair and sat down beside her. 'Do you feel up to talking?'

Jesse nodded, tears in her eyes. 'I lost the baby?'

'Yes. I'm sorry.'

'It's . . .' Jesse's words caught in her throat.

'I know this is hard for you, but there's something else. It's about your husband.'

Jesse took a sharp breath. What had Steve done now? Caused a scene in the hospital? Abused the doctors?

'Steve's fine. That is, he's going to be fine, but he's also in hospital.'

'Did he have a car accident too?' Jesse asked, feeling panicked. 'My children?'

'They're fine. They're with your parents. I'm afraid your husband overdosed.'

'As in drugs?'

Mike nodded.

Jesse's eyes filled with tears. How much more could she take?

'But he's okay?' she asked.

'He will be.'

She sighed deeply. Whatever she thought about Steve, she certainly didn't want him to die. He was the father of her children. They didn't deserve to grow up without their dad.

'Are you all right?' Mike said. 'I know it's a lot to take in.'

'What drugs?' Jesse asked.

'Cocaine. We're running tests for other narcotics as well.'

Jesse turned away. She was embarrassed, humiliated and so, so sad. Life wasn't meant to be like this. Her poor children. How would they ever cope?

It seemed like hours before Mike spoke again. 'Jesse, can I ask you something?'

What now, she thought, nodding ever so slightly.

'The afternoon of the accident . . . can you remember what happened?'

'I was angry and upset,' she whispered.

Mike said nothing.

'I felt like everyone had let me down. My husband, friends. I was shaking so much it was almost impossible to drive. I could barely see the road through the rain and my tears.'

'And?' Mike prompted gently.

'I knew I had to pull over.'

•

After Mike had left, Jesse thought some more about that afternoon. The shaking had become so bad she'd had to stop the car, like she'd told him. With minimal visibility because of the rain, she'd chosen a spot on the long, straight stretch of road, a grassy area where she could pull over safely and take a few minutes to calm down, collect her thoughts and do some deep breathing.

As she sat there, the rain eased. Across the road, she noticed a man in a lightweight raincoat walking his dog, a labrador. He looked content, at peace. That was what she wanted, to be at peace. She focused on the man, the way he held the dog's lead, then on the animal itself, its even gait. Watching the lab, Jesse felt her breathing slow down. She didn't feel quite so anxious or panicky.

She wiped her eyes, then started the car again. Before heading off, she pulled a lipstick from her bag and turned the rear-vision mirror slightly so she could see her face. It was red, blotchy and sad. Despite appearances, she had to believe she could get through this. She certainly wasn't going anywhere without her children.

As she went to apply the lipstick, she dropped it on the floor. Her leg jerked and her foot tapped the accelerator. She slammed her foot on the brake and bent to retrieve the lipstick. As she did, her foot jerked again and this time it hit the accelerator. Hard.

Now look where she was . . . in hospital. She was so sad—about losing the baby, about Steve—but at least she was alive. Imagine if she never got to see Ollie and Emmy again? They'd be in to visit her soon and the three of them would get through this together. Jesse was going to come out of this a much stronger woman: secure in her beliefs and the direction she wanted her life to take.

As for Steve? It was a *fait accompli*. She was leaving him, no doubt about it.

When Jesse was finally allowed to see Oliver and Emily, she couldn't hide her delight. 'My darlings,' she cried when they tentatively entered her room. 'Mummy's missed you so much. Come and give me a big hug.'

They barged at her with every bit of their nine-year-old energy. The impact almost wiped Jesse out, but she'd never admit it.

'So, what have you been up to?' she asked once she'd caught her breath.

'Mummy,' said Oliver in an exasperated tone, 'we've only been thinking about you since the accident.'

'And that's been like forever!' said Emily.

Jesse smiled at them both, determined not to cry. They'd seen enough tears these past few days. 'Thank you. I knew you were thinking of me. I could hear you. I missed you both so much.'

'Did you really hear us talking to you?' asked Oliver.

'Of course,' she replied. 'And then especially when you squeezed my hand, Ollie.'

He beamed. 'I knew you could feel it. I just knew. But Mummy,' he was suddenly serious, 'I was very worried that you wouldn't wake up.'

'Thank you, darling,' she said. 'I know you were but . . .' She faltered and started tearing up. 'You know Mummy loves you and would never leave you . . . will never leave you?' She kissed her son's cheek. 'I love you, Ollie.'

Dot appeared in the doorway. 'Come on, Ollie, Em! It's time Mum had a rest. And Grandpa needs an ice-cream.' Dot winked at Jesse before leading her grandchildren out into the hall. Moments later, she was back. 'Love, how are you doing?'

'Fine, Mum.'

'About Steve . . .' She hesitated for a moment. 'I'm so sorry. I had no idea.'

'Neither did I, but the good news is, he's going to be okay. He and I aren't going to be together, but we'll both get through this. I'm very sad, but . . .'

Jesse couldn't help herself. As the tears came, Dot rushed to her side.

'You have a family that loves and adores you,' she said. 'We'll be here for you. Speaking of which, Louisa's here. Are you up for another visitor?'

'Am I!' Jesse said, wiping her eyes as Louisa walked in. 'Sis!'

'Darling,' said Louisa, tears streaming down her face. 'You had us all so worried.'

Jesse smiled. 'Thank you so much for keeping me company while I was asleep.'

'Oh, Jesse,' Louisa said. 'I've missed you so much. Can you ever forgive me?'

'Probably not.'

'Oh.' Louisa looked stricken.

'I'm joking. But you should have told me, Louisa. After all, blood is thicker than water and all that.'

'God, Jess, I'll never forgive myself.'

Jesse sighed. 'You have to and you will, because if I hadn't been with Steve, I'd never have had Ollie and Emily.'

'Oh,' said Louisa again, remembering. 'Do you know about . . .'

Jesse sighed. 'Yeah.' Tears welled in her eyes. 'But obviously it wasn't the right time. Maybe in the future . . .'

'Yep,' said Louisa, fighting back tears as she kissed Jesse on her cheek.

'Anyway, I'm sick of talking about me,' Jesse said. 'Tell me about Philippe.'

Louisa grinned. 'You're unbelievable, you know that?'

'Enough with the stalling. Tell me about this Adonis of yours, and you'd better have pictures on your phone or there'll be trouble.'

After Louisa had shown Jesse several photos of Philippe and Ziggy, she said, 'Can you ever forgive me for running away six years ago? I'm so sorry. I was scared and ashamed and I didn't want to ruin your perfect life.'

Jesse looked at her. 'My perfect life? Really?'

'Okay, it doesn't seem so idyllic now, but back then . . .'

'Back then, I was living a lie.'

'I'm sorry. I didn't realise the extent of it—Steve's drug taking and everything else.'

'Hello?' came a voice from the doorway. It was Stella, and Carly with her. 'Do you have room for a couple more visitors?'

Jesse smiled. 'I sure do.'

Louisa left Stella and Carly to catch up with Jesse while she went outside and made a phone call.

After her text yesterday afternoon, she'd received one back from Philippe simply saying: *I love you. If you need me, I'll be on the next flight.* She'd read the words and wept. She hadn't known it before but those were the exact words she'd wanted to hear. She loved Philippe. She just needed to tell him.

'Hey,' she said when she heard his familiar voice.

'Lou, I've been so worried. How's your sister?'

'She's going to be okay.'

'Babe, I'm so glad. I haven't been able to concentrate on my studies since you left. Might need you to write me a note—'

'Philippe,' Louisa said, interrupting him.

'Yeah?'

'I love you.'

Silence.

'Philippe?'

'I'm still here. Could you repeat that, please?'

Louisa smiled. 'I love you. Can't live without you. Want to be with you forever.'

Philippe sighed. 'Well, it's about fucking time.'

Louise got off the phone feeling happier and more content than she had in years.

Was it really possible that, after all this time, she could truly be in love?

As happy as Carly and I were to sit with Jesse, we knew she was tiring. It would be days, maybe weeks, before she was back to her old self. Mike had told me that Jesse's accident had been exactly that. Thank God. The hospital didn't believe she was a suicide risk but she was still fragile and we needed to take a softly-softly approach for now.

'You sure you're okay?' I asked.

'I think so,' she said quietly. 'Stella, I'm so sad for Ollie and Em. And I'm sad for Steve, too. But I'm relieved he's going to be all right.'

'I spoke to Mike before,' I said. 'Steve'll probably only be in hospital for another day.'

Jesse nodded.

I glanced at my watch. Carly and I had been at the hospital over twelve hours. I was wrecked. It was time to leave. Besides, Jesse was starting to nod off.

Just as I was about to kiss Jesse goodbye, Louisa reappeared.

'How about I get us more coffees?' she said.

Carly and I glanced at each other.

'Sure,' I said, yawning. 'And then I've got to go home. I reek.'

Carly laughed. 'I think we're way beyond that.'

Louisa left to fetch the coffees, and I took the opportunity to ask Carly about the situation between her and Brett.

'You two going to be okay?'

Carly shrugged. 'I don't know. But I do know I'm going to talk to him when I get home, try to make sense of everything . . . Stella, I really lost my way the last couple of years, and then with Nicky moving overseas, I just fell apart. I might fantasise about fuck buddies and leaving my husband, but it's not what I want. I say and do things without thinking them through.'

I hugged her. 'You've always been impulsive. It's one of the things I love about you.'

She sniffed back tears. 'Thanks.'

I reached for her hand. 'I like Brett.'

Carly smiled. 'Yeah, so do I. When I think back to how it was in the beginning for us—we were so in love. Maybe we could get back to that place.'

'Absolutely, hon.'

'I've been scared for a long time, thinking that love has gone. But maybe we can get back on track. It won't be the same, of course, but hopefully it can be just as strong. What about you?'

'I'm doing fine,' I said, and meant it. 'Though did I tell you Terry's having issues with Amanda?'

'No!'

'She's pushing for more commitment and he's terrified.'

'I bet. And?'

'His solution is to run back to me.'

'You're not serious?'

'I'm not, but Terry seems to be. I told him no, and that's about as far as I'm going to get involved. He needs to decide what's right for him on his own.'

'True.' Carly threw me a sly grin. 'So what's the story with Mike?'

I smiled. 'Nothing. I mean, he's nice.'

'And?'

'And that's it.'

'Hmm, you know meeting those guys the other week doesn't have to be all bad. Love—'

'Carly, enough. I am not about to fall in love.'

'Just saying. Besides, you have no control over who you fall in love with . . . it's destiny.'

'Thank you. Let's change the topic.' Thinking about Mike was making me feel a tad too excited.

'Talking of destiny,' said Louisa, walking back into the room with three coffees, 'I've just told Philippe I'm coming back to Australia.'

'Jesse will be ecstatic,' said Carly.

Louisa glanced at Jesse, who was still asleep. 'I know. San Francisco is wild and crazy and I love the place, but I think I could love Sydney, too. Anyway, I'm giving it a shot. It means bringing my beloved Ziggy out here and putting him in quarantine for six months, so I wouldn't be doing that if I didn't have serious long-term goals. I just want Jesse to know that it's not because I feel obliged. I want to be here. And . . .' She trailed off.

'Come on,' I said. 'And what?'

'Philippe's coming out, too. We'll see how it goes.'

'Wow,' I said, almost spilling my coffee. 'That's great. I'm so happy for you.'

Louisa smiled. 'Yeah. Perhaps I haven't been entirely honest with myself about my feelings for him. I know it might end in tears, but if I'm ever going to take the next step with him, now's the time. We'll see out the academic year at USF, then come over. I should be able to pick up work here. Anyway, it's an adventure.'

'Absolutely,' I said, raising my coffee cup. 'Here's to life. It's definitely one hell of a rollercoaster.'

27

*C*arly was finally home . . . and she was wrecked. All she wanted to do was shower and fall into bed. When her phone rang, she assumed it would be Brett. She hadn't spoken to him except a very brief and tearful conversation letting him know Jesse was awake. But when she glanced at the number, she saw it was Nicholas's. She hesitated about whether or not to answer it given her tired and emotional state, but he rang so rarely.

'Hello.' Her voice was croaky and uneven.

'Mum? Are you okay?'

She felt herself tearing up. 'Yes, darling. It's good to hear from you.' She told him about Jesse, then said, 'I'm worried about you, too.'

'Yeah, I know. That's why I'm ringing. Mr Sinclair said he's going to email you and explain everything, but basically this kid, Jeremy Middleton, doesn't like being away from home. He makes up stories about the other students, the assistants, the ground staff, everybody.'

'So he made up the story about the towel flicking?'

Nicholas laughed. 'No, we were flicking towels, but there were loads of us involved. He made a big deal out of it because he wants his parents to pull him out of school. Fair enough—he hates being a boarder, and his parents only live two miles away. Seems a bit weird, but it's the way the Brits do things.'

'So you're not about to be kicked out?'

'Of course not. The guys think I'm great.'

'I'm so relieved.' Carly hesitated a moment. 'Nick, there's something else. Your dad told me about Mr Busby—'

'What? I told him not to.'

'I'm upset that you felt you couldn't tell me.'

'Why would I? It's embarrassing. He was a lunatic sending me crazy letters.'

Carly took a deep breath. 'I found the letters. So you didn't—'

'Mum! Gross. I knew you'd freak, that's why I told Dad. He dealt with it. He had a word to Busby and the principal, and next thing I knew he was gone.'

All these revelations were doing Carly's head in. 'So you're not . . .'

'Mum! I'm not gay! And I don't have any trouble finding girls to sleep with either.'

Okay, thank you. Too much information.

'Nick, I've been so worried. I had no idea all this was going on.'

'You're not supposed to know everything about me. I have my own life.'

'I can't help worrying. I'm your mother—it's what I do best. So you're okay? I didn't fail you?'

'How?'

'By not picking up on the Mr Busby signs.'

'Mum! There weren't any Mr Busby signs because nothing happened. Sure, he was annoying and sent me gross letters, but he was harmless and unhappy. There was never a time when the two of us were alone.'

'You're sure?'

'I'm sure. Look, if I need therapy later on, you can pay for it.'

'It's a deal. And Nicky, you're not really sleeping with girls, are you? And if you are—'

'Hanging up now. Bye, Mum.' He ended the call.

On autopilot, Carly walked into the kitchen and opened the fridge. There was a full bottle of wine in there and she pulled it out. So much had happened over the past few days; she was finding it hard to digest it all. It was so strange how a single action like meeting Toby and going to that party could have caused so many lives to veer off in directions no one could have imagined. Carly's behaviour that night had set in motion a chain of events that had led to her friend lying in a hospital bed in a coma.

She stared at the bottle's label for a minute, Steve's words from a week earlier playing in her mind: *I can recommend the Oyster Bay Riesling this week. It's on special for a hundred and thirty bucks a dozen, and since you buy your liquor by the crate, you'll save a bundle. Or rather, Brett will.* Wine had been a crutch she had relied on for too long. Now, Carly had a picture in her mind of what her future looked like and it didn't include her passed out every night from too much alcohol consumption. She put the bottle back in the fridge and closed the door.

What she needed right now was sleep, not wine. She walked into her bedroom, took off her shoes and fell into bed. She woke when Brett sat down on the bed beside her.

'Carly,' he said softly, 'are you okay? I'm so happy about Jesse.'

She opened her eyes slightly, adjusting to the dim light. 'Jesse? Yes . . . so happy.' She closed her eyes again.

'Hon, are you okay?'

She nodded. 'So tired. Spoke to Nicky.'

Brett sighed. 'I'm so sorry for not telling you. I was trying to support Nick the best way I knew how, but I stuffed up.'

Carly forced herself to wake up fully. 'No, I'm sorry. I know you were trying to do the right thing.'

She sat up, and Brett stroked her hair then put his hand around the back of her neck. 'Are we okay?' he asked.

She shook her head. 'I don't know. After everything that's happened with Jesse, I'm an emotional wreck.'

'I'm here for you, you know, and I always will be.' When he pulled her into him and kissed her on the lips, she felt instantly comforted.

'What did Nick say?' Brett asked.

'You were right. Everything's been sorted with the sports master.'

He smiled. 'See, I told you.'

He lay down on the bed and wrapped his arms around her, drawing her in close. When he kissed her, she felt herself responding to him in a way she hadn't for months. The kissing was slow and intimate and felt divine. Carly pulled back and glanced at the door. 'What about Will? What if he comes home?'

'He's at basketball practice till eight. Let's live dangerously, hey?' Brett whispered, massaging her breasts through her dress.

'But I've been so stupid.'

'We both have. I know you've been unhappy. I was trying to wish it away.'

'With all that's happened to Jesse, I realise how selfish I've been. I do love you, Brett.'

'I know. I love you, too,' He said as they both shrugged off their clothes.

Brett pulled her down on his chest and kissed her neck. Carly knew every inch of his body. He was so familiar; his scent, the freckles on his stomach, the perfect way their bodies fitted together.

'Feels good,' she said, positioning herself above him so Brett could enter her. A couple of thrusts and he was inside.

He smiled. 'Just good?'

Carly stared into his deep brown eyes, her pleasure obvious.

'Fucking fantastic,' she said finally as they found their intimate rhythm and rocked together, revelling in the moment.

I was home, tired and exhausted, but happy to be with Hannah, Ben and June. All that had happened over the last week had made me even more aware of the importance of family. I was so grateful for the love and joy my children brought me, and for the loving marriage I'd enjoyed with Terry, and the continuing presence of June in my life. That's what got you through in the end: the love of family and friends, and a belief in yourself that you were doing the right thing, or at least the very best you could.

I thought back to my conversation with Jesse that evening, just as I was preparing to leave. She'd woken up briefly and motioned me to move closer to her.

'Steve and I . . . finished . . .' she'd whispered. 'Feeling sad but strong, too . . . How do you do it?'

I'd taken her hand. 'One step at a time, one day at a time, angel. When Terry and I got together, he told me he'd love me forever and I know he meant it. But forever is a long time and maybe it's just too much of an ask.'

Jesse had nodded slightly.

'We're all here for you, Jess,' Louisa had added.

'Yes,' I said softly. 'We're all here. I'm leaving now, but I'll be back, darling.'

'Tomorrow?'

'You bet,' and I'd kissed her lightly on her forehead through the bandages before heading out the door.

Now, I sat at the kitchen table, drinking tea and enjoying June's company as she filled me in on the last few days of family life. She'd been marvellous while I was spending so much time at the hospital. She'd organised the kids, supervised the making of their school lunches and had even made sure they stacked their dirty plates in the dishwasher. Not only that, but the past few nights she'd persuaded Hannah to log off Farmville and do her maths homework.

'But only after I agreed to sign on to Facebook,' she told me with a chuckle.

'Facebook?'

'Don't look so surprised. I'm not that ancient. Besides, it will open up a whole new world to me. I've already got two friends,' she said proudly. 'Hannah and Ben.'

'Really? Well done. They keep rejecting me but I'm trying not to take it personally.'

'Sweetie,' she said wisely, 'they're never going to accept you. You're their mother. I'm a harmless old lady. I pose no threat.'

'So you'll spy on them for me?' I asked with a smile.

'Of course, my dear. Why else would I join?'

We were laughing together when the doorbell rang.

'Expecting anyone?' I asked her.

She shook her head, and I walked down the corridor to answer it.

I opened the door to see Mike standing there. He was looking tired but still gorgeous, wearing denim jeans, a collared blue shirt and a big wide smile. I was surprised . . . and then I was delighted and excited. Until a split second later when I remembered. 'Is it Jesse? She was fine—'

'Shush,' he said, putting his forefinger against my lips. 'In my expert opinion, I'd say she's doing very well. Better than expected given everything that's happened.'

My heart skipped a couple of beats—relief or desire, I wasn't sure. But I was enjoying the warm erotic sensation of his finger on my lips.

'How are you doing?' he asked.

'Okay, though I'm a bit puzzled as to why you're standing on my front doorstep.'

'Yeah,' he said, kissing me lightly on the lips. 'Must be confusing for you, because I know you're definitely not looking for romance.'

He put his hands around my waist and I couldn't help melting into his arms. Still, I stuck to my guns. 'That's right.'

He moved in towards me, his body close against mine, and I could smell his fresh woodsy scent. 'We need to work on that,' he said and kissed me again, this time with greater ardour.

It had been a long time since I'd kissed someone new and I wasn't disappointed. Despite sounding like a fifteen-year-old, all I could think was what a good kisser he was . . . passionate, forceful, arousing. He tasted like peppermint. I wanted more. A lot more. In fact, my legs started to go wobbly. If I could have whisked him up to my bedroom right then, I would have.

'Mum!'

I heard Hannah's voice in the background and pulled away. 'I guess we should stop,' I said half-heartedly.

He smiled, still holding me in his arms. 'I guess. After all, we've got time on our side.'

I liked that.

'So,' he said, stealing another kiss, 'dinner tomorrow night?'

I smiled. I'd said no to him before and instantly regretted it. Now I was going to say yes and dive into whatever lay ahead. Rather than hover around the periphery, worrying about whether I was making the right decision, I was going with my heart—and my heart was screaming at me to seize the moment, to accept what the universe was offering me.

It was one of the lessons I'd learned over the past few days.

'Why don't you come in?' I said and took Mike's hand and led him inside.

Acknowledgements

Sincerest thanks to all at Allen & Unwin, especially my publisher, Louise Thurtell, to whom *Stella Makes Good* is dedicated.

Thanks to Christa Munns for your insight and guidance, and to the sales, marketing and promotion team. To Nicola O'Shea, huge hugs for your ongoing, outstanding editorial suggestions. I feel exceptionally privileged to have had your input for all four of my novels.

And to Ellie Exarchos—another stunning cover! I love it. Thank you. (I want that woman's shoes and dress . . . Oh, and the balloons. In fact, I want to be that woman!)

Finally, the continued support of my family and friends has been outstanding. I spend an obscene amount of time living in my head with my imaginary friends, so thanks for your understanding and combined resistance to have me committed.

A special shout out to Anjanette Morton, Dr Anita Heiss, Dr Jeremy Fisher and Lloyd Christison. You guys rock!

And, as always, thanks to Betting, Josh, Noah and Mia for everything. I couldn't have written this book without you on my side.

The characters in *Stella Makes Good* are fictional, as are the sex/swingers parties I've invented. Sydney's North Shore is a perfectly respectable part of town!